Death on the Wing

A Nocte Mortis© Novel

Antony M Brown

Published by Antony Michael Brown

If all else fails,

immortality can always be assured by spectacular error.

John Kenneth Galbraith

About The Book

Harvey Taadpole was a tough son of a grumble mother, on the run from some of the most seasoned bounty hunter's death can throw at you. His escape run was now as fast as a horse drawn carriage could travel. A fellow passenger was sitting in the shade, and looking like he had overdone the sunblock a bit too much. But what a smile? A smile like that could open doors, or punctuate your day to a full stop.

Treacle for his part was an undercover agent from the vampire guild, open to adventure and ready for action. Their adventures lead them into conspiracy and political intrigue, way beyond who stole the Queen of Hearts gluten-free vegan tarts!

Introducing Nocte Mortis

In the higher plains, there is a magical place by a lake of the deepest blue, where award-winning blood pudding with red wine is a traditional dish. The old traditional vampire families had called this place home for several centuries and had moved into banking as a natural progression, as they sucked the life out of their customers one copper coin at a time.

Vampire clans competed for power and wealth against each other from the shadows, where all nefarious nosferatu types lurked.

There are many stories from such a place, and this is but one.

Contents

300 Year Prologue

CRACK, YELP and SNAP.

Trappy, the driver of the coach and horses could not swear it occurred exactly in that order before a jury, but he could think of some good profanities. It seemed to happen to him all at once. Lightning had played staccato across the mountains; it chased his coach further eastwards than he had really intended to travel, though he preferred to travel a few miles out of his way and be dry and cold, rather than cold and mostly moist under his seat. So a few hours earlier, he had steered his horses towards the line of blue sky and hoped for the best. But the storm had decided to stop playing that game and had outmanoeuvred him, and was now directly overhead dumping the contents of a small ocean upon him, drop by drop. In no time he was pounded and soaked from raindrops the size of sheep eyes, and he could feel the dampness slowly seeping into his boots. The driving rain penetrated every layer of clothing he wore, and the CRACK of thunder, accompanied with its flash of lightning, had startled an already spooked team of horses. He was sure Rudolph had reared up a bit at the front, and that was never a good sign.

A YELP of instant pain emanated from within the confines of the coach, as the flash of lighting illuminated every corner of its dark interior. The sound was not what he had expected to hear from the well-turned out gentleman such as the one he carried. He knew his passenger was a man of taste -- the traveller had asked for the best driver and horses money could buy, and had paid Trappy handsomely for his time and expertise without niggling over the fare. Strangely though, the horses became jittery as soon as his passenger climbed aboard; after ten miles on the road they had still not calmed down. As for the SNAP? That was supplied by an old overhanging oak tree. A few minutes earlier it had sheltered the whole road to just beyond the oncoming fork which split the thoroughfare in two, much now like the tree. To his left the road was totally obscured by a cottage-sized pile of branches and leaves. Thereupon, Trappy chose the route clear and unobstructed to him, and pushed his horses on to the village of Nocte Mortis, located at the near end of this mist-filled valley which marked the start of the upper plains of the central continent in the Old lands of Tres-Leones. Why it was called Tres-Leones no one could really recall, so the name had fallen out of fashion. Anyway, home didn't need a silly name; it was called home, after all.

Trappy had travelled to this so-called Nocte Mortis many moons ago, and found a village just surviving on the edge of existence. It should have disappeared long ago into history (during the Mulberry Plague two hundred years past, the local pig population had become so depleted that it almost became impossible to maintain the local blood pudding industry, the staple food source and income in these parts) and his opinion of the place was less for it not having done so. Most of the local forms of finance accepted in this hovel were not based on coinage, as one would expect, but instead around existing agricultural produce, or that which might exist sometime in the near future, or the lending of tools to harvest the agricultural produce.

The coach rattled down the road past the milestones buried in the hedgerow, resembling headstones for miles long since passed. Trappy noticed that the village sign had rotted away since his last visit due to the neglect of the few remaining residents. The main road ahead slowly curved on the ridge line around the water's edge, bringing the coach to a collection of stone buildings that had survived mostly due to the high quality of the original building materials rather than anyone bothering to spend money maintaining these remnants of better times.

Finally the coach came to a stop, and Trappy jumped down, creating an instant puddle beneath him as every drop of water on his waxed clothing became dislodged. A rolling cloud of smoke confronted him upon opening the coach door. Whatever this gentleman traveller had been smoking smelled none too pleasant, especially compared to the blend of Old Sailor Trappy preferred in his pipe, and Trappy's nose could appreciate a sweaty horse. As the gentleman traveller stepped down from the coach, Trappy was sure the smoke actually crept out from every gap between the man's clothing. However, the smoke quickly disappeared in the howling gale blowing around the traveller's nether regions.

Trappy sought shelter behind a wall and opened a small brown paper parcel containing a meal of two hard-boiled egg sandwiches, while his employer for the day quickly ran across the cobbled street to the only inn in the village for what he no doubt would consider to be a very stiff drink indeed. Inside the warm and well-shuttered bar, the traveller, much to his surprise, found he was treated to both a warm welcome and a side order of cordial respect, courtesies he had not recently seen, and he felt much the better for it. Upon scanning the menu, the traveller exclaimed, "You don't really serve 30 award-winning blood puddings do you?"

"Yes sir, we could have more but they wouldn't bloody well be award winning, now would they?" stated Rowena, the waitress for the day. "Would sir like a nice red wine with that?" she asked.

When the wine arrived he discovered it was a very young red vintage, grown in the valley's unique microclimate, and so freshly squeezed that it suffered from bottle-shock. It could have been pressed yesterday, he reflected. By the time the now-contented stranger had finished his plate of "Pat's Plump Porkers" -- a tasteful, triple blood sausage selection worthy of its gold medal from the local connoisseurs -- he had decided to make this place of culture his home. First, however, his business trip must be concluded. Many of the locals who saw the gentleman that night considered him to be someone important in an operatic company. He dressed just like the pictures in the paper suggested opera fans should be adorned this season. While there was no local opera hall for comparison, travellers had graciously left behind the odd bit of gossipy reading material that was read aloud by the local priest when he was giving one of his late night sermons from his mount on the rickety legged bar stool that was avidly re-quoted in the long, dark winter nights.

The traveller left the next day promising to return once his offal trading had been concluded in the Low Countries. Several years later, his black coach returned with an entourage of hanger-on's who set about building his new country mansion and, to that end, his first act was to invest ten thousand rather exotic gold coins in the name of Count Drak of Ula in the local bank, thereby instantly propelling it to one of the most influential banks on the whole continent. The Count, it was rumoured, had been the target of persecution in his home country and had been granted political asylum. He wanted somewhere to call home where he found the locals inviting. It was a welcome change to find a place where the only heads threatened by scythes, pitchforks and assorted sharp agricultural instruments were attached to the stems of corn growing in the local fields. The Count quickly put down roots of his own on his return, building a large home for himself along the banks of the Great Drin, the large lake on the river that ran through these parts.

Other great displaced families from the old country also found enticement to relocate to Nocte Mortis by what was quickly becoming an excellent banking system, which kept a good distance from prying eyes. Each family found that land was cheap and plentiful -- perfect for building grand houses of their own. They placed their residences along the Great Drin, suitably distanced for maximum privacy so that they could visit their bank manager in style. Those individuals who didn't understand banking believed that what was now quickly becoming a city would sink all the way to hell under the weight of the vast sums of gold stored within its vaults. They didn't truly understand that the money never sat still. -- It was out in the world earning favourable rates of Interest on loans for everything from wars to the neighbour's new privy door. The bank had so many customers from a particular stratum of local society that it gained a motto: "Achieving Wealth from Compounded Interest." This credo arose since most of its special investors expected to easily live long enough to see their 100 year bonds mature.

1 Week Prologue

Ruud Darknight, Lord High Protector of the clans, was sitting at his opulent desk inspecting the daily reports and letters that had reached him from all three corners of the known world. He had already ordered a meeting of his own particular "Lamia" clan the following week in Lower Inferior, in response to some of the documents already held in his hand, and the first guest on his list to attend was a one Treacle Tanner, his young nephew who had demonstrated an uncanny knack of placing himself right in the centre of any investigation the clan had instigated recently. That sort of good fortune needed to be nurtured or exploited when playing for high stakes such as these; rumours were abroad of large arm sales - which was nothing new in these times of escalating political cat fighting, but when this was coupled with a large amount of new loans secured against troop ships, it all pointed to a possible invasion plot and, if that happened, Ruud didn't want to find out who had won in the paper.

Half an hour after receiving his summons, Mr Branch was standing in Ruud's office, waiting for his master to get around to acknowledging his existence. As Mr Branch sat and waited -- by now he was accustomed to delays while waiting for an audience with this Lord High Protector -- he studied the office, which always had a new insight to discover, there was the wall of pictures of the rich and the powerful, which seemed to always be moving around the wall, the movement of which, he was sure, was based on some strange equation. Mr. Branch would have loved the chance to read the documents splayed across the desk in front of him, but several years ago Ruud had installed a small glass screen especially designed to distort and obscure the contents of the desk. So he settled for a quick scan of the hierarchy of clans pinned to the nearest wall, which changed weekly depending on wealth and influence, and which treaty was being invoked or ignored.

Suddenly, Ruud noticed his expert had waited long enough. "Mr. Branch, it's always a pleasure, and I must apologise for demanding your presence at such short notice, but we will be needing your talents," he began. "I require a special collection to be created or gathered together for a city adventure. Whatever you think might be required should be supplied, and you have a week to deliver."

"The three magic questions as always, sir: size, weight and location.' Branch stated briskly.

"Sorry, Mr. Branch, I forgot I'm dealing with a professional in a world full of amateurs. The size must be normal for a journey on the mail coach, its weight must be comfortable for a man to carry for an hour without wanting to place it on the ground, and delivery should be in Lower Inferior within a week."

"Very good, sir. Anything else? I do have some rather pressing experiments under way. Oh, while I remember sir, we will be requiring a new south wall for the workshop. We had a little accident involving rapidly expanding gases."

"I will make the necessary arrangements with the local builders, Mr. Branch. No need to apologise. These things happen, I am sure; you do work on the bleeding edge of science."

"That also reminds me, sir. Gerald will not be in for a few days, not until the worse of the burns heal a little anyway," Mr Branch said, with regret couched in his tone.

"That's a great blow to the team, Mr. Branch. I hope you can deliver on time. We are so counting on you. Now don't let me detain you any longer."

As Mr. Branch left Ruud made a note to send a card and flowers to Gerald and to increase Mr. Branch's budget for incidental costs yet again.

High up on the mountain trail, a stranger grasped a self-made staff cleaved from a willow tree which had, a few hours earlier, been growing quite happily on the far side of the mountain ridge. He glanced at the deathly quiet and dark building in front of him with the sign hanging above the entrance, and used the end of the staff to tap on the door. The owner Soi Nyi woke up and lit a rush light next to his bed. A light appeared in an upper window above him, casting his long shadow up towards the mountain peak he had just crossed. A few moments later the inn door was opened by Soi Nyi wearing nothing but a night shirt gathered together by a large belt of assorted weapons, just in case the stranger wanted a bit of trouble with his drink.

"Come in, come in," the innkeeper said as he surveyed his visitor. "You must be freezing. Here, come sit in front of the fire. You're a lucky man. I dare say if you had been fool enough to continue along the high pass at this time of year and at this time of night it would be your certain death."

"I, I, I've--" the stranger struggled to speak.

"Don't speak lad, let me get you a nice hot toddy. You do have some money, don't you?' An affirmative nod was offered and hot drink was fetched from a large flask by the fire.

A long time passed before the stranger regained the ability to speak without his teeth chattering together as if a castanet player were rattling them. Finally he said, "I have travelled the high pass in the hope I could catch the first mail coach out of here."

The inn keeper had witnessed this scene before. If a man was determined enough to cross the pass and take risks no sane mortal would consider, he could cross the mountain range and disappear so quickly it would be as if he had never existed. "I never said this and you never heard it from me but if you catch the ten o'clock coach from the village down the hill and swap coaches at the Long and the Short Inn for the 'Upper Plains Runner,' it will take you through the mountain pass to the lower plains in about a week. A couple of days later you could be in the Great Smog. It's not the fastest coach but it travels the back roads and stops at none of the common locations someone would look."

"Why?"

"I have a whole set of selfish reasons really, because if they catch you here I would be in trouble with them again. But if they have to chase you they will need supplies and a nice warm meal before they even consider moving a step further down the hill in hot pursuit."

Soi Nyi thought that this short and stocky man had the build and determination to survive great hardship. If he survived the pass in this weather, he could likely survive anything life would throw at him.

The Coaching Inn

Treacle says yes – Harvey says hello

- Fred Bent gets his head turned -

Harvey gets propositioned

The light streamed through the cheaply-made window. The window had a unique construction, being made entirely from the little square bases cut from numerous Urgh-Wright's gin bottles. As light passed through, it became a pale green hue that now danced across Treacle Tanner's face as he sat up in bed. His mind was filled with the excitement of the previous days' adventure travels across the upper plains within the comfort of the six horse-drawn mail coach. He had watched the pink long-haired pigs that were common in these parts feed upon the lush pastures of the valley floor. The coach had stopped briefly at two nice coaching inns -- the 'Galloping End' and the 'Trotting Bend' -- which catered to the locals' specialised finer taste in blood pudding and red wine. These indulgences could easily be accommodated from the permanently cooled basements dug into the permafrost below. Then, as dusk fell and by the magic of a correctly calculated timetable, the coach reached the one and only mountain pass to the lower plains and an inn of distinct character.

The atmosphere here was different from the previous inns; it was more robust, more heavy-handed, more military in nature. The name of this inn, according to the sign hanging outside, was 'Whoa, You Buggers, Whoa.' Treacle had come down from his room with its sloping floors, cold running jug water and lumpy bed and entered the bar for an evening meal, taking a booth by the window. As he looked around the establishment he had noticed that all the space on the walls, even behind the bar, was decorated with a complete collection of wild boar heads, man-traps and weapons. Nowadays the use and ownership of man-traps was supposedly illegal in the upper plains, due mostly to the amount of farm animals needlessly injured by them. Having people maimed by them didn't really seem to matter much, but when it came to damaging a prime porker, someone had to pay. Pigs were someone's property, after all. Treacle found it interesting that the owner of the bar could keep them all in fully working order as long as they were for decorative purposes only. He could smell fresh blood emanating from a few of the traps and wondered if that too was also for show.

While he had waited for his meal to arrive he watched the serving staff. The inn-keeper had the dusty look of someone who didn't get out much, or who had died but didn't let it inconvenience him while running his business. As the inn-keeper, bent from many years of service, stooped over the table across from him, Treacle let his inquiring mind get the better of him, and he just had to ask "Where did that rather interesting name for the inn come from?"

The inn-keeper glanced up.

"It's a famous quote around these parts," he replied. "They say you can hear it on the wind sometimes. Some say it's the last words from all those poor souls that died riding the haulage carts during the creation of the mountain path." The inn-keeper continued with the offhand manner of someone trying to surreptitiously slip something outrageous past an unwary innocent. "That was also many a last word of the coach passengers that went over the edge on a regular basis too."

As he left the table, the inn-keeper whispered a sentence mostly for his own benefit. "It's strange no driver has ever died on the pass. Maybe they have a guardian angel," he spluttered for effect. Tourists, the inn-keeper had decided, liked that sort of drama -- a nice bit of character acting always brought them back for more. Treacle thought to himself that any driver going down the mountain pass who could see the track disappearing below him would easily decide to make the six-foot jump to ground level long before the cliff edge and its 600 foot plunge to bloody doom, no matter how fast they were travelling.

Treacle got himself out of bed, waved the green light away just as one would brush away a fly from one's face, and prepared himself for the day that lay ahead. He took just a quick wash; no need today for the fragrant talcum powder that everyone used due to the exceedingly high amount of human - pig interaction that was found in these parts.

This magic powder was sold with the catchy phrase 'Put it where you smell.' Those canny salesmen! Treacle thought. A phrase that doubled as instructions. What would they think of next! When Treacle perspired, his scent was sweet with a hint of flowers -- something he had always attributed to a genetic trait that invariably enticed young maidens to fall under his spell. He gave the mirror a quick glance. Did he need a shave? As he held his chin, he looked this way and that in the mirror. No, he was still clean shaven as always; it was another benefit of his genetic disposition. The state of his hair? Well, that did need some work. Just in case, he decided, if some aeronautical adventuring into a young maiden's windows was in order. From his coat pocket he extracted a small jar of 'Extra Hold Hair Cream' that proclaimed "Just like Granny Used to Make" on the label. It was the only product that really worked and was recommended by everyone he knew, including the women whom he squired. It was disheartening that prolonged use of this product turned one's hair jet black, but he could live with that, Treacle thought, as he rubbed his fingers back through his locks. Either he looked good or... well, it wasn't worth thinking about. As for his choice of clothes, he thought heavy tweed would be highly suitable for dealing with the internal condition of these coaches, as their comfort really did leave something to be desired. If he picked up a splinter at least he wouldn't feel it. After he prepared himself for the journey ahead, a knock at his door took him by surprise. At the threshold was the morning maid -- he forever would remember her as succulent.

Treacle entered into the courtyard of the inn as the early light broke over the hilltops and slowly rolled down the valley. Somewhere over there in the half-light (he wasn't exactly sure precisely; continental geography wasn't his best subject) was Lower Inferior and then the higher city of Nocte Mortis. But now he was far from home, and still two days of travel awaited him on the mail coach. The coach didn't actually travel down the mountain passes any more, not since a rather quick thinking little child had surmised the mail would travel much quicker and without interference from stamp collectors if you threw it off the cliff or lowered it down with a rope.

The passenger coach presented to them as today's transport looked to have been designed to be everything yesterday's mail coach was not. Treacle noted the wheels were made from materials three times the thickness compared to the ones on yesterday's coach. Also, the windows were not large and draped with satin such as yesterday's coach had been (if satin could accurately describe this material, in which you could happily store potatoes in over winter, and had once been used as such). The windows on today's coach had wooden shutters with small slots only large enough for a crossbow bolt to pass through. The driver's seat had a sort of makeshift waterproof cover of draped fabric covered in pig's fat and some sort of animal innards not worth looking at too closely if one had just eaten. The brass work --in fact all bright work on the coach -- had been painted black. Some sort of effort to camouflage it, he presumed.

Raising his arm to grab the rail to pull himself up onto the step and inside the coach, Treacle felt something poke him. As suddenly as if from a childhood dream, he felt the familiar feeling of a sharp elbow hitting him in the ribs. While a quick mental flash of happy family meals bent over lunch passed before his eyes, he looked down at the elbow and let his eyes slowly travel along its owner's arm to a man's face whose look screamed, "I may be small mister but I would kick your teeth in if you don't let me get on first." "Or I will die trying" should have been added to his look, Treacle thought. Nonetheless, he kindly let his new travelling companion precede him into the coach without a fuss. Such things in life were not worth the effort of explaining to the police after the fact, he considered.

Treacle sat opposite this impolite short and stocky man and looked backward through the window to survey all he was leaving behind. The other passengers were the normal lot of pig "oinkment" salesmen and pig wranglers. He could tell that a lot of body fat was a job requirement for pig farming -- he wasn't exactly sure why, but guessed that body fat was needed to survive the harsh winter months up in the valley while looking for lost pigs once the snow began falling. He supposed his fellow passengers were chasing the next meal and a warm bed, or running from their past in a romantic sort of way.

As the journey began, Treacle thought on how this new adventure had started back in the austere surroundings of the Clan's meeting house in Lower Inferior. A stream of images started to play itself back to him and how he attended "That Meeting" the day before. He was certain that, to his dying day, he would always call it "That Meeting" even if he lived for 200 years, and he would never forget that dreadful topic concerning their knowledge or lack thereof about the politics of the new world, which was Uncle Ruud's current pet subject.

It was the sort of pet you let out and it pissed all over your prize daff's if you were lucky or, if you were unlucky, as he considered himself to always be, it would piss over your new shoes with your feet still in them. He remembered his nervousness of sitting for the first time at the head table instead of working security detail, and how that annoying habit of tapping out a tune with his fingers (in this case the death march) had got him into trouble again when the question arose about who would be willing to spy for the Clan council in the city of the Great Smog. Treacle remembered everyone turning toward the tap, tap, tap, and he could hear himself saying:

"Yes?"

On looking back, it was obvious his habit had thrown him into the deep end again. No wonder he had drawn everyone's attention his way. How stupid he was not to have realised the query two seconds before saying "Yes?" But now, but now he had volunteered himself and was on his way to the city with the Clan's blessings and good wishes filling his pockets. Gold, he thought, would have been better and more practical on such a journey, but he was footing the bill himself, in which case he was not going to skimp on the finer things in life.

Harvey, a fellow coach passenger, looked at the rakish stranger in front him, a man nicely dressed when compared with the local pig farmers. Hell, Harvey reflected, in the scheme of things the stranger was nicely dressed for any situation that might arise. The locals all carried their possessions on these coaches within a pig case (a case which was extremely strong and capable of rendering a pig unconscious, if required, due to its weight) but not this man. Back in his home town there was rumour of people being killed by a single swing should one of these cases connect with their skull. No wonder -- the case was constructed with some depth and could hold any manner of weapon or weapons. He also noticed his new travelling companion had not turned that paler shade of green, which commonly afflicted the travelling public due to being rocked back and forth on these mountain roads. Come to think of it, Harvey recalled, this elegant man had not moved from his seat during these last three back-breaking hours. The bone-crunching ride required either a backside of steel, a complete loss of feeling or something a little more dangerous, a will of iron. The question arose in Harvey's mind: Why would someone with money, who could afford to buy nice clothes, travel like this? The clothes were not stolen; nobody steals clothes that well-tailored with a perfect fit. The locals had hand-me-down clothes, some spanning several generations -- it was practicality disguised as tradition. Anyway, who earns enough for a tailor in these parts where a half a potato had entered the currency system? This stranger travelled without any form of protection, not even a sword disguised as a walking stick, unless maybe he had someone in the carriage protecting him like a guardian angel. But who? Their fellow travellers seemed to pay no interest to this guy. Harvey made a mental note not to mess with him or, more notably, not to mess with the person protecting him. He then added a postscript: Maybe this guy would be good to know if trouble started. Then a second postscript was added quickly: I will get to know this guy. I can only benefit; what do I have to lose? He dismissed another postscript as he hated letters or anything longer than a sentence. He leaned forward and addressed the stranger.

"Hello, my name is Mr Harvey Taadpole. Let me apologise for our first meeting but I do like boarding first. I like to see the road ahead. One never knows what ruffians (a word he thought would appeal to someone posh or posh-ish) could be waiting round the next corner.

Treacle looked at him. "Excuse me, Mr Taadpole, but what is a ruffian?" he said -- or would have if that inner voice hadn't reminded him what Auntie Gertrude had said: "Ignorance signs your death warrant." Instead, he used Uncle Puuse's default tone of voice.

"Really, Mr Taadpole, you expect ruffians on this trip?"

It's amazing what relatives teach you if you bother to listen. Uncle Puuse was an expert in nothing in particular but he could give a fantastic impression of someone who was worldly wise. He had the knack of stringing along a conversation until he could extract exactly what was being discussed. This worked especially well with Treacle when he was younger, but he had learnt a trick or two in dealing with his uncle since. So Mr-Kick-Your-Teeth-In turned out to be really a pleasant chap called Mr Harvey Taadpole. Some would call him a rogue of the road, he thought, but underneath that tough exterior was a very decent apologetic chap. For a second Treacle could see the decency glimmer within him; he could also see that it was completely misplaced. Taadpole had a tough exterior and a killer's heart to boot but there was a sliver of something there like loyalty, although what it really was and for how long it would last, Treacle couldn't tell.

"I think ruffians are guaranteed," Mr Taadpole remarked, glancing out of the window. 'Normally we can outpace them but if they are more creative than the usual type that stand in the middle of the road shouting 'whoa,' as those ahead of us seem to be, we will have to resort to some sort of violence, I'm afraid."

Was that a wink? Harvey asked himself. Yes, I am sure that it was. It was so fast as to be unseen by anyone else but he was sure he had seen his new-found friend acknowledge the situation that was rapidly approaching.

Treacle smiled and held out a hand to shake in the few minutes left to them as he said, "My name is Treacle Tanner. I find it's good to know someone's name when you have their back in adversity."

At one of the tightest inner bends on the mountain pass which swept to their left next to a small plateau of woodland, someone stumbled as he moved. He said, "Bugger, I think they seen us, Fred." The horses were now quickly slowing as the bend approached. Normally the drivers kept up a breakneck pace, as fast as enthusiasm would allow.

As the horses slowed, Treacle saw his new-found friend Harvey Taadpole slip his hands into his pig case and, with the skill of a practised hand slide something silvery up his sleeve. It was also totally unnoticed by his fellow passengers who were all concentrating on not being sick, or trying to get as much fresh air in their lungs as possible in a vain attempt to keep down their breakfast.

The horses stopped and the driver spoke some choice words about someone's mother's easy virtue of a road block ahead or would have, if the conversation had been completed. At least the silencing of the driver had saved any delicate souls on board from blushing, as his language was as completely ripe as a late summer strawberry. Treacle thought some of the words the driver used might have had foreign origins; whenever Uncle Ruud said them he always added, "Pardon my Franco-side."

The smiling face of Fred Bent or Bent Fred, as he was casually known in these parts, arrived at the window. His unkempt beard appeared to have half of his lunch stuck inside it and his hair was not much better. His clothes smelled of damp leather and sweaty horses. He really was a rough looking fellow, Treacle thought. No wonder they call them ruffians; he was as friendly as someone who believed they held all the aces, and the weapons too. Fred could be described as a local entrepreneur and a family man, if your family consisted of about twenty grown men whose career progression was measured in their value on dead or alive poster. His professional title was 'Bent as five and five eighths note Fred.' He would always say that if you were going to rob or lie, make it a whopper.

Harvey was the first to step down from the coach. As he glanced back into the coach, he said, "I hope your protector or protectors are professionals."

"Possibly, Mr Taadpole, possibly," Treacle replied.

As Bent Fred lined up the two of them on his side of the carriage, he thought of how clever he was to separate the passengers. Separation creates the possibility for the imagination to work wonders, and that was more cruel than any blade could ever be. Once all of the passengers were outside the coach, he made his demands very clear. "Your money or your life," as he was a great one for tradition. What he really meant was "Your money and your life" but he didn't like giving away the game so quickly. Fred guessed this short stocky man he had forced down from the coach and who now stood before him was trouble. He appeared to have the capability to move quite quickly, as he looked like a coiled snake ready to pounce. Then again anyone would look short standing next to this posh and lanky but mostly posh travelling companion.

Bent Fred wasn't wrong; the little fellow had exceptional speed when he released his knife. But his speed was not so exceptional when compared to Bent Fred's almost uncanny ability to read people's eyes and react with a cat-like instinct. The knife had flown from Harvey's sleeve into his hand as he had lunged forward. But Fred blocked the knife from entering his ribs with his left hand as he punched the short fellow as low as he could with the butt of his sword that he held in his right hand. The low blow knocked the wind out of Harvey and he crumpled onto his knees at Fred's feet, fighting for breath. He was already positioned for Fred to deliver the coup de grace. Fred moved closer to Treacle, for he wanted to see the look of horror in this posh man's eyes as he delivered the killing blow -- he loved watching the rich squirm and hoped the violence would affect this man just like all the others. Fred hoped he would cough up whatever was left of his breakfast that the road had not claimed for its own. There was something about this posh passenger's eyes -- they showed sadness, not fear, but Fred dismissed it as his imagination playing tricks on him.

Treacle would have wished for the darkness of night or a dark corner somewhere, or even not to be in this situation at all, but this ruffian was the type who would push and push until you made a mistake, and then he would cut you down where you stood, just for the fun of it. He hoped his expensive education would pay for itself today, but one never knows. There was always someone faster, someone cleverer and sometimes those who were just plain lucky. He had kept back one small secret which would work to his advantage -- he too had a weapon or two up his sleeves. His hands moved so fast that Fred didn't even see them hit him. All he felt was the sharp points of pain that seemed to be emanating from all across his body as Treacle's strikes hit nerve clusters and major organs alike. The sixth blow against Fred's neck was enough to make him drop to his knees next to Harvey. At school Treacle had been taught to respect all life, but life had taught him otherwise. A hand came down with the force of an executioner's axe, leaving Fred with one last mortal thought -- Why had the eyes not stopped staring at him or shifted focus, or just gave him a hint of what was to come?

Fred stood up and dusted down his soul. Looking around with fresh eyes, he saw everyone as if for the first time for what they really were. He then looked down at his lifeless body at his feet, and saw Harvey for what he really was. Oh, you're a naughty boy, Fred thought. He had pulled some strokes in his time, and turning with his finger raised to berate this posh lanky beanpole of man, he saw something he wasn't quite expecting and so let his finger slowly drop. Even in death Fred had respect for his betters. He now saw his so-called "friends" as the hideous and ruthless individuals they really were. He now knew his "friends" had stolen not just from the innocent strangers their career paths had brought them into contact with, but from him personally. It was the sly way a ring or coin "accidentally" slipped into their pockets before the divvy. What about the code? He wondered. What about the bonds of blood? -- mostly someone else's but even so, it was still valid. Then there were so many other times they had taken advantage of him. Once or twice he had drunk himself unconscious and had slumped across a table. His so-called "friends" had always used such an opportunity to go through his pockets looking for change. If his soul could have manifested itself at that moment he was sure he would have discovered if a man could survive to the hundredth cut, or if that was not a myth also.

In front of Fred a set of muddy stairs appeared. They led down to a large well-lit door, and the warm red glow of the sign illuminated his face. The sign read "Hellfire Club" and in smaller letters just below it "New members always welcome." Fred knew he would one day go to hell -- it sounded more like his sort of place with debauched parties and all you could drink at any time day or night. Hell sounded better compared to his and the church's belief that heaven was full of prim and prissiness. Fred wasn't going to be let down. In the afterlife he got everything he had hoped in total, never-ending abundance.

Bent Fred was dead. The now ex-thief's friends and partners in crime glanced at the broken body now face down in the mud under the carriage on the far side of the coach, then at each other, then the body again, and all at once their imaginations ran riot. They all had the same thought -- first, this was a sign from the gods. Second, the thought that everyone knew, death always hunted in threes and being second or third held no appeal. They all turned and ran as fast as their legs would carry them to become upstanding members of society, for at least a week or two until the heat was off.

Treacle helped the now smaller crumpled-looking Harvey up to his feet and congratulated him in his 'I really do not want to be overhead but if everyone could please listen to my voice' sort of way, with a heavy spin of extra volume. "Well done, Mr Taadpole. I have never seen someone kill a ruffian like that before. You are my hero. Here, have this reward, my brave fellow."

Treacle offered an open hand with a single silver coin nestled in the palm. It was a fortune in these parts -- in fact, a fortune in any place Harvey could think of. Yet Harvey knew his attack had failed miserably. He had not even landed a single blow, but who was he to argue? Hell, why would he, especially with someone who had just killed a man with his bare hands?

As Harvey regained his footing in the mud-covered track with the help of his new-found friend, he glanced down at the lifeless body and was horrified by the look on Bent Fred's face. It was an image that would never leave him, Harvey decided. The amount of "Old and Very Peculiar" -- a very intoxicating brew served only under the counter in these parts – it would take to forget he certainly couldn't afford. The look on the dead man's face was certainly novel to Harvey. He had seen many dead bodies in his time. With some, he had the misfortune to create their state of death. While many wore an expression of surprise, they never kept that look by the time death claimed them. Nothing had been as surprisingly quick as what had happened to Bent Fred, who appeared to still be gloating.

Deciding that an inspection of the body might upset his new-found friend or might come across as a bit ungrateful, Harvey deemed ignorance was the better course of action. But why had this man congratulated him? He himself had done nothing, but an argument about who killed whom was not in the cards when silver was concerned.

A life debt -- how could Harvey repay that? A man who could break your neck in a split second while looking immaculate doesn't normally have many enemies. If he did, they didn't live very long, he surmised. Then there was that small question of how he managed to do it. He didn't even look that strong. With that pale, pasty countenance he looked none too well, especially now that he was in the bleached sunlight and out of the dark carriage interior.

As the passengers resettled back into their seats they all gave Harvey a round of applause, and patted him on the arm in a very courteous manner. For the rest of the journey, everyone kept a very discreet distance and gave him a nod, the type of nod and distance a penitent gave a priest after his indiscretions had gone public before confession. The footman pulled himself up to the driver's seat and shouted some obscenity at the horses. They were then on their way again. No one stopped for the dead on mountain passes unless joining them was one's last goal in life.

Treacle sat and let his temper subside. He was angry at himself; he should have managed to talk his way out of that type of situation rather than resort to violence. He straightened his jacket from its bottom edge again, as if by doing so it would straighten his mind. Later he wondered why his new friend had not bothered to check to see if the ruffian was dead before getting back on board the coach. It wasn't what people did in these situations. He decided that his clan leaders could be right -- maybe they didn't understand the real world that lay beyond their hill country. The journey to the next way-station was quieter than before, with much more forced smiles and a nice nod whenever eye contact was made.

The journey took all day before finally arriving at the way-station at the foot of the cliff face. The way-station sat on a small outcrop of solid rock in a landscape of marshy wilderness. It was constructed like a small fort on the sides that faced the coach way. The side that faced the swamp needed no protection, as the marsh looked as though it could swallow men whole. The road snaked off into the distance and appeared to be the only other firm surface as far as the eye could see.

The coach was allowed through the gate into a large open courtyard and, as the footman jumped down to open the doors, he made sure to inform the passengers that the next mail coach would not wait for those who were late, no matter what the excuse. Their connecting coach was already out of the stables, being prepared. While porters double-checked the mail as it was loaded on board, exactly one hour was allotted for lunch. Every preparation was intended to get passengers onto the next coach as quickly as possible.

After his customary single glass of the local red wine and some blood sausage, Treacle sat and observed the chaos at the coach company's desk. It seemed that every traveller was being rebooked on a later coach or had made alternative arrangements for the next stage of the journey – except for his new friend Harvey. He was very healthily demolishing a bowl of sheep's head stew with the eagerness of someone who had been snatched from the jaws of death and didn't want to miss a single thing, especially his new generous guardian angel leaving on the next coach.

Harvey too, watched the chaos at the coach company's desk. He thought, what silly fools his fellow travellers were to negotiate travel by any other means possible. Would it not be safer to travel with the devil himself than without any protection in this bandit country?

When the coach departed, this time Harvey let Treacle board first with a sweep of his hand in a mock bowing motion, a wide grin on his face. But now Harvey had no worries when it came to a choice of seats. It was only just the two of them and he could sit almost anywhere he wanted.

"Travelling all the way to the Great Smog, Mr Tanner?" Harvey inquired.

"You can call me Treacle if you wish, Harvey. We are friends, I hope."

Never one to let an opportunity slip by, Harvey said, "Yes, I hope so. Maybe we can do some business together." But Harvey couldn't imagine what he could possibly offer a man with the skills Treacle had already demonstrated.

Treacle thought for a while and replied with the straightest of faces, "I think you can help me get started in the police force."

After Harvey's coughing fit concluded, he agreed to help. One never knows when a favour gets repaid, he reflected, and one favour in the bank with a police officer could pay off dividends later.

Treacle, seeing that the pleasant conversation could possibly turn from "Isn't it a nice day to join the police force?" to a full conversation about pets and family, to finally, "Where did you learn to kill someone like that?" pulled his collar up in front of his face and fell asleep. Harvey saw this for what it was -- a polite way of stopping the conversation stone dead, and decided that that might have been his outcome should he continue to inquire further.

Pigly Poke

Shiny Buttons – Memory Trick

Moral Compass

As the coach approached the night's layover, Harvey sat and watched the town of Pigly Poke emerge from the horizon and slowly grow in size. Pigly Poke was the sort of town Harvey liked. It had a high turnover of visitors looking for a good time – not that they really found it, but it was what they expected. The town's main income came from the trading of all manner of goods in its markets and had the enviable position of being the gateway town between the upper and lower plains. In fact, it was the only town for miles, positioned on a heavily silted river that flowed through and down to the sea, carrying rich pickings for those who knew what to find in its murky waters.

Treacle awoke a few minutes before arriving at the town's gate. He stretched his legs and peered through the coach window at the approaching town before turning to Harvey. "Would you please join me for a meal, Mr Taadpole, and we can discuss your future?" he asked. Treacle thought the meal would keep his new-found friend busy while deterring him from landing in any trouble or keeping trouble from finding him. He would be alongside him to help with some well-placed words of appeasement. Treacle didn't want to lose his newly appointed guide to the big city, especially since they hadn't even arrived yet. Deciding to err on the side of caution, he wanted to accompany him just in case, to steer him away from danger.

The carriage dashed into the courtyard of the "Well Pass Inn", and rattled to a stop opposite the front door. Outside the inn stood Ron, or as the locals called him, Running Ron. Due to the emptiness of his pockets and his stomach that morning, he had decided to undertake his famous ruse of grabbing a piece of luggage and running off before anyone realised it was gone. He would be almost to the bend in the lane before anyone noticed the loss of baggage; once out of sight, he could duck down the alleys and make good his escape.

Harvey noticed the old man in the doorway in his long red coat with two rows of shiny buttons running down each side, looking like new. He then noticed the old man's trousers that looked like their owner, about fifty years old, with frayed edges and a well-maintained look that meant the trousers were the man's only pair. His appearance said everything Harvey needed to know, including the old doorman's trick, something Harvey's father had warned him against as far back as he could remember.

Upon seeing this man and having a mental image of how the world should work, Treacle thought, *Isn't it nice to have a doorman to greet you? The inns must be of a much better quality on the lower plains.* He promptly stepped forward and thrust his large black bag that had been sitting on the top of the coach, unnoticed by all, into Ron's awaiting arms. *"My good man, take this to MY ROOM please."* Treacle wasn't totally unaccustomed to the ways of a good thief but he liked giving someone a chance to reform.

Ron looked at this stranger with his piercing eyes and felt his legs start to move, but to his surprise and a creeping sense of horror, rather than running at full tilt down the road he walked into the inn and right up to the bar. He wanted to scream; instead he politely asked for the room key. After receiving Treacle's room key, he found his legs were completely beyond his control. They propelled him up the stairs and down the hall to the room number indicated on the key. Letting himself into the room he watched his arms drop the bag onto the bed, then his legs quickly twisted round and took him down the stairs before he had a chance to grab the bag back. He heard the sound of the door locking behind him, echoing down the hallway. Arriving shortly thereafter at the table of this smart new stranger, he found his good deed rewarded handsomely with three copper pieces. Ron thought the reward was one copper piece more than his brother, the proprietor of the used luggage shop, would have given him for his troubles.

On his walk home from the inn, Ron felt an epiphany. What it meant, he didn't know, but during the long walk he decided that perhaps, at this point in life, being a legitimate doorman living off tips might increase his life expectancy and wealth. In any case, he was getting too old for all this running -- it was tiring and the cobbles were not doing his knees any good. As the adage goes, "Tomorrow is another day." When it arrived he would go straight round the station and inn and offer his services for all the tips he could muster.

Treacle and Harvey sat at a central table in the lounge bar. Harvey kept his eyes on the bar, where his experience told him trouble always started by someone spilling drinks or nudging someone else. Meanwhile, Treacle faced the door, as this small crowd could never amount to much worry. Only a mob bursting through the door, baying for blood would push him past the threshold of turning and running from trouble.

Treacle recalled a time back in the old country when a mob had reached the door of the mansion and Uncle Ruud had politely talked them down with his total agreement strategy. Yes, it was a disgrace. Yes, it was awful; in fact, it was terrible that the old coachman had been killed and, with each agreement, Uncle Rudd incrementally drained the mob of its anger, particularly when he said he would kill the guilty person himself if he knew who it was. Soon they had dispersed and he undertook a thorough investigation, exactly as he said he would. After six months of investigation, covering hundreds of interviews, everyone agreed that no one could make a proper living with these constant disturbances in their lives and asked the local mayor to quietly ask Uncle Ruud to drop the case. Then Uncle Ruud had the gall to state that he still had several lines of inquiry he really wished to pursue but, if they insisted, he wouldn't continue and would consider the case closed, as so should the mob. With a humble bow, the mayor took his leave, thanking Ruud for such an exhaustive inquiry. As the door closed on the contrite mayor, Ruud announced aloud as a warning to nobody in particular, "That's how to stop the mob and have them thank you for it. But the person who did kill the coachman better never say it in front of me. Otherwise it really will be the last thing he ever says."

The bar conversation was exactly as any other bar you might find on the lower plains at the edge of the mountain pass -- a lot of salesmen and talk about pig farming and the odd interjection regarding the newest pig oinkment treatments. Pig oinkments would cure anything if you listened to the salesman long enough, including the winter chill, if you drank it yourself. Treacle thought one normally had to pay for an education such as this, but here it was totally free if you listened intently and long enough. As he drank his customary glass of red wine following a day's journey overland, Treacle overheard a conversation on swine flu and how a farmer could catch it by staying out with his herd overnight in the cold, or standing in a damp environment. After hearing a salesman discuss one of his more remote journeys and his belief that swine flu could even be caught by standing next to someone with a cough, Treacle turned to Harvey and said, "I'm looking for a good man to be my assistant. Well, not an assistant. What's it called? Cat's...."

"...Bits," Harvey interjected without following or even listening to the conversation.

"no, no, cat's torso. That's it -- my cat's torso."

"You mean dog's body, I think,' Harvey corrected after a couple of seconds of trying numerous sentence combinations in his mind.

"Well, if that is the case, a dog's body will do. That's someone who does the dangerous jobs when there is a good chance that any mistake could get you left in an alley resembling a dog that's gone under the cart wheels," Treacle said with a smile.

"Stop pulling my dangly bits. It's not really my sense of humour, my new found friend," Harvey said with an edge of acceptable annoyance in his voice.

"Yes, a laugh is always good fun, don't you think, Mr Taadpole? Especially at the beginning of a discussion on paid work, don't you think?" Before he could pour scorn, Treacle waved him off. "But seriously, I can pay a single silver piece a week. I know it's not a lot for someone with your talents but it's a regular income for a man of your...." He suddenly felt every eye within the bar turn upon him. A single silver piece was a year's wages in these parts. By mentioning a mere few words, he now was targeted by half the bar's clientele. Treacle could hear plans being made in every corner of the bar with scenarios involving a dark alley and the involvement of assorted weapons ranging from swords, lead pipes and, he was sure, he heard talk of a two-by-four, whatever that was. Following so many simultaneous conversations was hard work and most were blowhards talking a good game, but the three at the bar, he could smell their adrenalin rising. They were not going to wait for the anonymity of an alley somewhere, when stealing everything right here would do just fine. Treacle quickly had to speak the words to control their memories before the adrenalin stopped him from having any control at all.

""*Please forget everything I have said except you of course, Harvey my old friend.*""

The bar snapped back into its normal routine and Harvey felt he had known Treacle all his life. It was a good trick from the old country which had fallen out of fashion due to the lack of clan members who would be susceptible to such influence.

Harvey didn't need to run this career opportunity past his moral compass. Once, he had been so lucky to obtain three silver pieces in a crooked game of happy pig family and spent the next two months so drunk that he still didn't know how he ended up in the middle of the road, tied to a stuffed sheep carcass, but what a story to tell your friends, if you had any. He already decided to say yes and to put the moral compass back in its box for a less well-paying job in the future. He replied in the affirmative and saw Treacle's smile -- a big, broad smile that showed all his teeth. He immediately regretted saying yes; he should have asked for danger money or maybe a garland of garlic.

Treacle, now fortified with the knowledge that he had a rather streetwise individual in his employ, was rather happy with himself, even if the expense was on his own account. A successful outcome in this mission for the Clan elders could elevate him to full membership. It could even move him into the executive where he would be above orders or clan duty and enjoy a nice, bother-free life for a while.

Harvey appeared to drink copiously to his good fortune, yet all night his glass never emptied -- a trick he learnt from less hospitable bars where the locals would watch you drink yourself stupid and then strip you of everything except your life. Many a morning he had awoken naked, dumped in some ditch miles from the nearest town. While his skill did not go unnoticed, it was completely unmentioned by his new employer.

Mrs Higginbottom's Academy

School Expenses – White Feathers

Ivana rob you

In the city of Great Smog it was the day of the debutante's ball at "Mrs Higginbottom's Finishing Academy for Young Ladies." The academy was world renowned even while the Great Smog remained shrouded in obscurity. The academy lessons invariably included needlecraft, speaking in public, How to win friends and influence people and budget management for young ladies. Due to their extremely high station in life, the students were expected to grasp that these lessons had evolved over the years to reflect the more modern times in which they lived. Needlecraft started with darning socks and progressed to suturing soldiers or personal guards in a running field battle. Speaking in public covered the finer points, such as winning over locals by fluently speaking any one of five languages, to what to say when accepting your crown at your coronation. Lady Aggy, whose lesson in how to win friends and influence people was, in itself, considered worth the academy fee, steep as it was. Her model for peace- making between years five and six over their tuck shop privileges had been used by politicians for the last 20 years to the betterment of all, due to its ability to get a lasting peace. Professor Smyth, another instructor, taught accountancy and law at the academy and had set records for the longest and most complex employment contract in history. A forensic audit several years ago had managed to track his wages through several tax loopholes before the money trail disappeared completely. All that was found seemed to have been spent on the academy's school supplies.

Professor Smyth was also famous for his home, which had to be seen to be believed. Its name, "Pencil Case Hall," was carved in a marble plaque built into the front wall. Just next door was "Fountain Tip Stables," the home of many exceptional horses including "HB Pencil," the favourite in the running of the next steeplechase. The Professor's lessons taught the young ladies the gamut of economics, from balancing meagre budgets of small countries, to trading in international option derivatives. The graduates of the academy possessed business acumen unknown anywhere else in the civilised world.

From this hotbed of education Mabel Stirrup was matriculating today. She had not been born into wealth but had it fall upon her; more precisely, an extremely rich merchant visiting the city had fallen on top of her by accident. The merchant, wishing to appear a generous fool with his money, had paid for her treatment and schooling as well as numerous column-inches of newsprint announcing his charitable works. Recently, she had read that her benefactor had forced his competitors on hard times with his extremely complex, three times more costly, buy-one- get-one-free offer. She considered that the population of the city always liked getting something free, and that the feeling of getting one over Johnny Foreigner was an absolute winner of a business model.

At the moment, Mabel was readying herself for the grand ball. She had no choice in the matter; the only home she knew was here in the school. Much to her dismay, no excuse was acceptable for not appearing at such a prestigious event on the school's calendar. She also had to tolerate these vulgar white feathers in her hair, all because some bloody girl eighty years ago wore them, thinking they were cool. Then the next year everyone copied her so it became a tradition. She was sure if she was in charge, stupid traditions like this would be the first to go. The second worst problem in her life at the moment was the fact her benefactor had just made his final payment to her, which only covered her academy fees. So she had nearly nothing left for a new white dress, another traditional item. She tried her best with one of bed sheets but it wasn't her best creation.

As Mabel looked in the mirror, she decided white feathers weren't really the right colour for her fiery red hair that fell around her shoulders in light curls. For the ball, she had attempted to create a dress that replicated the classic design seen on most of the famous statues in front of the academy's finer buildings. But unlike those statues, she made sure she didn't suffer from a wardrobe malfunction and expose herself, especially if she needed to carry a large jug of pouring water.

Sadly, the effect of her dress, due to her stick-thin figure, made her look more like a piece of confectionery, she believed, called a lollipop.

Since she started at the academy, her money never went far enough, so she had to create half of her clothes herself to keep her dignity intact. One of the local fabric shops had hired her for holiday work in the summer for which she was paid by the yard. One lucky day, while on the shop floor, she was "discovered" -- she thought she knew exactly where she was, but that's how the fashion industry phrased her revelation. The agency that "discovered" her supplied the 'IT Girls' to the fashion industry. They offered to take her on a trial basis and see where it led. Mabel held high hopes that this income could at least feed her and keep a roof over her head once she left the academy.

The ball turned out to be the dismal event she expected. The rich girls competed with each other for the most expensive dress and drove their fathers mad by ignoring all the wealthy, eligible bachelors in attendance that had travelled several days at the insistence of the girls' parents. To maintain their crumbling grand homes, those who would inherit titles and large estates chased wealthy bachelors for their money. As for Mabel? Well, everyone knew her history. Some of the more spiteful girls had made sure of that, and who wanted to date a street girl who had luck fall upon her?

The morning had started slightly overcast in the town of Pigly Poke, but Harvey's appetite had been totally undiminished by his revelries from the night before. This fact was proven conclusively when he ordered lots of everything by pointing at the cooked breakfast on the menu brought by the young serving girl. For once, he didn't worry about the cost since his new found employer had offered to pay.

"For you, sir?" the girl asked Treacle.

Treacle turned and gave the girl a smile that could have wooed birds out of a tree. "Some blood pudding and red wine, my dear, if you don't mind, and please stay close. I might want a bite just before we leave."

Their large reinforced carriage had been replaced with a much more elegant "Plains Runner" model. Both Treacle and Harvey were pleased to see cushioned seats and large windows as they entered the carriage of the lightweight mail coach.

Already on board was Cornelius Smidgen, the tax assessor. He was a man who could judge at a glance the real worth of anything he saw and underestimate it, which had won him many a friend in these parts. With his pleasant nature, he only slightly undervalued everything in his extra special way that let one know he was doing a favour, so don't argue or he might have to do his job a bit more competently. Next to him was Mrs. Miller, on her way to see her sister -- a right "Smoggy," as the residents of the Great Smog were known. The two centre seats contained Mr. and Mrs. Etherington, an attractive couple looking for domestic positions in the city. To their surprise, they both were hired by the time they finished describing the reason for their journey. Harvey was shocked to hear Treacle offer them half a silver piece a month for their services. During the course of the journey, Harvey gave the offer some thought and came to recognize that it was an exceptionally good wage, but also demonstrated a much more secure grasp on Treacle's value of money and the value Treacle placed on his own special skill set.

The Etheringtons had embarked on their journey after a very unsuccessful adventure in turnip farming and spent their remaining money, which amounted to their entire life's savings, on one-way tickets to the Great Smog, in the hope that Mrs Etherington's brother Tenacious could put them up for the night if no live-in jobs could be found upon their arrival. Their hopes turned out much better than the couple could have imagined. Three hours after being on the bread line, this extremely well-mannered and immaculate young man had saved the couple's bacon and landed them in clover. His first job for Treacle upon arrival was to find a house of at least six bedrooms with a large cellar for a wine collection, which Treacle planned to start immediately. Mrs. Etherington's task was to order the necessary supplies from the local shops and await delivery once the house was ready.

Upon arrival in the Great Smog, the Etheringtons watched their newly discovered benefactor disappear down a side street, leaving them entrusted with fifteen silver pieces that felt very cold in their hands. They glanced at each other with the look of small children asking for permission from the other to run. This notion was quickly dismissed, as the wealthy can afford to get the law on their side. Next would have been a final remedy handed down with the sentence normally delivered by someone called "Hang 'Em High" or some other name of finality. They had no choice but to do their duties by their new employer as best they could. Mr. Etherington quickly discovered a talent hitherto unknown to him and his good wife, by the discovery of the greatest property crook in the city's history. Ivana Gazump had had a property sitting on her books for the last three years, and every time someone had made their first step inside its hallway, a strange feeling of dread would fall upon them, and only the sound of their feet running down the street was proof that she had shown this property to anyone at all. To her amazement, that morning a stranger had walked in from the street and asked for a house of historical significance with at least six bedrooms.

"It's your lucky day, my good man," Gazump proclaimed. "I just so happen to have a property with sixteen bedrooms."

"How much?" Mr. Etherington briskly asked.

"Well, since it needs a bit of tender loving care, it could be let out at 50 silver pieces per annum or it could be purchased for 25 gold pieces...."

Before she could finish, Mr. Etherington almost snapped her hand off to snatch the keys, no questions asked.

"My employer will settle the fee, Ivana!" Etherington shouted as he exited the building and ran down the street.

Ivana began to wonder why the man was so keen for this standing death trap. Surely he wasn't doing anything underhanded. Was there something she'd missed? She was sure she had sold every fitting and fixture and some structural parts of the house. No, she couldn't possibly have missed anything.

Likewise, Treacle's day was proving to be very successful. With a little help from Harvey's navigational skills, he had found the main police station located at the main junction of several major roads. The station appeared to have won awards for its architecture but from which century, Treacle wasn't quite sure. Maybe all of them, he reflected; the building had been extended many times as events and policing had demanded. He pushed open the huge brass doors which, due to the current market value for brass, would have disappeared long ago if they had been mounted on any other building in the city.

Stepping into the station, Treacle immediately felt at home. The layout of the building was exactly like his bank back in Nocte Mortis; the main counter had a reinforced steel cage around it that ran along the back wall. Next to the front door, a large reception desk overlooked events. The desk was mounted so high on a pedestal that its occupant would completely disappear if he leaned back in his chair -- an option always open in times of trouble. On reception duty today was Samuel Pickett, a bear of a man who was now too large to walk the city streets and so just let the city orbit around him. Sitting upon the desk next to him was an extremely heavy crossbow loaded and waiting, ready for trouble. When Samuel Pickett leaned forward and asked if he could help, Treacle had responded with a request to see the Chief Constable about a job in the force.

Samuel's copper brain rejected the question out of hand and he had to repeat his query to Treacle. "How can I help you?" he asked again, stupefied.

"Yes mate, I am here for a job on your coppering squad," Treacle said in a phony, dumbed down conversational voice.

After taking a long, hard look at the posh gentleman before him, Samuel decided that this man had more money than sense. He must be a deluded fellow for asking to work here; no doubt an officer would be required to take this guy down to St. Bart's, the local hospital for the insane, lame and the not-quite dead yet.

After Samuel ushered him down many a corridor, Treacle arrived at length to Chief Constable Quern's office, which smelt of stale coffee and much staler cigarette ash. Quern lived up to everything Treacle thought a chief constable should be. He had white, wavy hair that seemed to be a little out of his control and, as for his big bristling moustache, it was obviously stained by tobacco smoke because it emitted a golden sheen. His suit of gold braid was obviously not worn by choice. It was most probably a demand of the office, Treacle surmised, because it looked as though it was bought without its wearer being fitted.

As they shook hands, Treacle wondered why policeman and soldiers always tried to break your fingers when they greeted each other. Maybe it was some form of initiation rite, something he felt he needed to correct the next time someone shook his hand. As for the Chief Constable's eyes, they seemed to be weighing Treacle's soul or more precisely, judging his morality. Chief Constable Quern dismissed Samuel, sat back down in his large and extremely well-worn leather chair, and put his two hands together at the fingertips as though he were making a temple out of his fingers.

"How can we help you, Mr. Tanner?" he asked in a voice calibrated for special visitors, just in case he had misheard Samuel saying this young man wanted a job.

"Chief Constable Quern, it's my wish to join your esteemed force," Treacle began. "My Uncle Ruud has heard so much about your no-nonsense yet flexible approach to law enforcement that he requests I spend a year in your employ before returning home to Nocte Mortis to start our very own crime unit based on your principles."

Great, Quern thought, a bloody nob's son is putting me in a very tricky spot. If he refused, there could be hell to pay diplomatically. While diplomacy was not really his department, Quern recognized that the subsequent screaming and possible grilling quite literally over an open fire might not only warm his cockles but totally incinerate them. But if he said yes, he would be providing a year of protection duty. In this city there wasn't a policemen's job that wasn't dangerous; even Samuel had his moments of excitement on the front desk. Well, they were very brief moments until one of his tree-like arms crashed down on some mouthy thug's head and knocked him out till Tuesday.

After considering the situation for a while, punctuated by lots of puffs on his cigarette, he noticed the young lad in front of him had not squirmed or tried to fill the silence. In fact, this youth was creating more of a damn silence than he possibly could, which was quite an art form in itself. Perhaps a test, Quern decided. Something observational maybe, and when he fails he will be sent home with his tail between his legs, better disappointed than dead.

"Tell me what you see, young man," he said as he spread out his arms to encompass his office.

Treacle glanced this way and that and said, "Bright-white."

"Pardon?" Quern asked, moving forward in his chair, not quite believing his own ears. This guy is really one cup short of a tea set, he thought.

Treacle smiled indulgently and said, "Would you like me to expand on that a bit, sir? I think you will find it quite interesting." Following a sceptical nod from the chief constable to proceed, Treacle continued. "The sink in that corner is a Bright-white model Six built about 150 years ago, mostly used in stables. Normally utilised by stable boys for cleaning their boots, it has the extra high taps for filling buckets and other such tasks. So I surmise this was the stable boys' washroom back in its past some time ago."

If Chief Constable Quern wasn't the longest serving officer on the force, he wouldn't have remembered old Lord Potts gifting his stable for use as the first police station, which happened during the first or second year he was on the force. This boy looked like a chinless wonder, Quern observed, but with a head like this he actually might be able to keep it on his shoulders.

"I have made a decision, Mr Tanner," Quern said. "We will take you on for a month and we will see what we shall see."

Treacle gave him a firm handshake, hoping it was just the right amount of force to instil confidence. As the door shut, Quern leaped to his feet, shaking his hand vigorously to return feeling into it. In his younger days, he had shaken hands with Officer Bone Crusher Smith, but that didn't compare to the vice like grip Mr Tanner had just given him. He was probably a foreign officer, Quern concluded. Some sort of military training obviously lay in that young man's past or maybe he was once trained to kill the enemy with a just a handshake.

As they walked away from the police station, Harvey felt a sense of extreme relief that it wasn't him who had to enter inside. In his experience, people with his experience who entered such a place usually found their careers come to a dead stop, quite literally.

He and Treacle made their way across the Great Smog while he pointed out the major parts of the city as he remembered them. They slowly made their way back to their previously-agreed meeting place with the Etheringtons. Harvey had insisted to his companion in the nicest way possible that the couple would have done a bunk, scarpered, vamoosed, run away but Treacle was adamant that their trustworthiness would win out.

The Etheringtons met them halfway across the Temptation of the Mermaid Square (which famously possessed a statue of a shipwrecked mariner with his head in his hands as he rested against the lone coconut tree of an extremely small island -- some of the locals affectionately called it by its nickname "The Thinker") with the keys to their new property and Ivana's word that it only needed a little bit of loving care to bring it up to scratch.

They all set off to find this dream property to prepare it for that night's habitation. Once they had found Higher Reach Lane, the property in question became blatantly obvious, as there was only one property not tended to by an army of servants at their owners' beck and call. Their new digs looked as though a century had elapsed without anyone even removing the cobwebs from its creaky structure. It was the only building on the street that looked like it was not worth a fortune. In fact, it looked ready to be condemned as unfit for any living creature -- even dead rats littered the property grounds. All that was required for the property's total demolition was a small hammer. Maybe a good knock on the front door would have completed the job.

As Treacle entered the property, a huge force blew past him, nearly knocking down the three servants standing behind him. Either the house had let out a large sigh of relief or its present occupier had decided it was time to move on before the street really went to the dogs. Harvey wondered if Treacle had flashed his pearly whites at the property and a spirit within had quite rightly fled. Certainly the house no longer had that feeling of dark foreboding; it now had a welcoming feeling, light and breezy. It was almost possible to describe it as homely, if your home looked like a long, lost crypt covered in cobwebs, with creaking and wonky floors and an off-chance you might plunge through a piece of rotten flooring to your death.

'Harvey, see to it the builders come in here and just smarten things up a bit tomorrow, would you?" Treacle said.

Harvey considered this the understatement of a lifetime and this was compared to a lifetime of understatement, including the time he and his mates painted Martin Snodgrass's cat pink and sold it as a sick hairy pig -- ah, happy memories.

Half an hour later outside the offices of Ivana Gazump, a stranger pointed at her through the window and entered by the main door. He appeared at her desk before she had time to stand and slip out the specially installed trap door just behind her desk.

"My good woman, I am Mr. Tanner, Mr. Etherington's employer," he announced. "I am here to purchase the property on Higher Reach Lane, as agreed."

"That would be 25 gold pieces, please." Ivana said assertively. She found that by drawing a line in the sand, verbally speaking, she stopped the haggling and informed everyone as to who was in charge.

"Twenty gold pieces I think would be a sufficiently generous sum, Ivana," Treacle intoned. Returning to his normal voice, he said, "I can call you Ivana, can't I? It does say that on the door."

Ivana's mind started to fog -- she had told so many lies over the years that she didn't know where the truth lay anymore and then there was that voice again. *"Twenty gold pieces will be acceptable, Ivana."*

She felt the voice reach her very soul and squeeze a modicum of truth or a little grain of honesty from her. It's said you can't con a con artist, but that only held true if they could think coherently without having a tightening singular thought running forever around and around in her mind. It was worse than when she drank a copious amount of fermented apple juice and imagined she was spinning around and around in her bed. It was much worse than... than.... She couldn't think -- that all-consuming thought had pushed every other idea out of its way. "Yes, yes, a hundred times yes!" she cried. "Whatever you think is acceptable." she cried.

"Thank you, Ivana," Treacle said warmly. "It was a pleasure doing business with you and I am sure you still made a respectable profit on this transaction." He pressed twenty gold pieces into her hot, sweaty palm and closed his hand in a tight ball around hers. "I think you won't regret your decision."

Strangely enough, Ivana never did. Treacle left "Ivana's Elegant Property Auctioneers" feeling that he had paid a fair price for a fair property, which it would be once about fifty more gold pieces had been spent on improvements.

On the walk back to his new residence under the hazy glow of the noonday sun, Treacle looked around and thanked a god -- whatever god happened to be listening to him at the time – for the choking, smog-filled streets where no direct daylight had fallen for decades. The filtered, bounced and reflected light had taken an extremely long path to reach nowhere in particular. He decided he was going to really enjoy the Great Smog; it was his sort of town.

On his arrival at the house, Treacle found that Harvey already had Mr. Wren, a builder, touring the property. Mr. Wren made extensive use of the builder's standard conversational technical terms -- "um," "tut," and "oh." After several hours of noting everything, double checking his figures, then adding to his notes again, Mr. Wren submitted a bid of forty eight gold pieces and nine silver pieces to secure a dream property in record time. Included was the most advanced security system money could buy.

Treacle looked at the builder and, in a flash, measured the man's honesty. He offered the same money without the trained death hound serving as a security system. It was easier to say "I am allergic to dogs" than to tell the truth, and much more acceptable than saying the dog would never stop barking and growling in my company, and I would most probably be the first person it attacks if I let it loose. Thus Mr Wren was employed to start work immediately, with a very hefty bonus upon early completion for a very modest retainer, paid in cash.

That evening, three rooms were found to be habitable enough to sleep in. Treacle, being the master of the property, had first dibs: his choice of the cook's room, the butler's room or the basement. He chose the basement, as it contained a large packing case which he considered an ideal starting place for creating a comfortable bed for the night. Too, the idea of falling through the rotten floor in the middle of the night did not hold any appeal to him.

There's a First Day for Everything

A Handshake - Three rules of Policing

A Slap to Sobriety

Each morning Treacle's day started with his almost fanatical requirement of blood pudding, which he claimed stirred the blood. Harvey understood this to be a joke posh people said to each other over breakfast, or at least he hoped they did. Treacle waved his fork with its blood sausage hanging off the end at Harvey and, between bites, inquired of his new employee what he would be doing today. Harvey couldn't really be considered servant material since he was so very skilled at what he did.

Treacle already knew the answer before it was even asked, but there is such a thing as manners and giving the impression of free will. Harvey shrugged -- his duties with the builder had been completed and Mr Wren's site manager kept everything running smoothly. Anyway, Harvey felt he should find an excuse to get out of

61

this mad house of builders working on top of each, but could not think of one fast enough.

"Then in that case, my friend, why don't you go down to the docks and find out a few things for my uncle?" Treacle suggested. "He's thinking about creating an import-export company and wants to purchase some wine in bulk to fill the cellars at Nocte Mortis. He was wondering about sailing timetables, the ships' capacities and the prices that would be involved in the rental of such."

So it was agreed Harvey would go down to the docks and find out about the ships that sailed and their destinations. What else Treacle's uncle was planning to export and import other than wine was not exactly clear but, Harvey decided, it was prudent to ask some questions so as to look intelligent and to find the right answers for his new friend. "So do you know how much wine exactly" he enquired

"Oh, several casks I guess" Treacle offered before realising his mistake "Several Barrels maybe, it does come in barrels doesn't it"

Harvey didn't know the answer to that, but still wanted to know more "I will find out. How frequent does he require delivery"?

"Who? Oh my uncle requires delivery once a month I suppose, maybe a whole ship could be rented, what do you think?"

Harvey was no fool -- he knew his employer was up to something. He didn't know what yet, but he damn well was going to find out and get a piece of the action.

Treacle arrived five minutes early for his shift at the city's main police station. It was against his nature but a show of enthusiasm was better than appearing precisely on time. Chief Constable Quern was duly impressed, as most of his staff on their first day usually turned up in the evening. New officers thought six thirty only occurred once a day rather than the customary twice. Treacle learnt very quickly that on the force there was a lot of paperwork requiring his signature. He had to sign for every accoutrement he was individually given. The first signature was for his shiny, nearly gold badge which he noticed had been manufactured by the world famous alchemist James Flash, who had cornered the market on his patented "nearly something materials." The reason why James Flash enjoyed an element of fame, so to speak, was because once he had nearly converted one material to another, he simply stopped experimenting. On the other hand, his more crazy contemporaries would use increasingly exotic methods of conversion with more combustible materials. He could have used substances that glowed and were as hot as the sun. Instead, he reasoned, such a creation should be used only if one wanted to create the sun in your basement and wanted a suntan this side of crispy. He considered himself an old fashioned alchemist, more interested in making one material appear as another just long enough for him to get paid and get out of town.

Then it was down to the stockroom to meet old Bill, who worked in the cage, as it was called. Treacle wondered why the police force needed to lock away their equipment, when they were normally several decades behind in weapon technology compared to the most ill equipped street urchin. Bill looked Treacle up and down as he descended the stairs and disappeared round the back before he even reached the counter. Sometime later he returned with an armful of armour which he dumped on the counter with a "there you go, your stick on a leash" as he pushed forward the truncheon.

Treacle picked it up and swung it around, almost hitting Chief Constable Quern standing behind him. "I suggest you tie it to your wrist to stop someone using it against you" Bill suggested. This piece of advice didn't really help, as anyone willing to use your truncheon against you didn't consider it much more work to use your own arm with your truncheon firmly in your hand against you, but it stopped the lost property chits in the mornings.

Then Bill pushed the armour forward in that way all stock controllers since time immemorial had done, in a large pile on the long counter in front of him, "it's not very nice and a bit old but it works", the armour consisted of a breast plate and helmet, and everything was one size to big. Bill had always subscribed to the words of his dear old mum who said that it may be too big now but you would grow into it.

But Chief Constable Quern was gobsmacked by what his new recruit said next "Excuse me my good man, I wish to make a complaint, this will not do at all". Treacle pushed the armour back across the counter. Nobody had done that before; most were happy to protect their soft bits from hard steel and, the palpable look of shock across the face of the resident stock controller, who went from a king of his own domain to that of a bespoke suit salesman, was plain to see.

Chief Constable Quern decided to let his new charge have his way in order to see what the lad had in mind.

Treacle picked up the cone-shaped helmet with ear flaps, designed to redirect blows away from the occupant's head, and waved it at Bill. "This, what am I to do with this, one blow on my head and it will be redirected straight down onto my shoulders, don't you have a helmet with a flare around the neck." If truth be told, Treacle didn't really know armour that well but he was quite aware of rain's tendency to run down one's collar. With a job described as 90 percent standing around while waiting for something to happen and 10 percent standing around and dealing with what did happen, he didn't need to deal with a soggy collar.

Treacle considered that the body armour presented to him must have been intended as a joke, a little jape for the new boy. For some reason, it covered his body -- in fact, its width was designed to cover two people across the front but at the sides there wasn't enough depth. So a large gap was left on the side, by which some rogue could dice the wearer's kidneys, but Treacle knew that for all practical terms he would have to be stony dead for some rascal to slice and dice him. He indulged the observers by showing that he, the new lad, could take a joke. "Armour shouldn't bend like this should it" he said as he pushed it with his finger. Bill laughed "Ok lad I will get you another". As he took the armour back to its dusty shelf he tried to flex it but found it as solid as any other he had supplied.

The body armour he finally settled upon had a decorative black brass lion's head mounted on the chest. He deemed it perfect, as the arms could easily move while protecting the body within a tube of steel. He also thought he could make it a lot darker, given a bit of polish.

Quern had never seen anyone ask to exchange armour before. As he watched his new ward make his protective sartorial choices, he had the sinking feeling that either he had hired an ex-soldier or a trained mercenary. Quern flat-out hated mercs; he believed they possessed a mind too morally flexible to be compatible with police work. Anyone who would fight and kill for money was little more than an assassin, in his book. Mercs didn't enforce laws; they ensured the survival of the richest. He sincerely hoped the lad was just highly educated in armour and was well versed on the subject. Then Quern remembered the Handshake. He summarily dismissed any fears that ran through his mind. A lad this serious needed to be nurtured, so Quern chose to team him up with a good, solid officer who had a no-nonsense approach. Thus, when the chief constable arrived at the front desk, he called Clump Hammerstone out of the tea room with a customary "Clump I have a new recruit for you to break in, now get out on those streets you horrible lot, oh, remember its good versus evil and we're the good guys, and let's be dangerous out there"

Clump Hammerstone was a solid police officer, built like a brick privy and bald as a coot. He wore a little black beard and moustache which he kept exceptionally well groomed. By the look of his creased and ironed shirt and trousers, Treacle guessed he must be married. Clump's body armour was tightly secured by a large sturdy belt adorned with a variety of useful policing equipment and, as Treacle observed, the belt served an even more practical function -- to hold Officers Clump's trousers up. A truncheon and a sword dangled from the belt and, on either side of the officer's body hung small leather pouches packed with god knew what. Treacle surmised from their size that the pouches held a light snack, maybe a couple of bacon sandwiches, to tide him over to lunch. Clump's hands also had the look of someone who wasn't afraid of a fight; he had small scars and cuts across the knuckles and fingers. If truth be told, Treacle concluded, Clump looked to be a good, solid officer of the law.

"Well lad, policing is easy as long as you don't mind interacting with the public verbally or physically" as he swung his truncheon into the palm of his hand with a thwack. As they walked and talked along the city streets Treacle discovered Clump held a very stoic attitude concerning life within the force. They discussed due procedure, when and where to use the truncheon and the best local places to stand when weathering a storm. Apparently the sword was just for show but came in very handy for cutting cake when one of the officers had a birthday party.

"Every officer has their own theory on how to do the job, but I suggest you are seen at all times and petty crime will generally relocate to somewhere a little darker, somewhere a little quieter, somewhere that was not around you"

This tactic served him well, leaving him only drunks and the stupid to tackle. He explained they were easy enough to control as long as you didn't jump into the midst of a fracas and shout, "Break it up, lads!" while trying to hold them apart. That was a sure recipe to get hit from both sides. Apparently, it was always best to pick one and get them out of the crowd and under control, and continue in that manner and the problem would easily be dealt with. Treacle failed to see the logic of this approach -- if he was in the middle of a brawl, any blow he threw would hit someone. Even if the first guy ducked, sometimes that was even better as the second guy would never see what hit him. Also, Clump informed Treacle that punching out the lights of any miscreant was considered terribly bad form without first following something called "due procedure" -- whatever that meant. He was sure he would find out soon enough.

They had walked a couple of streets when they were approached by an attractive young girl wearing a slinky outfit best described as the accumulated foliage of a couple of bushes. She wanted to know the directions to Tin Plate Hall. While Treacle had only glanced at street signs on his return from Ivana's property shop, he could still accurately work out a route from their present location. As he began to describe to her the shortest route, Clump gruffly interjected with a harrumph.

"It's just up there, miss," he said with a wave of his truncheon. The girl, obviously in a hurry, raced down the street while still trying to maintain the impression of gliding serenely, with what could only be described as the sound of rustling leaves. "You get a lot of that in our job," Clump flatly stated. "It comes with the territory. Don't worry; you'll soon know the city as well as me."

Five minutes later, the girl found herself at the dead end of Angel Street, cursing the oaf of an officer for his useless directions. Why hadn't she listened to the younger one? He at least seemed to know where he was. So she turned around and doubled back to find the sign directing her to Tin Plate Hall. It hung on the alley wall about four shops down on her left. The small alley was a local cut through and opened onto Deane Street, the main thoroughfare to anywhere interesting in this area.

Towards the end of their shift, the market stallholders' lunchtime drinking activities began to spill out onto the street. The sight prompted Clump to recount to his younger companion the three periods of the city's police work. As far as Treacle could discern from the highly over-descriptive examples, there were lunchtime drunks, evening drunks and things that go bump in the night. The night shift normally had the most experienced officers, ones who didn't need to ask their commander what to do, especially when those type of questions arose at about three thirty in the morning after their sergeant had only just got to bed at midnight. Their shift only had to deal with the lunchtime drunks that always caused trouble in the afternoon and, to that end, they arrived at the Barley Sack Pub at exactly three in the afternoon, as if by some stroke of luck or, more likely, by years of Clump perfectly timing his beat. Treacle soon discovered that the daily occurrence was accurately called "Chucking Out Time." The stallholders in the local markets always seemed to cause trouble due to their hard working and hard drinking lifestyle.

"You know" Clump said "I think all this trouble could be solved by paying the men that work on the stalls in the local markets weekly, but it's not to be, and now they get paid by the day, so always have something in their pocket to pay for drinks about this time of day. So get yourself ready, trouble's heading our way."

As the sound of a scuffle broke out, Clump held Treacle back with his sausage-like fingers. The disturbance started from within a bar on the other side of the street, when its noisy conversations abruptly vanished, as if severed by a cleaver. Suddenly, a roar came from pugilists screaming and thumping each other. To Treacle, it seemed the phrase "Fight, FIGHT" grew progressively louder.

"Wait, lad," Clump advised. "We don't want to enter a place where we won't have enough room to swing a truncheon, let alone a fist, at a wayward individual. Let the fight come to us."

Seconds later, the fight rolled out onto the street. Clump, utilizing his lifetime of experience on the beat, circled the battling men like a wild animal searching for prey. Much to Treacle's surprise, Clump didn't pull the smallest battler from the pack. Instead, after deciding on his target, in one great swoosh he slapped a bigger man across the face. It sounded like a thunder clap. As if a ringside bell had sounded the end of a round of boxing, everyone immediately stopped fighting.

Clump held a now-unconscious stallholder by his collar. "Gentleman, I will give you minute to walk away quiet and dignified-like before I choose someone else to slap into sobriety or tomorrow morning, whatever is sooner," he announced.

Two men decided to tackle Clump while the other men ran, fell, picked themselves and ran some more. Treacle would have helped his partner if he had looked like he needed it or had he called upon him, but Clump appeared to be enjoying himself as he quickly exchanged punches with his assailants. Soon the two belligerents, brave from their beer, fell to Clump's sobering hands.

Just as the last man fell Treacle stepped forward with his truncheon in hand and a smile across his face. "Need any help?" he asked.

"Let's get this lot home," Clump laconically replied. "We can't leave them here or we'll be charged with littering." Both officers piled the unconscious men into a readily available wheelbarrow supplied by the barman, who kept one at hand especially for such occasions.

"Why couldn't you find a lighter one to slap?" Treacle queried. "This lout here must weigh eighteen stone."

"It's simple, my lad," Clump replied. "This one lives only a street away on the ground floor of Mrs. Bloom's boarding house with these two idiots. Whereas those other buggers' live miles away and I would like to get back to the station in time for the end of the shift, the customary sticky bun and a nice cup of tea."

Treacle could not find fault with the logic of his senior officer, and his opinion was only confirmed as they easily dragged the man into his lodging and dumped him on his bed. As for Clump, his opinion of the new chap had greatly increased over the last couple of minutes. He was very willing to help, especially with the heavy lifting of the stallholder. It seemed to him that the lad was quite prepared to carry most of the weight in their partnership, even offering to take the shoulders when they lifted the men from the barrow. After leaving the lodging house they made their way back at a pace that could only be described as orderly, arriving at the station's door just in time for the clock to sound the shift change.

Chief Constable Quern was standing at the door like an expectant father hoping his new officer had survived the baptism of fire. Clump gave a nod to his senior officer confirming Treacle had had a good first day on the beat. Quern gave Treacle a pat on the back in acceptance, and pushed his worries that his new officer might have never made it back at all to the back of his mind.

Fair-well to Arms

It Girl – Mr Paisley

Splash of Fame

Today was the day Mabel Stirrup started her job as an "It Girl" or, in the words of the more impolite members of her school, "That Girl." She really couldn't see why they looked down on her for choosing a life that allowed her to wear nice clothes, talk to interesting people and wave a lot at photographers. Meanwhile, her erstwhile classmates were returning home to become princesses and future queens. From her perspective, she couldn't see much difference between their career paths.

Her first assignment for her new employer was to work the international arms fair at Tin Plate Hall, whose previous owner was one of the most successful arms dealers on the continent. The rumour around the city fountains was that his weaponry was constructed from very cheap materials but, since not many customers survived to reclaim their money, he had grown fat along with his wallet.

The designer who was too busy to drop the item off himself had posted a roll of material in the post, with a letter instructing his model to wear this material to the fair, his intention was for it to be draped over her shoulder as a shawl, a fact he forgot to mention in his rush, but Mabel read the letter and got a totally different impression on what the designer required of her. Seeing as the material could be seen right through, except for small leaves strategically scattered across the material had driven her to be creative. By wearing multiple layers of the fabric, she created the effect of it becoming totally opaque to the eye. It imparted a certain allure, hinting that one might see everything while she actually showed very little at all. Her dressmaker tried to explain that sexy was all in the mind and the less you showed while making it appear that you were showing everything was the greatest form of sexy you could achieve. It didn't make sense to her. She was wearing more than she did last night at the debutante's ball, but today she was sexy and yesterday she was described as frumpy.

Once she had arrived at the visually stunning Tin Plate Hall after asking that very nice policeman for directions, she was required to find her client Mr Paisley for her day's agenda. She soon found the stall owner, who was readily identifiable with his pot belly, red cheeks and even redder nose. These were all indications of his dedication to his work, accomplished over numerous years of business. How he forced himself into such a bad physical shape for the sake of a few sales. Was it the money or his employees who drove him to entertain clients in bar after bar? she wondered.

Barry saw his battlefield camouflage first before realising it was covering his new model. "My girl, you look absolutely, what's the word? in season, yes absolutely in season. Can you stand in the middle of the gangway within the main hall and wave, smile and just be nice and keep pointing as many people as possible to my camouflage stall."

It was no coincidence that the arms fair had been timed to fall exactly during the same week as Mrs Higginbottom's debutante ball, as most of the influential members of royalty and their assorted ministers were in town to collect their daughters from the academy and could easily extend their visit for couple of days.

Mabel's day at the arms fair consisted mostly of standing around and looking pretty but this soon became boring, so she added some lazy swaying to demonstrate the way her dress material appeared to resemble a shrubbery. This certainly eased the heavy feeling in her legs from standing all day, but she passed the day's monotony by inhabiting her own little private fairy daydream. She started to notice all the people attending the fair were requesting directions towards Mr Paisley's stall. Oddly, most were women, who wouldn't ordinarily seem to be interested in anything military.

The stall suddenly discovered they were doing a roaring trade, with most of their business in fabric sales for fashion houses, and not a lot of military enquiries, but a sale was a sale, and fashion houses had a tendency to order more material than arms merchants. Barry had never been complemented before on the delicate cut of a leaf; he normally received compliments along the lines of "It looks like a real bush" or "From my tent I could have sworn that was a tree over there." But now he was becoming the talk of the town in certain circles.

Fashion designers began offering him money to print his design on silk in various colours, all of which were much too shockingly bright, in his opinion, but if real money was being offered he decided to give way to progress. How his design in shocking reds or purples was going to camouflage anyone in the jungle was beyond him, unless they needed to hide after an explosion at a paint factory.

Lady Jane, a famous fashion writer, had asked Barry several probing questions concerning the name of the design. His reply of 'Large leaf with curl" was not really acceptable for her decidedly up-scale clientele. Everyone seemed to agree it should be named after the designer or at least part of his name, so the awaiting fashion journalists had all asked him his name. "Barry Paisley," he had replied. The attending fashion reporters had gathered together to officially agree on a name that would do their columns justice and give the name some distinction.

Barry kept insisting on the "Large leaf with curl" name but no one listened. From that moment on it was called "Barry-Cuda." Thereupon, all the customers seemed to have heard of the Barry-Cuda design or knew someone who had told them about it ages ago. They all seemed to be asking for it by name with phrases such as "It's the must-have thing" or, "It's tomorrow's fashion today." Barry's fashion designs for the military went from dusky desert to jungle foliage; in fact, those two types of camouflage were his complete fashion knowledge and comprehension of what his customers required or ever needed to purchase.

Mabel was allowed to keep her newly conferred Barry-Cuda dress in the aptly named collection of "Shades of Nature" to take home with her, but this was more to do with the fact that she was required to wear it again tomorrow at the fair for the last day of trading and the closing ceremony.

The walk home took much longer than the one to the arms fair, since all the young ladies in the street kept stopping her to request the name of her designer and where they could buy a dress just like hers. It did suddenly seem to be smashingly popular.

As she was passing a bit too close to one of the many fountains in the city, a man running up the street and carrying a large black box obscuring his face barged into her. She stumbled on the cobbles in her high heels and tumbled into the fountain. The young man stopped and set his new-fangled camera on its tripod legs before helping the now-drenched Mabel to her feet.

The young man humbly apologised and introduced himself as Davy Hailey as helped her back on to her feet. "So sorry, Miss. I was on my way to photograph you at the fair but I was delayed by a rather gruesome accident at Cooper's Corner back there." He explained he was on assignment for the 'Gazette,' the leading newspaper in the city and he had been dispatched with due haste to get an image of her famous dress for the gossip column before the paper was sent to print.

"Never mind," said Mabel primly. "You will have to photograph me splashing about in the fountain, otherwise I will look totally like a bedraggled cat." Davy duly obliged; he had always wanted to photograph a wet ankles shot, quickly snapping picture after picture of Mabel trying to splash his boots in revenge for earlier soaking.

On his return to the paper, the editor quickly wrote

'Barry-Cuda, Makes a Big Splash'

and sat back in his large leather chair chewing his pencil for about thirty seconds before writing the whole of the front page, pushing the unfortunate death in a barrel story to page three, as it wasn't really front page material without a picture. Mabel, now soaked and cold, ran home and got her feet into a nice bowl of warm water. After an hour of thoroughly warming herself she decided to have an early night, as she just didn't know what tomorrow might bring. Hopefully, not a fever.

Evening of Walking Shadows

When it won't do – Me and my shadow

Treacle came home to find the builders had been busy working on renovations: there were so many of them that he couldn't get an accurate count. His house vaguely reminded him of an anthill -- workers walking this way and that, their belts full of tools, with stacks of flooring planks perched on their shoulders. Treacle couldn't help but be impressed. It appeared to him that Mr. Wren must be employing half of the city's craftsmen on this project. A ten-man team of carpenters had been deployed to the basement, replacing the main support pillar at the centre of the house for an identical pillar without the rot. Milled from a special species of Ironwood, the new pillar would sit where the ghost of the previous pillar had existed. Ironwood was well known for its extreme density, its ability to stand in water for decades without rot or pests getting into its fibres. The builders or "artisans," as Treacle sardonically called them, were ably skilled in the ancient art of wood carving. They drank tea from an earthenware pot; any metal would have been eroded by their over-brewed concoction. In fact, the beverage was so strong they painted it onto the pillar as an extra pesticide control before permanently securing the support into place.

Everyone inside the house had noticed the difference, once the jacks that supported the floors, which had been taking the full weight of the house, were removed. Meanwhile, the corpse of the previous pillar had been removed by giving it a quick sideways blow with an axe, snapping the pillar in two. Now that the imminent danger of the house's collapse had been averted, the builders fell into the habit of half-jokingly informing Treacle that he had barely escaped disaster by telling him again and again "lucky escape there, guv"."

Nonetheless, Treacle was annoyed by the builders in his employ, particularly the end of day justifications they kept giving him for their excessive pay and lack of work. The builders hid the fact that they turned up late and had a two hour liquid lunch before nipping back to be seen when the owner returned home from work. That attitude had to change, and Treacle knew that a little discussion about customer satisfaction was going to be required. *"hey lads, let me tell you something..."*

Treacle hoped that after his little chat, his so called artisans would maintain their newly discovered work ethic, as it was very impressive. Everyone had noticed the drastic change in the house since the new pillar had been installed. Now, if you put something down, it tended to stay where it was placed. Before, the item would slowly slide away toward the dip in the centre of the house.

Once Treacle had pulled up a chair at his dining table, Ethrington slid up next to him with a newly practised ability and said, "With Mr. Taadpole's compliments, sir." His voice was beginning to share the resonance a butler always seemed to collect when in service. Ethrington sat down a large silver tray at Treacle's side of the table. Sitting upon the tray was a bottle of rather expensive looking Franco-side red wine. Next to it, a very generously sized empty glass sat upon a folded piece of paper.

Treacle gazed at the price-label of the bottle next to him. It was a very cheap Franco-side wine, if the price had anything to go by, he decided. It was a bit decadent to have one of those medals pressed into the glass like the more expensive versions to which he was accustomed. But after one sip he discovered that a cheap bottle from a direct shipment delivered this morning was worth many more times on the lips, than an expensive bottle that had travelled by cart for three hot days across dirt track. I must congratulate Harvey in his superb taste, he thought to himself as he opened the folded paper.

The message read:

The Wake My Day –

Direct from Franco-side returning once laden with trotters.

The Sea Knight –

Direct Franco-side returning once laden with turnips.

The Neptune's Cutlass –

Spices and fabrics from the Far East.

The Katchen Diner –

Fishing boat.

The Fisher King –

Fishing boat.

The Knot Big Enuff –

Assorted goods returning to Porta.

The Lady Marie Jane –

A private yacht.

Harvey had been busy, Treacle concluded.

Harvey's day started with a simple set of instructions -- go down to the dock and find out where the vessels sailed from and maybe enquire about cargo costs with the captains, the ones who were still independent and hadn't signed with that Count Alexander. The few remaining independent ship captains who still sailed the seas were trying to pick the meat from the bones of what was a very profitable industry. They tended to specialise, and used their personal contacts and friends to get an advantage over the Count's fleet, which sucked the profit out of every deal. Thus the captains were extremely keen to discuss new business and let slip a lot of secrets about good routes and products that were keenly traded in faraway ports to anyone with the financial wherewithal. As for Count Alexander's fleet, his ship captains knew their employer believed that bleeding edge technology pressed to one's family's throat was a good incentive to provide timely delivery, and stopped people from taking little jobs on the side. The Count had also demanded that the town improve the security around the docks after they started to ask for a ten per cent import duty on all of the goods. Of course there were payoffs and hidden shipments, but the cost had risen dramatically.

In an effort to maximise the import duty and stop the tax from just walking out the door, the docks now had an impressive eight foot high wall with guard towers to watch everything going on, not only within the port area but outside its walls as well. The two tax collectors chosen to run the place hated each other with a vengeance and were always double-checking each other's work, looking for a minor error that could be used as proof that the other was corrupt, or worse, enumerate. The more successful of the two would be rewarded with the position of head of tax collecting -- on appointment; such a position had a little perk slipped under the counter consisting of a few percentage points of the tax income. In fact, both were considered far too ruthless for such an office. If given half a chance and unlimited funds, they would try to take over the country for their next promotion.

To distract them from cutting the council's throat, the sage councillors had wisely placed the publicans at each other's throat -- a ploy that had worked for several years. The council maximised the tax collection by appointing guards to check the goods at the gates to the port. The gates of the port were patrolled by a rather slow-witted cadre of guards, but they always checked and double checked the goods and carts as well as the people moving in and out of the port. Too, the guards used a unique cart checking method and not the customary pitchfork in a bale of hay. The lads had discovered that a large plank of wood easily deflected the thrust of a pitchfork, but their method of fitting everything through a small hole not large enough for a whole person quickly dispelled any attempts to surreptitiously stow-away in or out of the port. The last person who tried had been hammered into the hole with the inevitable consequences to his health. Harvey sat outside the Frog and Toad bar with the largest newspaper he could find. For one reason, he could use it to obscure his face if required and, for another, it gave him a reason to sit there for hours overlooking the port's entrance. The boats could be seen through the open gate, slowly rocking from side to side as their precious cargo was loaded or unloaded. When any of the ships' sailors happened by his most advantageous position, Harvey would give the sob story of his brother the sailor who had gone on to meet his maker, and in his will left a certain amount of money for a drink in his memory. Once the sailors were expertly lubricated, they tended to talk about their time at sea. With his practised cunning and aplomb, Harvey could easily steer the conversation toward events of the last fortnight.

He wandered out of the bar into the darkness of the night, totally drunk by his standard, having managed three drinks all night. He hoped the boy he had paid so well to deliver his message had arrived back at the house, as keeping Treacle happy could mean a totally new and prosperous life.

Walking down the cobbled streets of Portsmith Lane, he could hear the two shadows following behind him. They were good -- in fact, very good -- at not being seen but to not be seen in the light of a full moon meant walking very close to the front of the shops that lined the street. There, rubbish gathered, the type of rubbish that was easily crunched underfoot.

He quickly gathered pace to give a little bit of thinking distance between himself and his pursuers, while still trying to give the appearance of being drunk, until an opportunity could present itself along the road. Opportunities always presented themselves to those who looked for them, and he could see one just ahead in the form of the alley's shadow.

As Harvey drew near to the alley's entrance, he straightened himself and ran inside as quietly as possible. Climbing up the crates at the end of the alley, he pulled himself onto the veranda above. Kneeling now in the shadows of washing to hide his shape and to prevent him from being seen, he could watch the two men below attempt to hide while trying to maintain a new faster pace to catch up with him.

He saw two men -- one large and the other stocky. The first looked like he had never refused second helpings of anything in his life, and the latter resembled a member of the weasel family, full of cunning and years of street fighting wisdom. The moon overhead reflected some sort of weapons glinting in each of their hands. By now they stood within the centre of the street. "Wilf, what are we going to do?" one of the shadowy men asked. "You know we can't return telling them we lost him."

"Let me think," Wilf replied. After a moment, he said, "Got it. We'll tell them we hid his body where no one will find it. It will take days for the corpse to be discovered, and if we see him again we can deal with him then." "Okay, Wilf," the other concurred. "But I think we shouldn't mention him at all." "Right, but if they do mention him he's been dealt with right."

As Harvey watched his pursuers leave the alley, glancing quickly backwards every few steps just in case their prey broke ground, he heard a familiar whisper behind him. "I had your back, Mr. Taadpole. You had no need to worry." Harvey didn't need to turn around, but his curiosity got the better of him, so he slowly swivelled himself around to find Treacle kneeling beside him, wrapped in some sort of cloak as dark as night with no reflection or shimmer. "I wanted to catch you for the last drink of the night, but then I heard someone drunkenly walking toward me followed by two stalkers with a determined sound in their step, so I was curious, and thought I would hide here and see what happened. Surprise, surprise – you used the exact same route on to the veranda as I did." Treacle pointed to two static shadows lingering at the end of the street. "Keep me company on the walk home once our friends have well and truly departed," he directed. "You can tell me later what you have discovered on what was obviously a successful adventure." Harvey felt much more secure on the walk home. He didn't feel the need to bother looking back because he was sure Treacle could hear everything.

Settling In

Working Sounds – Death Flowers

Wine Tasting

Next morning at breakfast, Treacle had two requests for Harvey: one, to find an excellent wine supplier, preferably with a selection of Franco-side wines in stock and two, a blacksmith that could repair the basements wine-cellar's cage. It had fallen from the wall when Etherington attempted to open its doors. As Treacle sat down to enjoy his usual helping of blood pudding, the sound of the workmen could be heard drifting in through the window from outside. It sounded like people actually working rather than the impression he previously had of the crew sitting around over mugs of hot tea, thinking about working. Now the workers found that the moment their shift started they could not stop themselves from starting work. It was as if they were being driven by some sort of internal voice forcing them on, screaming at them to finish as quickly as possible.

At the conclusion of his meal, Treacle caught himself tapping out the sound of the death dirge by the famous composer Reggie Ortis. As he read the story on page three of the morning paper, he thought to make a note of that habit -- first, to stop doing it and second, there must be something lingering in the back of his mind regarding the story he was reading, but what, he didn't know.

The long case clock in the reception area struck the half hour as Treacle made his entrance at the station. He was greeted by Officer Clump, who asked him for a left handed notebook and pencil from the storeroom (an inside joke played on all officers, and considered more sophisticated than requesting a left-handed truncheon). Once these valuable items were procured, Treacle was to proceed outside to meet Clump, who would be catching a breath of fresh air and the pleasure of some fine rolled tobacco.

Treacle equipped himself for the day's adventure and stepped out into the early dawn with Clump by his side. "You have my notebook?" Clump asked with a smile. To his pleasant surprise, Treacle handed him one.

"I'm afraid I could only find a right-handed pencil," Treacle apologised. "I'll try my best tomorrow to find the one you asked for."

Clump was speechless by the resourcefulness of his new underling and decided to keep the little notebook. One never knew when such resourcefulness would be needed and a left-handed notebook might actually be in demand. They both walked at the same steady, exact pace down the road from the station, with Treacle letting Clump lead the way -- a fortuitous decision, as his partner chose a different route this morning.

"Today is Market Day," Clump explained, "and our job is to observe all the crimes that were committed, and their perpetrators. We'll make a note of who the perpetrators are, and let the evening shift pick them up once they've had a few drinks at the bar. But any criminals too slow or too stupid to run away from us are fair game for arrest. And the ones that elude the evening shift are left for the night shift; they've perfected the art of picking up their man from some gutter when he's too drunk to walk."

Their route along the cobbled streets today was an intricate one but, as they neared the market, Treacle detected the smell of the mystic east on the wind, on the wind -- a term employed by the locals, but to his nose it was unmistakably the stench of the death flower. Maybe more than one, Treacle decided, judging from the pungent odour with its near-instant gag reflex. The flower took its name not from the smell -- a fragrance very reminiscent of a dead creature in a privy -- but more from the fact it was used by seagoing vessels below the water line of the ship's hull. It killed all of the burrowing worms and rats. Treacle never ceased to be amazed at what scientists would discover when the topic involved three square meals and the funding for a life of further study. Every sailor in the street knew the rats were really killed by the flowers' fragrance and the stories mostly told in the far side of the Upper Plains mentioned the effects the flower had on the crew, especially when bad weather forced them to stay below decks.

As far as Treacle could gather, the flowers worked on the skin, drying out one's body. The smaller the body, the faster it dried. The time-worn adage "Old sailors never died, they just dried" he thought summed it up completely. The odour became stronger as they arrived at the corner of a street that entered the centre of the market. There, they took a position standing on the steps of a rather smart shop selling cheeses whose smell, although pungent, still didn't cover the flowers' overpowering fragrance.

The view from this slightly elevated position, Treacle quickly ascertained, was highly advantageous. Clump started to describe what a crime looked like, a gesture Treacle considered somewhat fatuous, as up to this point he thought he knew what a crime looked like. One minute something was there, the next it was gone and no payment had exchanged hands. By Treacle's definition, a payment by any medium covered anything of value -- it was either eaten, worn or spent.

"Oh, no," Clump demurred. "In these parts, only money is acceptable -- no matter if a family could eat a week on a basket of vegetables being offered in exchange of payment."

Treacle let the remark pass. It wasn't that he didn't understand money; rather, he recognized its relative value and worth, and knew that when the crops failed, a starving man was not fattened with copper coins.

According to Clump, a crime consisted of several distinct parts. Using an authoritative tone, he informed Treacle that each of these parts could easily be spotted by a trained professional. First, there was the targeting, when the prospective thief looks for the opportunity and goods to steal. Second was the vital act of robbery, which creates the crime, and third was the thief making good his escape.

"Making good the escape and the associated pursuit is the bit everyone believes is full of adventure and scrapes, with fast chases across the city, but I can tell you it's more like a slow walk down the back alleys to the usual suspects' residences," Clump explained. "People are creatures of habit, see? They like the familiar and they feel safe, see?" Clump looked Treacle in the eye to emphasise the point.

As he listened to Clump expound upon the parts of a criminal act, Treacle thought this spiel must be a highly practised and polished statement for use in bars and other social venues designed specifically for when Clump talked to people about what he did for a living. What other social occasions Officer Clump would find himself in, Treacle couldn't imagine.

After about two hours, the officers, as Clump had implied, had become a total fixture of the market. Anyone looking with a quick glance would not even see them standing on the cheese shop steps. Treacle found it difficult to believe that their armour didn't all but shout out their presence but as they stood on the steps, Henry Light Finger entered the market and started to furtively look around -- as Clump had described, the first step of thievery. The officers, hiding in shadows on the half obscured steps of the cheese shop behind a stall selling hand-crafted blankets, did not even enter his mind. That he had seen the officers standing there in the past still hadn't registered with him as a fact, to which he should pay particular attention.

What attracted Treacle's attention to this little man was the movement of his head and the look in his eyes -- it was just a little different from everyone else in the crowd. He looked more interested in the direction the stall holders were gazing instead of their wares. This shifty individual could have been an officer of the market, but then he would have carried something like a check list and would have been interested in each individual stall, one at a time. Instead, Henry's eyes darted this way and that. Treacle was sure he was building a mental picture of all the blind spots and escape routes across the whole market. Then the little man suddenly started to move at quite a quick pace, and a small bundle of goods that once sat upon the stall display suddenly disappeared under the cape draped over the man's arm and into his clothing.

Clump slowly leaned forward so only Treacle could hear him and murmured, "That's Henry Light Finger, that is. Why don't you try and catch him by the street's end?" Clump enjoyed such moments. It's what he lived for; seeing a young officer fail totally in his endeavours was a sight to behold and confirmed to him that all his years of experience wasn't for nought. Treacle looked in front of him at the market in full flow, with all of the pedestrian areas along the sides, edges and centre at full capacity. There was a wall of people between him and the ever-increasing distance Henry was putting between himself and them.

Treacle straightened his mind and his uniform and set forth, as the crowd parted before him like a ship cutting through the sea. In his entire career Clump had never seen a crowd separate with such little care or concern for who made his way through them. As Treacle stepped forward, many lucky moments of coincidence started to weave themselves together, and a little circle of emptiness in front of him would appear, just as, and when required.

Treacle, Clump decided, was a man with whom never to play cards. The amount of luck he displayed today was more than one man should have. It was a freak nature that created people like him, Clump reflected. No matter how much luck they used, they always had an inexhaustible supply on which to call upon.

Treacle was now picking up speed; there was no submission or even an acknowledgment of the existence of the crowd in him. By now he had almost managed to get level with Henry and within a few strides. Henry felt a hand on his shoulder and a voice in his ear: "STOP, I have you bang to rights." Henry felt his will to break free and dodge and weave his way out of this mess drain from him, and he stood meekly awaiting further instructions.

Clump forced his way through the crowd, bumping into nearly everyone along his way, all to give his own "dun up like a kipper, my son." After reading Henry his rights in a clear and precise manner that only Treacle could possibly give, they dragged him off to the station. "Dragged" was an inappropriate word, since "Henry just had the demeanour of the condemned man and he even walked right up to the custody sergeant's desk with no running or nothing," as Clump later described it to the shift in a way the other coppers could comprehend.

After a short break in the canteen it was back to walking the streets but the market had now closed for the day, due to the fact that the inns had opened, and the porters were not fit to push anything else but their drinks.

"Those criminals who slept-in this morning will be wanting to steal something today, just to keep their hand in, and that's when they make mistakes. Let's see who we can catch, my fellow officer," Clump said with a new found respect for his partner. With someone as lucky as Treacle, they might catch some of the biggest criminals on their most wanted list.

Clump steered them onto Cherry Street, a venue where officers had seen many crimes committed, but had never been fast enough to catch the culprit before the crowd would surround them, and chase them back to the station with their tails between their legs. But this time might be different. Treacle felt the tension rise from the cobbles under his feet, right up to the back of his neck where the hairs stood on end. For his part Clump dismissed the growing sense of risk he felt as just the normal part of the beat while walking Cherry Street. However, he was now aware the crowd was balefully staring at them. It was not the look reserved for the new stranger in town -- it was more the look assassins have just before dropping the hammer on a victim. "Right lad, we're looking for Damien 'The Shark' Guppy for extortion," Clump said. "He's done a lot more but sadly, that's all we can prove. However, he didn't get that name for nothing so come on," Clump encouraged.

Ahead of them Damien Guppy was a bit preoccupied, as he was quite literally stamping out his competition. His rival was trying to crawl into a side alley while Damien and his crew used their interpersonal skills to get ahead in business. If they couldn't get his head, well, a few swift punches and kicks to the body would do. After all, it's only business -- nothing personal. The object of their attentions, Richard 'Two Girls' Lovelock, had managed to crawl and drag himself to the mouth of the alley as Clump and Treacle came into view. Clump lifted his arm to urge Treacle into a run only to find his partner already making distance between them, truncheon in hand.

Treacle grabbed the gutter on the corner of the alley and at breakneck speed swung his full body round into the alley.

The flying pancake leap assault rammed Damien's face right into the centre of Treacle's chest where the protruding face of a lion on his armour made swift work of his nose. Damien sagged back, unclear as what had just happened to him, other than his nose had just exploded in a cloud of bloody mist. Now that Damien had fallen aside, Treacle saw his two henchmen, twin brothers Crunch and Munch. They were mountains of men who had grown into their names, breaking people's arms and legs for sport. Well, everyone needs a hobby.

A quick roll and a swift kick to the side of Crunch's knee dropped the large man, screaming in pain, to the cobbles. Munch, who now turned faster than Treacle had almost not given him credit for, found a truncheon returning the other way with more force than a man of Treacle's size should possess. It occurred to Munch, as he lost consciousness, that this small guy hit him harder than his brother had ever done in their violent past.

Clump arrived at the mouth of the alley just in time to see the full results of the body slam and watched Treacle twirl his entire body as his foot made full connection with Crunch's knee, as well as the sickening haymaker that connected with Munch's face. He thought the event was more like a dance than fighting, except for the blood and pain. Then again, Clump heard that ballet was pretty gruelling. Munch's legs folded like a cheap card table as the blow took its toll, throwing him and especially his face for a second horrible connection with one of the alley's walls. Thereupon he slowly proceeded to slide down as if made from molten wax, coming to a complete, unconscious stop.

"Damien, Damien, Damien," Clump tsked-tsked. "You're nicked, son." He threw a glance around the alley. "The locals don't like one of their own getting arrested and all hell's going to break out around here, I am sure." Clump tried his best to be heard above Crunch's screams of agony as he rolled around on the floor, holding his knee, repeating a litany of choice comments about the occupations of the officers' mothers. "Not quite yet," Treacle said, grabbing Crunch's damaged leg. "One last thing to take care of." "Now lad, there's no need for blood sport," Clump quickly interjected. "The red mist of violence can do bad things to a man's mind. Old Crunch is already in a world of hurt. He'll be...." Clump's voice trailed off as Treacle twisted and snapped the leg back into place, totally correcting the displaced kneecap.

A sigh of relief escaped from Clump's throat, eclipsing Crunch's whimpering. "Well done, lad," the officer said with a nod of approval. "He will walk away from this with a better appreciation of our own self-control and the law."

"I don't think so," Treacle said in a cheery voice. "I doubt he'll be walking any time before Sunday with the amount of force I hit that kneecap."

As Damien Guppy was led away, no one in the street lifted a finger to help him. In fact, no one even dared to twitch. Instinctively, the crowd knew when the weight of numbers meant nothing -- the possibility that the top dog had been dethroned only cemented their decision to let the dust settle, before making a hasty decision one might later regret at leisure from a hospital bed. Each onlooker decided this was one of those times to watch the show and so they stood as motionless as statues. Only their heads moved as their gaze followed the prisoner along the street. Treacle thought the crowd resembled a parliament of owls as they watched Damien go by.

The two policemen quickly dragged their collar back to the station. The distance wasn't far and Damien appeared to be more worried about his future good looks or lack thereof to put up much of a fight. Indeed the prisoner seemed more interested in stuffing a handkerchief up his nose to stop the bleeding.

On reaching the custody sergeant's desk Damien started to recount the story of his arrest. His words pained an unprecedented saga of police brutality, as he floridly described in minute detail the extreme beating he had received at the young officer's hands. Conveniently, the fact he was trying to maim someone for life failed to enter the narrative. Just as Damien's story reached the first mention of the word "brutality," Chief Constable Quern arrived behind them.

"All right, men," Quern brusquely said. "Your prisoner is making some serious claims about the propriety of your behaviour. Hold both of your hands flat out in front of you and let me take a look." Obligingly Treacle and Clump complied with Chief Constable's request for inspection. Quern looked very carefully at Clump's hands -- he knew this officer over the years had been involved in too many fights to leave a bruise yet the massive quantity of blood Damien was depositing across his station must have left at least some trace on the guilty party. But to Ouern's surprise Clump's hands were clean except for the remains of a hastily eaten egg sandwich left from lunch.

"Well, Mr. Tanner, what do you have to say for yourself?" as Quern suddenly remembered the young lad's display of force in the handshake Treacle had given him earlier. In reply, Treacle merely lifted his hands slowly, turning them over and over for Quern to get a better look. With a firm grip Quern grabbed the hands offered to him, only to be surprised by their softness -- they were as dapple as the hands of a girl at the moisturiser factory down the road. Not one bruise or one drop of blood was visible. Turning to Damien, he shot the prisoner a look of disbelief. "Do you wish to check yourself? There's not one speck of blood or one bruise on my officers' hands."

"They must have used their truncheons then," Damien said. With a knowing smile both officers held the truncheons before them as Quern ran his nice, white -- well, it was white (and nice) once -- handkerchief down each weapon. Both times Quern turned to Damien and the rest of the gathered officers in the theatrical way of a magician, and displayed the handkerchief to them. Not a single smudge of blood could be seen. Damien was sure one of these characters had beat the hell out of him, but not being able to remember too much about what actually happened to him didn't help. Where exactly was the proof? His only witnesses Crunch and Munch, if sworn into a witness box under oath, might actually tell the truth for once about his business dealings. So now it was a case of protecting himself from a secondary charge of making a false accusation against an officer. Thus he had no choice but to agree to withdraw the brutality story from the record.

Treacle and Clump made the long walk under the heavy stare of Chief Constable Quern, who knew his officers had got away with something -- he just wished he knew how they did it. Clump gave Treacle a friendly punch on the arm. "You're a fine one, lad," he said. "Here's a rag for that lion on your chest. I suggest you use the rag and throw it in the stove." Clump walked all the way home, chuckling to himself on a good day's work.

Meanwhile, the desk sergeant slowly led Damien away to see the police surgeon to be patched up. Every few feet a drop of blood seeped from his swollen head to the floor. The doctor had a look up Damien's nose, which still dripped blood, but now across the surgeon's dark wooden desk.

"So prisoner, how long have you been bleeding?" the doc idly asked. As he heard the story of woe he flicked the edge of his sandwich sitting next to him on its crisp china plate, exposing its delectable filling. Listening to Damien's answer, which he knew could not possibly be true, the doctor merely nodded his head in agreement and proceeded to peel away the top layer of the crusty loaf of his sandwich, exposing the rather generous helping of salted ham his wife had chosen as a filling. Personally he would have preferred a pickled egg and a pint; today's circumstances gave him an excuse to dispose of his sandwich and go to the pub for lunch.

The doctor opened the large, black medical valise beside him. Removing a scalpel, he proceeded to quickly shave the ham and stuck a slice up each of Damien's nostrils. "Old war remedy that is, my lad, and it works, so don't remove them until tomorrow morning," the doctor instructed. "Now off you go to the cells with you."

Harvey found himself in a thoughtful mood of reflection. He had been sitting and thinking over the day's events. Once in a while he found it necessary, if one wanted to stay alive long enough to see the morrow. The realisation began to dawn upon him that his boss was already a competitor in the wine trade, or was having the suicidal thought of maybe going into the wine business in direct competition against the ruthless Count Alexander. It was only a feeling, but a feeling based nonetheless on the nature of his employer's requests. One thing was sure -- Harvey knew he should start wearing body armour, as he was the perfect target if someone wanted to send a bloody message to his boss.

He decided to visit one of his secret sources of information, a street trader friend who stood and watched as he served the culinary needs of his clients. "Feeling Dodgy Dick" was the seller who sold his own very famous "Something Like a Chicken Wrap." He had been forced to adopt that name so no one could complain later that he had lied to them. The filling was always something that tasted like chicken -- the only problem, it just never was chicken, never not once. Accordingly, the town's rat population lived in fear of him. Dick had earned his nickname due to the strange combination of ingredients and odd spices he used in his food. One special feature his food magically possessed was its ability to stay down once consumed but could also stop any feeling of sickness or nausea from the dodgiest alcoholic night out.

Dick's 'Morning-After-the-Night-Before' totally outsold the evening before sales due to the fact the medical fraternity was very keen on using the strange liquid that normally poured out of the food as you ate it, a very hung-over medical student had made the random discovery that the cold remnants of last night's special, when eaten for breakfast, could keep even the most disgusting medicine down.

A wide assortment of the city's doctors queued and ordered in bulk every day; they were forced to go to these lengths since Dick would never sell the recipe. So the medicos themselves had to extract what they wanted from the 'Something like a Chicken Wrap.'

Harvey purchased the 'Morning-After-the-Night-Before' special to keep Dick happy and in his confidence, while they talked about wine suppliers around the city.

"Your employer should know that wherever the local wine industry is, Count Alexander's men are sure to be lurking close behind." The street vendor focused a curious eye at Harvey. "Why are you asking all of this?" he enquired. "Do you have a beef to settle with the Count? These people don't like having their business interfered with personal vendettas."

"It's my boss, Dick," Harvey said. "He's the one making enquiries."

"Well then, my advice to you is to start saving as much of your wages as possible because your boss won't be around for very long," Dick said. "Strange and mysterious tragedies happen to the Count's competitors. First, it was Maximilian's 'accidental' drowning. Next, Captain Hanover drowned in his bath, and he was a competitive swimmer. Then, as I recall, the owner of the building that is now The Wine Cellar, which is a wholesale wine shop, he died when his front door fell on him. There are more, but I think you can guess the endings."

After a few more casual comments, Harvey bade goodbye to the street vendor and made his way toward The Wine Cellar. Due to the oenological knowledge of his employer, Harvey had become aware of the establishment and its manager, who wasn't very imaginative on anything other than describing wine, of which he was a specialist. The story Harvey heard was that the manager once described a certain vintage of wine as liquorice and banana in flavour. The shop was located in an advantageously high position within the city, where the building's large cellars always stood above the level of the area's groundwater and thus remained dry all year round. The building was specially designed and constructed for the storage of wine; its walls were built from very thick stone that kept wine cool during the summer while preventing it from freezing in winter.

The front of the shop was workmanlike but nothing fancy, and Harvey needed but a few minutes to realise from the class of customer in the shop that wine was only being sold in casks or by the case. The buyers at the shop worked for the city's most prestigious families or the best restaurants, purchasing wine in bulk in the hope that it would mature into something palatable in the future. The cheap kegged wine was put aside, mostly for vinegar, to be sent to the mountain regions of these parts. Strangely, the wine normally arrived already fermented after the long journey, aided by the change in temperatures and conditions and the slow undulations of the local roads. The centre of the shop had a yellow floor, while the edges on both sides were red. By the way the customers acted at the division of the colours, Harvey quickly understood that the yellow floor was for customers, and red was reserved only for the staff. Harvey slowly walked into the store, stopping at every cask and barrel, admiring the rather exotic locations from where they had travelled. He believed that any one giving more than a passing interest to the label's small print was likely an expert in their field, so he methodically continued along the yellow walkway as if he were checking the wine casks against an imaginary list. The further back into the store he went, the fancier the writing on each cask became and the dustier the casks appeared. However, Harvey thought the dust looked slightly false compared to the state of the barrels, the floor and the surrounding area, all of which were spotless.

After a time, a tall, well-dressed gentleman sallied over to Harvey and introduced himself as a Monsieur Garcon -- in truth his name was Bob Sprocket but the name "Garcon" automatically lent an aura of omniscience concerning the vagaries of the fermented grape, and thus people on this side of the sea had a greater tendency to believe without question what he said about wine.

After a short tour of the shop, designed to show the salesman's best wares to his new potential customer, Harvey could immediately discern that in the learned opinion of Garcon aka Bob Sprocket, the salesman considered any wine with a hefty commission to be the best. Harvey also noticed Bob was eagerly keen to gather as many details as he could about Harvey's master in order to extract the greatest amount of coinage possible. Harvey, for his part, was very impressed with Bob's ability to glibly talk about a single product in a thousand different ways. He had no doubt Treacle would enjoy this place; it was just what he thought Treacle appreciated about a big city.

As Bob guided Harvey towards the front payment area in a vain effort to get his master's details or, more importantly, access to the master's wallet, Harvey espied two characters entering the shop to whom he instinctively knew he should give a wide berth. With a quick turn of his heel Harvey made some silly comment about delivery dates, as the two passed him by and went down the staircase marked 'Staff Only' to the basement. Harvey made his excuses to Bob Sprocket, announcing that he would tell his master what he had discovered, and try to get him to return forthwith, before beating a hasty exit.

Repairing the Entrance

The Squeak – Poison Oak

Knocking at the door

Harvey reached the house just as the builders had finished fitting a new front door; he couldn't help but notice it was constructed from extremely strong ironwood, with metal bindings across the entire front for extra strength. No doubt his employer was making a hefty investment in protection, he surmised.

But the builders had been busy above and beyond the installation of the front door. Harvey was amazed at the results of the builders' labours as he surveyed their work. Most of the ground floor had already been refitted. He did, however, note that just as he reached the bottom of the stairs the wood squeaked, and the squeak was tuned to a pitch that set one's teeth on edge. Behind him he heard Mrs. Etherington vocalise exactly what he was just thinking – the builders had deliberately put that squeak in. "They say the master specially requested it, as well as the creak directly in front of the door to the cellar," she said. Harvey walked across the floor which was as silent as the grave, yet just in front of the cellar door a loud creak sent shivers down one's back. It was as though the sound was tuned to some subconscious frequency that plugged directly into the fear centre of one's mind.

Harvey found a place to sit down and read the local paper. He wanted to get a better feel for the area. For one, he felt he lacked some insight into street crime. He wanted to know who was going up and who was on the way down. Harvey was of the opinion that mostly the only way to keep a good thief down was by hanging him at the end of a rope. His prime suspect for the leader of the city's largest criminal gang was the notorious Count Alexander, who seemed to enjoy making people homeless, especially in the docklands area. Harvey reasoned that anyone who did this on such a large industrial scale enjoyed it far beyond the additional profit. If it was just for profit, the Count would have thrown one family out as an example and force the others to pay a higher rate. But the Count threw all of them out; that was just not good business.

From what Harvey ascertained, the Count's numerous business dealings had managed to upset a large percentage of the population, whilst the rest seemed to be employed by him, which amounted to the same thing. He also had an unusual amount of interest in the wine trade, travelling numerous times a year to Franco-side, refreshing the stocks of his numerous wine businesses. Franco-side, as everyone knew, was a single day's journey by boat across the Gurgling Sea. In the past, the country had been at war with the city but that was a century ago. Since peace treaties and trade deals had been signed several years earlier, the city had become the bigger trading partner of the two. That's not to say that both sides had not benefited disproportionately from the peace dividend reducing their navies -- now they simply concentrated on the trade that brought wealth and influence amongst their neighbours.

Harvey methodically constructed the story of Count Alexander's ascent to power, gleaned from his conversations with the numerous street sellers around the city. Alexander had come across on a merchant ship as a stowaway when he was in his early teens. He had been taken under the wing of an exceptionally fair trader named Maximilian Trollop, who treated him like his own son. Maximilian made his wealth while helping people along with the odd meal here, a missed rent there. It all added up to a great mass of philanthropic work. The local poor worried about their future when it was reported that he had been washed overboard while taking the young Alexander back to his home country. Then Alexander returned to a large inheritance and bought the title of Count. At the time, he pledged to continue the good works his mentor had started, but money freely given quickly changed to small loans, which later became large loans, until whole families had been enslaved by the repayment of the debt.

The Count had upset many working people within the city, with the large number of Franco-side labourers he shipped over to work for him, undercutting the local wages and driving down the living conditions of the poor. Harvey couldn't work out if the population hated the exploitation of the cheap foreign labour, if it just hated foreigners in general, or if they were just jealous of anyone who was doing better than they were. It was Harvey's opinion that the city had transformed the working people into a hardened lot. They always had two points of view, and would show the side they thought would extract the greatest amount of coinage from whomever might be listening.

Over the evening's meal Harvey discussed all of his findings with Treacle, who thought it all needed further investigation, but it would be best if Harvey was not seen around the docks for a while. A good alternative was to allow him to take some letters to the post office tomorrow. The post office was located some distance outside of the city gates so that the coaches that travelled to and through didn't need to worry about dealing with the city guards. The guards were duty bound to inspect everything coming into the city -- not that they did every time, but one couldn't tell when their commanding officer might visit and enforce the rules. Immediately after eating their evening meal of ham in blood sauce -- a recipe Mrs. Etherington had discovered from the local butcher, and which both Treacle and Harvey found tasty -- Treacle wrote two letters, one to uncle Ruud and another to his cousin Aleasia.

Mabel was finally home after another exhausting day from being an 'It Girl.' Her ankles hurt from all the different shoes she had to wear. They all seemed to have been made with one size in mind: bloody painful. The modelling sessions for the 'Olive' magazine shoot was for the "Girl-About-Town" section which, in the past, had some of the best models in the business appear within its pages before they became famous and too costly for the magazine. She knew the 'Olive' was very respectable, and that nothing too revealing would be shown, which wasn't hard as the frocks she had been given to model were full evening wear and designed for the winter season of a frozen country.

The catch-phrase or the tag line the photographer had been instructed to use for the day's photo session was "Warm in Your Woollies." So the photographer tried to catch the very essence of the phrase, whatever that meant, and she thought they had achieved that goal, since hardly any skin showed with these clothes, not even her hands. Then there was dinner at the 'Poison Oak,' the place to be seen in the city. Mabel thought it just as well that the food was served on such small plates -- any diner would be left hungry, and in disgust demand their money back.

Mabel had guessed quite correctly that if one wanted to be photographed leaving the 'Poison Oak' it was always handy to inform the photographer before entering so he could have his camera ready. David Hailey, the photographer, had also promised to give her a percentage of his earnings if the picture was published. He offered this courtesy to her for remembering him, as well as making his life easier for not having to chase her down for a story. Then after being "spotted" entering the restaurant, it was back to the offices of 'Olive' for an exposé interview about her favourite colour and which shoes she liked best, before picking up a very handsome cheque and retiring home for a substantial home-made meal to stop her stomach growling at her.

She made a quick change into her only party dress and, picking up the gilt-edged invitation that had arrived early that morning by special courier, she hurried out to the new nightclub opening, the invitation had a flourished gold script that the rich appreciated, and the fact that the little card stated it was by special invitation of Count Alexander himself meant that a large amount of money was to be spent, making the evening very memorable indeed.

The new nightclub on Speckled Street was called 'Le Castile' and had just been rebuilt. It was said that the building was made to Count Alexander's exacting design to give it more cachet. When Mabel entered the marble hallway, one look told her that the Count had good taste and deep pockets. The building was nothing short of fabulous, with a large dance floor in the centre, and separate small individually-styled bars ringing the floor. Each bar had a fancy lady's name written above the door -- that is to say, a name you would hear in polite company. These bars certainly were not dressing rooms for dancers stepping from a stage with a pole mounted at its centre.

Mabel noticed the name "Mirabella" above one of the bars matched her own invitation. When she presented her card to the uniformed man at the entrance of the small bar, he gladly opened the velvet rope and allowed her to enter within.

A sumptuous sight to feast the eyes awaited her. One waiter smoothly glided through the throng of guests, pouring wine at the merest hint that their glass had touched lips. Another waiter offered small finger food from gilded plates of the finest china. Within her segregated bar area Mabel could see Sylvie Dogwood from Uplands, one of her best friends from school and a good gossip to boot. Mabel manoeuvred her way across the room to her school chum and said hello. "Hi Mabel. Have you the Count yet? There he is. Doesn't he look simply marvellous?" She pointed across the floor where the Count sat on a gilded throne. Mabel thought he looked very suave in his silver suit. In his left hand he held a long black cane with a head of gold encrusted with fine jewels, which caught the light and cast colourful reflections around the room. His hands were bejewelled with rings inlayed with precious stones, and his face was long and thin, hidden by a well-kept moustache and beard. The Count slowly spun his cane as he spoke to two roguish characters who seemed to have never worn a suit before. The two men kept adjusting their collars and cuffs, looking around as if trying to just miss the glance of someone, or to be the first to see someone whom they wanted to purposely avoid.

As Mabel turned back to her friend, her eyes instead met those of that nice young policeman from whom she had asked directions a day or two ago. "May I introduce myself?" he politely asked. "My name is Treacle Tanner and tonight I'm here as the acting cultural ambassador for the citizens of Nocte Mortis, on special attachment to the constabulary of these parts." Mabel noticed that he spoke with the assurance of someone who was firm in his beliefs. While Treacle knew he didn't have to include all the information he offered, he found that presenting such facts upfront helped to clarify people's thoughts for them rather than inviting them to try to arrange their own thoughts for themselves.

Both girls smiled sweetly at him; maybe a bit too sweetly, Treacle noted, as they both seemed unattached and appeared to be on the prowl for someone of status. Mabel and Sylvie introduced each other and enquired why he was walking the streets as a policeman.

"Isn't it dangerous for someone of your high position to be patrolling the streets like that?" Mabel asked.

"I've been assigned a most capable mentor, Officer Hammerstone, one of the finest officers on the force, and one who is most capable of protecting me," Treacle replied.

"Well, I can't believe he can be as good as you make him out to be," Mabel said. "His misdirection wasted a lot of my time and sent me to the dead-end of Angel Street."

"Yes, that could have been true, but I am sure the cut-purses following you were really caught out when you turned and came back at them," Treacle mentioned in an off-hand tone. Mabel looked stunned. "What cut-purses? I saw no one' she said, a tone of alarm in her voice. "I'm sure Officer Hammerstone did not want to worry you, my dear, or make you feel uncomfortable," Treacle said soothingly. "There was no evidence to arrest anyone or hold them against their will from following you."

Mabel found herself impressed by this polite, well-spoken man as she coyly ran a forefinger through her hair. "So did Officer Hammerstone point them out to you then?" she asked. "No, he let me work it out for myself," Treacle replied. "It is a lesson I don't think I will forget very quickly." "Well, well," interjected Sylvie, a look of scepticism on her face. "I didn't know the police officers were so clever in this city. I think you need a mind like a steel trap to catch some of these criminals."

"I think you should have a drink, Mabel," Treacle suggested. "You look a bit pale, but if you're worrying about what the cut-purses might have done, not to worry. They wouldn't have touched you with me and Officer Hammerstone following you at a discreet distance for your protection."

After a pleasant evening chatting about the cultural differences of Nocte Mortis compared to those of Great Smog, Treacle noticed the two characters he recognised from the other night in the alley with Harvey, leaving the party. He quickly made his excuses and left, after all the cultural niceties of his position had been observed, but took too long in making his exit. By the time he left the building the two men he had been watching secretly from afar were nowhere to be seen.

Treacle called it a night, and walked home as slowly as he could to draw out any lurking cut-throats, but no-one took up the bait, unlike Harvey who seemed to attract followers like a tethered goat. He knew it was wrong to use him that way, but Harvey was so good at seeing trouble coming, as well as staying alive once it was knocking at the door.

Old Mothers Ruin

Hot and spicy – Tea and cake – A Sea Voyage

The next morning brought its own dangers. Treacle was shouting at Mrs. Etherington for an explanation: "What's this white sausage on my plate, Mrs Etherington? You know I like blood pudding!"

"Sir," she explained, "this is Morcella -- it is a blood pudding, but comes from Porta and has arrived fresh off the boat. I thought the change would do you good."

With his most apologetic smile Treacle relaxed and, in his nicest voice explained that it was very considerate of her to go to the trouble, and next time it might be a bit helpful if she informed him first before surprising him with new exotic food combinations. The taste was very hot; in fact, he was sure it was almost eye-watering to him. Maybe it contained a hint of garlic or something very similar,

121

perhaps something from the same plant family. Its effects he found very interesting to observe, as it forced him to drink a lot of fluid and wipe the sweat from his brow several times during the meal. After finishing the contents of his plate, he knew he had eaten the hottest meal in his life. He took a while to compose himself afterwards, wiping the tears away and trying his best to lose the taste in his mouth. Treacle decided this sausage definitely needed to be imported into Nocte Mortis in bulk. It would go down a storm if you could get anyone to take the first bite.

Arriving at work perfectly on time in his ever present relaxed style, Treacle readied himself for the day ahead, and met Clump chatting to Budgie in the canteen, as the night officer gave him the low-down on the murder of Wino Jones, the last home-owner living down on Portside Road.

"Very lucky for Count Alexander that this fellow is now dead, don't you think?" Clump mentioned to Treacle. "Look, you haven't heard it from me, but Count Alexander has had many such lucky moments in his past, but we've never been able to get anything on him." Clump intentionally guided them away from the port area, using his well-honed ability for self-preservation. In Clump's mind, anything important enough to patrol the area required a directive from someone at captain level or above.

"Have you met Mr Easy?" Clump enquired of his new charge. "He has been asking to see you, I've been told. If not, I will take you there right now. I am sure he will be interested to hear a foreign student's point of view of the police force from you. They keep a nice cup of tea and a slice of cake awaiting for those of us who keep democracy running."

As the two entered the long thoroughfare that ran across the city, Treacle didn't need to be told where he was: he knew instantly this must be State Street. All the government buildings were located on either side of the road, and one could feel the belittling effect of the architecture built into each pillar and cornice. The main parliament building sat at the end of the road looking down State Street, like a parent overseeing her children at the table.

As they approached the parliament building, the gates were opened by two guards who looked to be employed more for their mental abilities than their brawn, especially when they said "Good morning, Treacle" to him as he passed. Clump gingerly moved around the outside of the building with the walk of someone who had been told off for not using the tradesman entrance once too often. He stopped at the end of the path and pointed to a side door. "After you, lad, third door on the right." Clump directed.

Opening the third door on the left (Clump, it seemed, was getting flustered) was like opening a pressure chamber, as all the candles in the room gave a nod to his presence. Treacle found himself in a large round room, with chairs awkwardly spaced around its outside edge. In the centre back of the room stood the secretary's table with an urn constantly brewing red hot tea, and next to it a cake stand laden with tasty morsels. The chairs looked like they had been chosen for maximum discomfort, and the spacing was just about right to make it impossible to speak to someone without everyone in the room hearing what was said.

Upon seeing them enter the secretary quickly ran to the door on the far wall and ushered Treacle though. As he crossed the room and drew level with the open door, Treacle leant over and tried to move the nearest chair toward himself, which was much heavier than it first appeared, and gave a horrible scraping sound capable of putting anyone off from moving it. The effect was everything he expected and maybe a little bit more.

Mr. Easy, the chief public servant, sat behind his desk, appearing to be busy with the problems of running the state. As he offered Treacle a seat, Treacle judged that his line of sight would be about two inches lower than Mr Easy once he had sat down -- the height would be perfect to give the guest a feeling that the person in front of them was of a superior position in life. But as he lowered himself into his seat, he was quite surprised to find the upholstery just kept sinking. The angle from which he was now looking at Mr Easy reminded him of being in front of the teacher at school. He was sure that the effect was by perfect design. Mr Easy was slightly bald, but this had not stopped him from tying his hair back in a ponytail. His clothes looked to be of the highest quality tailoring; they lasted longer, and expensive clothing never really went out of fashion. Then again, if they were very well chosen they never were "in" fashion. The expensive classic tailoring outlasted some of the more fashionable designers.

"Well Mr Tanner, there is no reason to hide your true self in here. I have a very large file on you," Mr. Easy said as he tapped out Treacle's favourite tune on a huge folder in front of him. Treacle smiled -- it was just the sort of trick Uncle Ruud would play on him. A name on a folder full of blank paper could make some people very worried.

In reply, Treacle smiled and said, "Then there is nothing I need to tell you." As he spoke, he watched the real Mr. Easy drop his mask of a respectable public servant.

"I believe they call you Treacle, so I will make it very plain, TREACLE, that while you are a guest of this city your status as a clan member will allow you certain allowances and privileges, but the moment we have a body in the morgue that shouldn't be there, with, shall we say, a rather anaemic look, there will be a garlic bath waiting for you, my lad."

Treacle again smiled. "How old are you, Mr. Easy? I have known some very old fellows, and you make them seem like spring chickens. I bet in your position you can control those who work directly in your presence and, with your so-called "bosses" being elected government officials who change every time there is a vote, you could remain indefinitely in your position without anyone noticing you're not ageing like you should. After many years I am sure you are reborn as your own son inheriting the family wealth.

"You see Mr. Easy, we know each other like we know ourselves. We have both read each other's files and I know I trust myself with your secret as I trust you with mine. For your peace of mind, I will promise not to kill anyone outside of my official duties of my chosen career, if that puts your mind at rest."

"That would be an acceptable position to have, Mr. Treacle, and may I suggest someone of your unusual talents might be usefully employed investigating the murder down at the dock-side last night, if you do not mind helping our little city."

Departing Mr. Easy's presence, Treacle closed the office door behind him, and saw Clump sitting uncomfortably, juggling a cup and saucer of boiling tea between both hands, as a plate of crumbs sat upon one knee. Treacle freed Clump of his plate of crumbs and handed it back to the secretary, much to Clump's relief. As the plates were designed to look very expensive, the poor fellow had felt unable to move; in fact, he felt totally imprisoned in his chair, all for the expense of a few pennies of china.

Once they had left the building and all of its listening devices Treacle undoubtedly knew were buried in its walls, he mentioned Mr. Easy's request. As he did, he watched Clump's shoulders literally sag with the weight of the assignment.

In an attempt to cheer up his partner, Treacle said, "I must point out, my friend, that Mr. Easy only mentioned that I should investigate this case for the city. There was no mention of your participation."

"Lad, all investigations in this city are undertaken by the police. You know that, and therefore, we as officers have a duty to the people to take this case together." After a moment, Clump continued, "But I do think we should speak to Chief Constable Quern before we do anything."

In Quern's office Treacle explained Mr. Easy's request in the least self-incriminating way he could manage. Quern looked at both of them, then stood up and walked around his desk in a mock attempt to appear to be thinking.

"Well lads, I don't think we should let public servants control police deployment, should we? By the way Treacle, aren't you from Nocte Mortis as, I recall?" Treacle knew he had never mentioned anything about his past. Quern must have glanced at Mr. Easy's file but this was neither the time nor the place to ask that question, so he simply replied in the affirmative. Quern continued, "We do have a murder to investigate at Portside Road of a Wino Jones, a previous resident of Nocte Mortis. I believe it may be something you may have some insight into. So for that reason alone, Treacle and Clump, I assign you to that case, and not because Mr. Easy assigned you the dockland murder, aka the death of Wino Jones." As Clump raised his hand, Quern rephrased his statement. "If anyone asks, you are not working on a case assigned to you by Mr. Easy concerning the dock murder, but working directly for me on a case concerning Nocte Mortis. Got it?"

Clump didn't understand politics but he did understand orders. Both officers left the station after a warm mulled wine which gave Treacle a new spring in his step as they navigated their way down to the docks. The docks looked very impressive when seen in the light, and much more accommodating up to a point, while wearing a uniform.

Portside Road was full of empty houses -- in fact, all of the houses were now empty since the mass evictions earlier in the week and the unfortunate death of Wino Jones. Wino Jones had lived midway down on the dock side of the street which now faced an extremely high wall, guarded by the type of individual of which one needed to employ at least two, one to guard the other. They had to enter Wino's house by stooping very low through the doorway. Treacle wondered if the builder couldn't afford a full-sized door or if he had found a rotten door and had cut the bottom off and built the house to scale around it.

Once their eyes had grown accustomed to the lack of light, the chalk outline on the floor seemed to occupy most of the available space. "Before you read the report Clump, let me guess. He was killed with a knife at close quarters in an upward movement," Treacle said.

"That's right, lad; it's like you were there," Clump replied with a wink of his eye.

"Come on, Clump -- we both know in a room this small with such a low ceiling you have very few options to murder someone if you're a stranger or even a professional for hire. There's hardly enough room to swing a cat, let alone a murderous dagger."

Clump agreed there weren't many options, and the more he looked around the fewer he saw available. Even the possibility of killing someone from behind seemed impossible in this small collection of bricks. When they left the house, they could see a demolition crew already pulling down the neighbours' houses at the far end of the street. As they passed the workers, Treacle thought it best to restate the fact that the murder house could not be touched, but the demolition foreman just stared at him.

"Does that instruction cover these houses?" he finally asked, waving his hand at the repossessed properties in front of them as the workers stood idly by, waiting to see what would happen next.

'"No, I don't think so," replied Treacle.

The foreman turned away. "In that case well, carry on, carry on lads!" he shouted.

Treacle looked at Clump. "I suppose that's the march of progress."

Clump nodded towards the dock entrance further down the dock. "Shall we question the guards that walked along that wall that night?" he asked.

"There's no point looking for the guards in there. The weekly shift has changed already and the guards have three days off and normally drink in the 'Old Mother's Ruin,' or so I have reliably been told." Treacle responded with the experienced sound of a twenty year veteran of the force.

Clump looked surprised at Treacle's insight. "Don't look at me like that," Treacle said. "We both know that a fool wouldn't walk these streets in a uniform if they hadn't walked it in civvies before. I haven't managed to walk the entire city, but in the few days I've been here I've completed most of the dock area and the little alleys that join it."

Despite himself, Clump was impressed. Chief Constable Quern had told him Treacle should never be underestimated, but this was far beyond anything of which he had believed a new recruit was capable.

The 'Old Mother's Ruin' was the sort of pub even the locals walked out of if they got the wrong look, a fact both men kept in mind as they entered. Being so close to the port, all sorts of rotgut gin and whiskies seemed to find their way into this bar's cellars, from which some of the city's most drunken and dangerous individuals would drink to excess. Treacle entered the bar with the confident stride of someone who owned the place, which was the equivalent of drawing a line in the sand then jumping over the line and slapping your opponent in the face. The room fell silent, as everyone looked toward the new occupants filling their personal space, as Clump did his best impression of a door blocking out as much of the available sunlight as possible. Treacle considered every possible option available to him while his audience watched from every corner of the bar.

Treacle nodded at the barman. "Two "Blue Slide" whiskies please," he said, joyfully sliding up to the bar. "I think extra-large." As he spoke he felt a large finger gently prod him in the back as Clump tried to remind him that they could not drink on duty. A "Blue Slide" was the most expensive whiskey this side of the continent, and two extra-large drinks was a week's wages to most of the occupants in this bar. The barman unlocked a large cage behind the bar and removed a bottle that appeared untouched for 500 years. Everyone watched as he measured out the two drinks with a precision unseen even within the alchemist profession.

With drink in tow, Treacle moved further into the inn and, as he touched the rail that ran around the bar, the magic of all public houses started to work on everyone, as the patrons snapped back to their own conversations. As Clump reached the bar he opened his mouth but Treacle, already knowing what he would say, cut him off before he could speak.

"My good friend, have you ever heard of Professor Nowl's theorems on 'A Shared Secret' psychology? In other words, if they know of our dirty little secret of drinking on duty, then we will not mention anything they say while we're drinking. That's how they perceive the reality of the situation." Treacle picked up his drink and said quite loudly, "Drink this slowly -- it's extremely expensive and worth savouring" and made a motion of someone drinking, but Clump saw his wink, and the fact that no liquid had touched his lips, as Treacle slowly put his glass back on the counter.

They both nursed their drinks, as illicit conversations swirled around them about a large delivery of terracotta being assembled in far off ports. But all the information was second hand and even sounded as if it had been translated several times, but it did contain certain themes consisting of the phrases "terracotta," "far off" and "will be shipped here soon."

As much as this mystery interested them both, Treacle thought it was time for them to steer the conversation with a well-placed statement only the barmen could hear. He said, "I really need this drink. Did you see all that blood in that house? Lucky we found that evidence under all that mess." Clump lifted his glass as if to admire the drink's colour and, in the reflection of the mirror behind the rows of bottles against the inn's wall, saw the barman scurry away to a confederate at the far end of the bar.

Treacle admired that about Clump: he had a cop's mind, always looking for those tells, that little angle, that little twitch in the corner of one's eye. When no one was looking, Treacle siphoned both whiskeys into a hip flask ever so slowly over a period of time to make it look like they were actually drinking the beverages. Once the transfer was complete Treacle said, "I think my nerves have steadied. Now, shall we try to make it back to the station before our legs give out?"

At the doorway Treacle turned to Clump and said, "You know what you are mate? You're the best partner I got." He thought it sounded right -- he had heard others say something similar when they rolled out of bars late at night. He propped himself up against Clump, as they staggered back toward the station until out of sight of the inn.

Treacle considered that the afternoons in the city always felt a little different. Most noticeable was the number of people who disappeared back to wherever they came. The streets were much quieter compared to this morning's crowd, and Treacle was sure someone would take advantage of this fact, especially against drunken men with secrets to tell. Returning from the 'Old Mother's Ruin' required them to walk up many of the more secluded streets, which meant the moment they were alongside a very dark alley, the inevitable happened: two crossbow bolts beckoned them inside.

Treacle recognised the two men immediately as his two favourite street hunters of drunken prey. "Well lads, you're going to give us the evidence you found and we will let you live," declared one in the knowing tone of somebody with a finger on the trigger.

Treacle fumbled in his pockets as he asked, "Have you heard of Master Toochme Toes? Famous words bend like a reed in the wind." He acted with a speed later described by Clump as "cat-like reflexes" to a select group of officers back at the station's canteen. Clump knew when he heard an instruction, words that the two men in front of them failed to recognize, as he quickly bent down to touch his toes. Treacle hadn't even waited to see if his heavy hint had been heeded, before his hands were pulling out two throwing stars hidden in his belt. He flung each one onward at their target. The bow strings of the crossbows now facing him twanged apart as the two stars found their mark before the triggers could be pulled. On hearing the distinctive twang of the bowstrings breaking, Clump, who, as instructed was touching his toes, launched himself towards the nearest street thug with a force that lifted him clear off his feet. The thug was now pinned against the wall, hanging from Clump's steel-like grip around his neck like yesterday's washing,

Treacle grabbed the crossbow of the one left standing, throwing it aside with his left hand as his right hand went straight to the man's throat. With a quick heave, he took the thug straight up level with his friend. Both men were now pinned against the wall, choking and hanging like dead meat in a butcher shop. Treacle gave a quick strike to each of their legs with his free hand and dropped his incumbent to the floor. Clump followed his lead but expected both of them to jump and run. The two men had the same thought and went to run, only to discover that one of their legs would not move. In fact both men had lost the feeling in one of their legs and had to sag back to the ground before gravity overpowered them.

"Well gentlemen, we seem to have a problem of communication, but I have you now for attempted murder of an officer of the law and street mugging, which I think you might want to trade for a more lenient consideration," Treacle announced. When both men stayed silent Treacle merely shrugged his shoulders, walked up to one, grabbed him by the collar and started pulling him along in the direction of the station. Clump picked up the other and threw him over his shoulder like a sack of potatoes. Minutes later they dropped both of them off at the custody sergeant's desk.

The chief constable, who always tried to make it to a booking, just shook his head. "Well, if it's not my very old friends Jack and Gill. Well lads, I thought you had gone straight or got clever, but here you are again." He turned to Treacle and Clump. "Let me introduce Jack the Sprat and Gill Hoony, two of the most ruthless little street thugs I had the pleasure of arresting when I was a street copper." He looked back at Jack. "I think the last time you got four years of hard labour on board a prison barge, but I see the hard work taught you nothing."

"Don't worry Chief Constable Quern, we will be free tomorrow, just you see. No stinking cesspit of a prison is going to hold us," Jack sneered.

"I think you will find, lads, we have actually reduced the stink and doubled the cess since you were last there. I hope it doesn't ruin the experience for you both," Quern said with a smile.

Treacle had a meeting with his builder to attend to, but Clump was very willing to stay and tell the story of the day's events, with a slant towards his good behaviour. Quern was mightily impressed with the story he heard, especially the bit about pretending to drink in the 'Old Mothers Ruin.' He was sure he had read such a tall tale in a book.

"Well Officer Hammerstone, if that is the official report you wish to file, you bloody well better be prepared to repeat the same story tomorrow at the trial without deviation." Quern thought if Clump's story was heard at trial, the old rascals will be looking over their shoulders for months to come, wondering what trick the force was going to pull next. He pencilled it into his notebook to make sure the prosecutor mentioned it if the defence did not -- just like any good copper would.

The moment Treacle turned onto his own road he could see Mr Wren his builder scratching his head and standing across the street, trying to see the whole house in a single view. "I believe we haven't met officially -- my name is Treacle Tanner. I'm the owner of the property and I'm very impressed with the level of workmanship your men are displaying."

"But it's not possible," Wren said in astonishment. "This is several day's work already completed. Who else are you employing here?"

"I can assure you, good sir, this is down to your employee's hard work, being -- how shall I describe it? -- given an incentive to complete. Yes, I think that certainly describes their situation extremely well, and when you're ready I will be inside. I'm sure you want to collect your money."

Chris Wren grabbed the first carpenter he saw as the worker came out of the house to collect eight lengths of two by four. "What has he offered you?" he demanded as he tried to hold the man back long enough from his work to have a conversation.

The carpenter turned, looked him straight in the face, smiled and declared as if he had learnt it parrot fashion, "I must complete my work as fast as possible. I cannot and will not stop until my full day's work is finished." Wren felt the carpenter pull himself free. "I must finish my work, sir; there is so much to do and so little time to do it in." And any question after that seemed to get the same response.

When Chris got the opportunity to dart onto the property in between the stream of workmen entering and leaving the property with a determination he lacked, he noticed the entire set of window shutters were on the inside, forcing the glass to be broken first by an intruder. This provided a clear warning that the reinforced shutters were next. The method of installation had been carried out to his interlocking military design in its complete form, without the usual compromise by the customer's budgetary considerations -- the effect was the same as one would find in the national bank, which never seemed to have a lack of funds, when keeping money secure was their business. Most people had considered the bank the most secure building on the continent, but after a quick inspection Wren considered the bank could have learnt a lesson or two from the work being undertaken in this private residence. Once this house had been completed the bank would then be the second most secure building on the continent.

Treacle ushered in his guest to sit at the main table, which had two glasses and a bottle of red sitting on a silver tray awaiting them. "Please sit and drink with me a while as my butler Etherington counts out your money," Treacle invited the builder. "And if you could enlighten me about your theories on the cantilever beam, which is

revolutionising architecture in these parts, I would very grateful."
After a long discussion on architectural principles, Etherington
presented a box to Wren full of silver, and a very large box it was, too.
Treacle knew it could have been a few gold coins but silver was large
and heavy and always gave a greater impression of wealth. "Mr
Wren, I will have your workers back to you in another week, totally
exhausted but in good spirits, and I will double your payment for
your silence on my domestic security arrangements. But I am a man
of the world and I know sometimes situations happen out of our
control, so if you cannot guarantee silence under pain of torture, may
I suggest an over-simplification of my internal security would be
advantageous for all of us."

Going Postal

Dead Drop – Mallow Hunting -- Plump Porkers

Harvey had two letters in his grubby hands but, as with all good employees who were employed seven days a week, and given one simple task and no standing orders, it was the equivalent of a day off. He knew that as long as his job was finished, his time was his own. To make the most of his day, at first light he departed to the post office. Its location outside the city meant the mail coach never dealt with the guards at the city gates who invariably managed to slow commerce to a crawl, as far as the post was concerned.

Having an out-of-town location had not stopped the city spending bucket-loads of money on the post office; it represented the power and the will of the people to have their "Wish You Were Here" postcards arrive home before they did. The post office would have been a prime target for attack by an enemy state, except it was located so centrally plain, any attackers would be seen from miles away. Once the postmaster dispatched runners in all directions, the word would be out. The city would then close its gates and sit tight for reinforcements to arrive.

The best feature of the post office was not the highly impressive building itself, but the fact that all roads from outlying cities were connected together at a central junction just in front of the stables. This arrangement also allowed a mail coach the most direct route away from the city without dealing with any of the city traffic. The post office building was built in the Romanic style, as all government buildings were, in a demonstration of power and prestige. However, for some reason the architect regretfully chose a dirty brown marble for the front of the building, which rather diminished the look he had hoped to achieve.

Stepping though the front door, Harvey felt a shiver down his back as he realised the inside of the post office also suffered from the same misjudgement in colour as the building's exterior. In fact, the interior was even a darker shade than the outside of the post office. His eyes were drawn to all of the building's dark corners -- they seemed to be everywhere he looked -- and the marble glistened, as any good marble should, in the early morning light filtering through the aperture of the post office entrance. But this eerie illumination only heightened his sense of unease. The counters were empty, especially since the post office had introduced the so-called 'Blue Penny' stamp a year before. As a result, the city's small shops and businesses cleverly started to collect letters free of charge, bringing customers past the front door directly to the counter with money in hand.

Even though Harvey appeared to be the only patron in the place, the counter staff still took ages to finally serve him. He didn't give it much thought; Harvey considered indifferent customer service the norm in post offices the world over. As the clerk began placing stamps on his two exquisitely scripted letters, they repeated the addresses back to him. He always wondered why, as the address was always clearly visible on the envelope for all to read. But on this occasion he was taken aback; he hadn't bothered to read the addresses on the long walk from Higher Reach Lane. In his opinion it was wiser to look over one's shoulder and savour life's little experiences in order to reach an old age, than concerning himself with the addresses on his employer's letters. The first letter was addressed to

Ryud Darknight

High Lord Protector

Dark Towers,

Nocte Mortis,

Upper Plains.

and the second was addressed to

Aleasia Stagnation

Dark Tower,

Dark and Lonely Moor,

Nocte Mortis,

Upper Plains.

"That's right," Harvey said as all his senses told him something is wrong -- something is seriously wrong -- he could feel the hairs on the back of his neck rise as he spoke. But now the letters were posted, his day was his own to use. What to do? He'd heard some of the local drinking establishments had old friends in for the summer, and he had a subconscious requirement to have a drink.

On the walk back across the city he decided to take the scenic route, passing through some of the more shadowy parts of the city's underbelly. Here the roads were narrower and Harvey felt the city's customary smog envelope him, like entering a cigar shop smoking room. As he ambled along, he was surprised to discover a little shop called 'Auntie's Armoury.' It looked to be a very old establishment, judging from its faded sign, but the door was open and he could see the store's shelves were fully stocked.

A lady attendant, who virtually sprinted from around the counter to greet him, gave him a vigorous handshake that almost yanked him from his shoes and through the front door. The "proprietor," as she described herself, had flowing brunette hair and wore a uplands dress of red which had always been sold as the "thing every young girl should wear if being pulled through a hedge backwards, nudge, nudge, wink, wink." Harvey took one look at the shelves that lined every wall of the shop, and instantly knew he would never shop for weapons anywhere else again. The items for sale in this shop were old; manufacturers had ceased making arms of this quality long ago. After closer inspection, he even saw weapons hidden at the back of the shelves that had not been made at all under punishment of death for at least the past twenty years.

After leisurely perusing the armoury's inventory, Harvey purchased some items for himself and a couple for his master, whom he was sure would appreciate them, as they would go so nicely with the house's new defensive modifications. Harvey's pocket bulged with his weapons as he left the shop with all those little necessary items a man needed close at hand on the streets of a big city. Rather, the pocket would have bulged if he hadn't paid a very costly bribe to his tailor to modify his jacket with specialised plates to flatten its appearance. Conveniently, the plates doubled as armour if needed.

Engrossed by the inventory he had found hidden on the back shelves in 'Auntie's Armoury,' Harvey suddenly realised it was nigh time for lunch, and hurried off to see if his friends were at the 'Old Mother's Ruin,' an old haunt of theirs from the past. As he entered into the bar, he took in the sight of his good friend, One Eyed Pew, sitting as always alone at a table in the shadows. At the bar stood two policemen; one of whom was none other than Treacle Tanner, who looked directly at him with no sign of recognition. He caught Harvey's eye for a brief moment before slowly turning away, a gesture that silently told Harvey that his master did not wish to be acknowledged.

"How've you been, Pew?" Harvey greeted his old friend.

"Hello yourself, Harvey. Long time, no see," Pew replied. He would have jumped up to give Harvey a great big slap on the back in greeting, but he thought the chance of surviving such an encounter to be slim. Harvey always checked his pockets after such close personal contact and didn't take too kindly to his friends rifling his pockets. Harvey pulled up a chair with his back to the wall and his ear as close to Pew's mouth as would pass for decency in a public place. Past experience told him Pew dropped his voice to a whisper when the conversation covered a topic the police would describe as "fruity." First they briefly spoke of their time apart; Harvey took care to omit his last twelve months on the far side of the mountain range. He didn't want to make the mistake of letting anyone know that the rogue wanted dead or alive for a hundred shiny gold coins was the same rogue sitting in the same bar with them. So the conversation mostly focused on the time when the two of them were hired to catch a pig rustler on the high plains.

They had been employed by the farmer Mc Donald to retrieve his herd, for the promise of a few hogs in payment. They were chosen because everyone knew they had no interest in anything agricultural, thus no possible conflict of interests could exist. It helped that they lived in that grey area between law and disorder, where things got done if the payment was acceptable. Harvey and Pew had liked it that way; the police never bothered them because they didn't rob the honest citizen. And helping the local constabulary catch the odd crook every so often always paid dividends as well. At times, the officers turned a blind eye to the exact amount of stolen property that would be recovered during the arrest, allowing a healthy reward to be extracted where none was offered by the courts.

They travelled to the numerous street markets and butcher shops along the trading routes around the victim's farm, stumbling across a leg of pork hanging in a butcher's window, with what remained of a branding from the "crazy reversed W" Farm marked upon its hide. For those with a keen eye, it was obvious to see that someone had attempted to obscure the brand by casually altering the mark. It would have duped a normal customer who didn't care, but it was fairly obvious to the trained eye of someone who could tell the length of time between burn marks.

When leant on, the butcher squealed like a fat pig -- especially when the leaning was done by Pew's elbow digging deep into the old man's chest. The lowdown given to them by the butcher put them on the heels of the Mallow family, a more aggressive, self-serving

147

bunch one would never meet. The family were the main instigators behind Pew getting his name of 'One Eyed Pew,' which caused him to curse their very name.

Both of them vividly remembered a time sleeping in a haystack for a couple of days, observing the family's movements inside their remote farmhouse, deep in the bracken-covered hills. They watched as lanterns zigzagged up the hillside following the ancient tracks laid by an ancient race whose name was long since forgotten. At the end of the track, they saw the lanterns quickly illuminate a cave mouth, before total darkness covered the ancient slopes. They guessed that the hillside cave was the perfect location to hide the pigs while they were re-branded and butchered for distribution.

To legitimise their actions, they enlisted the local police officer to help them place the family under arrest. But as they barged their way into the front of the farmhouse, the Mallows escaped out of the back. The ensuing chase resulted in Harvey and Pew falling face-first right in it -- quite literally, it took weeks to get rid of the smell. The episode only confirmed the reason why they normally didn't get involved directly in farming escapades, or anything else involving the countryside.

Now captured, the Mallows were judged by twelve good men from their community, all of which save one was a pig farmer. Truth be told, there wasn't really anyone who wasn't a farmer in those parts. The court's sentence seemed to agree with Pew, who had said the only good Mallow was a Mallow on the gallows.

At this point in the story, they were both leaning over the table in peals of laughter. Pew fought through their shared mirth to say "Remember the laughs we had when we found that second cave full of pork products, well before the remaining Mallow family members could regroup and get their act together to dispose of the evidence. Was it six or eight butchered hogs we found there?" "Six plump porkers, I think the butcher called them, remember his face when we walked into his shop again"? "I think he almost swallowed his dentures" Harvey laughed. "That was a picture, wasn't it? and a great price as I remember, and a couple weeks of fun", Pew responded. "Couple of weeks for you, couple of months for me you old goat". They both laughed uncontrollably.

As they wiped the tears away, the conversation came round to the awkward bit about the here and now and what the future held. Pew normally enquired at great depth into Harvey's plans; he had always done so in the past. Today, however -- luckily for Harvey -- he decided to brag about his next caper. "Do you know that a lot of little items of interest can fall into your pockets down at the docks". Harvey felt a wave of relief wash over him. He didn't want to mention his employer, standing only steps away from their table, and doubtlessly hearing at least part of their conversation.

Pew gave Harvey a nod towards the police officers at the bar. "Watch out for those two -- they don't look like much but they have a ruthless reputation," he confided. "I heard one is very good with his hands and the other is a right street thumper. Those two arrested Damien Guppy just by themselves, so I heard, and Crunch and Munch who were present at the time are nursing their wounds at their mums. That's the word on the street, mate. So steer clear of those two. Consider yourself warned."

"I will," Harvey replied, giving the officers at the bar the briefest of looks. "Thanks for the heads-up."

"But it seems they like to break the rules like the rest of us," Pew remarked, as he gave the "drinky, drinky" hand movement universally known across all the three continents. "If Chief Constable Quern catches them, they would be for the high jump. If I wasn't too afraid of being called a snitch, I would tell him myself." Pew retorted. Harvey found he needed all his concentration not to get fixated on Treacle, and his almost perfect pretence of someone casually enjoying nothing more than a good drink. He wondered if anyone had guessed that nothing within that glass had touched his lips. He so wanted to tell Pew what he really was seeing, but he knew Treacle would be in deep trouble if he did. Actually, not so much trouble for Treacle personally, but more than enough trouble for the person who tried to point out this fact, he thought.

As Harvey prepared to make his excuses to leave, Pew stood up from the table. "I know you've seldom heard me say it, but I really have to return to work. There's a big ship arriving today, and all the other ships need to be moved out of port as soon as they unload their cargo. And, as we know, a large ship has a lot to go missing. Be seeing you, Harvey."

"Take care, Pew. Don't get yourself Press-Ganged,'" Harvey said with a smile.

Treacle locked the house up himself, ensuring all of the crossbars and braces he had installed were in place. He knew the reinforcements were only meant for the ground floor, but the idea was to gain time rather than to keep out intruders. He still had his police whistle to summon help if needed. Treacle had to admit that the police whistle would have been quite an advantage if one had a life-or-death situation house-training a werewolf. Otherwise the whistle just antagonised an enemy to be more ruthless.

After the house had settled for the night, Treacle sat at the kitchen table with a plate of blood sausage and a glass of red wine and proceeded to read a letter the Etherington's had accepted on his behalf. It was from his Cousin Aleasia, who was as "keen as mustard," as she wrote in her letter, to get to the big city and shake it up a bit. Treacle was quite sure the city was shaken up enough. Adding Aleasia would be like lighting the blue touch-paper, which he didn't mind doing, as long as he could retire to a safe distance first.

After first reading the letter as any normal person would, he decided he still had time to decipher and read the second message hidden in the text of the letter as well. The cipher was very easy if one looked for it -- merely read the capital letters, or the letters after a full stop was encountered. The second message read that the clans had been informed of all of Treacle's discoveries, and they were acting on his requests. Treacle knew he had stirred the proverbial hornets' nest, but he had no choice; the consequences would be horrendous if events were left to run their natural course. As the darkness of the night deepened, Treacle blew out the lamplight. Sitting in the dark, he watched the expanse of Higher Reach Lane through a specially placed knot in the shutters.

The street was extremely hard to read tonight due to the long shadows being cast from the lights of the nearby houses that burned wax for illumination. Their owners had deep pockets that could afford large glass windows, and personal security that stopped someone from breaking them to enter.

Treacle had hoped that he had attracted enough attention to deserve at least a semi-professional hit man to fulfil a contract on him, but it seemed he had only got the attention of a complete bunch of amateurs. He sat watching them from his seat as they plotted their attack on his house from the shadow of the stable opposite. He felt a rising sense of offence; it was just plain rude, in his opinion, to send them, as it reflected that, in someone's opinion, he was hardly a risk at all.

The three men seemed to be common street thugs, who apparently held the opinion that General Gordon's famous pincer strategy worked in urban break-ins and murders. Having heard and seen their plan, as they discussed it and pointed it out to each other while they argued between themselves, Treacle knew exactly what was coming. He made his way up to the second floor, placing himself behind the master bedroom door to the hallway.

Soon he heard the window break and the knife release its lock. He then saw the shadow move across the bedroom and the look of confusion fall over the shadow when he found his target's bed was empty.

The second fellow was having trouble getting through his window. It seemed as though had intentionally nailed it shut. The third thug had discovered that the window he chose from which to enter opened a little too easily, as if it were greased regularly. This had totally surprised him when it almost jumped its rails at the top of its tracks.

While still worrying about the sound of the window, and wondering if the noise had alerted the occupants of his presence, he swung into the house and gently let himself drop onto the floor. Except he discovered there was no floor; in fact the floor and the beams had been removed by the builders earlier that day to replace the rot they had found a few days before. His fall was broken by a stack of chairs previously arranged, their legs all facing upward, ending his worries forever as he was skewered like a piece meat on a stick. The thug who entered into the master bedroom had decided to creep along on the tips of his toes across the bedroom floor towards the hall. Treacle was thinking to himself, what a bloody fool. These louts really were amateurs. Everybody knows floorboards make more sound when the weight of man was pressed onto such a small area. Anyone who crept around at night knew that, or at least should. Treacle could feel his heartbeat quicken, or it could have been indigestion, as the second man succeeded in opening the window. Now he had two men inside the walls, hunting him with daggers drawn.

Treacle wondered if he should wait for them to come to him or take the initiative by intercepting them. He found that the decision had been made for him as the man creeping along on his tip-toes quickly drew level with him. Summoning his full force of strength, Treacle used the edge of his hand to hit the intruder across the throat. The thug made a small cough-like gurgle as he fell dead at Treacle's feet. Turning round to locate the last intruder, he was confronted by the sight of a knife being thrust toward him from an outstretched arm. The knife stopped just inches before him; it did not move, it simply hovered in place, as if a spider sitting on an invisible web between two trees. Behind the blade, Treacle saw a smile, the unforgettable smile of Harvey, with one hand over the thug's mouth, and a second withdrawing a blade from the ruffian's overly exposed armpit, and it was a very long blade. With a wink, Harvey announced, "Mr. Coppet's exploding and extending dagger, banned on three continents. Once the trigger is pressed, the blade doubles in length. I hope it's the outcome you wished for, sir," he said with the respect he only gave to someone of Treacle skills.

Treacle drew an imaginary vertical line in the air with his finger. "That's one life I owe you then, Harvey. It won't be forgotten, my friend." Harvey smiled. "I think you underestimated them just a little, sir. To still be alive at their age in this city in their choice of career requires more than just a sharp dagger. It requires brains or speed, or an evil combination of both."

Treacle patted him on his back. "Well, shall we send Etherington to the local station to get the night officers?" Harvey looked at him, a shocked expression on his face. "That would be extremely unwise with that bowman targeting our front door. Unless you wanted a dead butler, of course."

Treacle now felt that at least someone considered him a serious threat if they were willing to back up the street thugs with an assassin bowman. It gave him back his dignity. So someone did respect his skills after all, even if it was his enemy. Harvey said, "We do have a few of Mr. Coppet's little toys. How about a flaming dart blowpipe or maybe a flying dagger bow? No? Maybe the siege breaker crossbow, or is that a bit of an overkill." "Overkill, Harvey?"

Treacle asked. "I don't think that's possible, but I don't think we should use all your toys. We might need everything in the toy box quite soon, if I read the circumstances correctly. Right now, I think it's a situation that requires me to have a private moment alone. Don't worry about our friend across the street. I think deaths on the wing."

Now alone, Treacle focused himself on the task ahead. Mind projection was a trick that vampires had long had in their arsenal, but every time he used it he always felt as though he irrevocably lost a piece of his soul. Placing himself in sight of the target area where he wanted to arrive, Treacle took a deep breath and felt himself slip away. A small, grey cloud floated out of the window and across the street, just above the cobbles. If the bowman had been thinking clearly, without the highly concentrated thought of killing someone, he might have wondered why the mist-like cloud was floating in a straight line against the gentle breeze. Then again, maybe not.

Behind the bowman, a smoky figure began solidifying in total silence and without moving, until it tried to squeeze its own hand to just check that it was solid enough for the job in hand. The bowman felt two steel-like hands grab him; the first over the mouth to stop the scream, whilst the second grabbed his arm with such force he suddenly couldn't feel his own fingers. With a twist of the head, his neck was exposed for a deathly thirst which had no remorse and absolutely no forgiveness.

Treacle looked down at what was a large, dead problem lying at his feet. What to do? he wondered, when he heard a discreet cough from the shadows. It was the type of cough that revealed the owner without giving too much information away. Harvey stepped out of the shadows. "I saw everything, sir. Total self-defence, I would say."

Treacle watched as Harvey cleaned the blood from his dagger. "Why did you leave the house?" he asked incredulously. "You could have been killed if I hadn't finished dealing with this fellow outside."

"But this is not the bowman I pointed to," Harvey replied. "I quickly realised just in time for you. Treacle, I think you would have been very upset with an arrow-like stake protruding from your chest, and I believe it was covered in garlic oil for your extra enjoyment."

"So we have two bodies outside the confines of the property border to explain? That's not going to look like self-defence, is it?"

"I think if you hurry to Officer's Clump's residence at 32 Upper Screw Drive, we might have another. I suggest you use every means of travel possible, sir. Time is of the essence!" Harvey shouted down the street as Treacle ran off.

Moments later a swarm of bats set off across the rooftops, carrying a large load beneath them who seemed to use its legs to hold itself up to steer around many of the larger chimney pots on some of the higher rooftops. Otherwise the passenger would have been slammed into a roof face first. Bats, it seems, never have a good sense of distance between themselves and the person they carry. In fact, they appear to have no perception of a minimum flying height which accommodates the safety of their payload.

In short order the bats arrived at their destination. They slowly released Treacle, letting him fall gently onto the street. While everyone thought people like Treacle could change into a bat at will and travel wherever they wished, that mistaken thought was due to the fact that someone had once recounted a story of what they thought they had seen while in a state of sheer terror. They obviously hadn't seen the truth directly in front of their own eyes, that Treacle could summon the bats at will, much like a personal taxi service. When and where they were needed, they just appeared. Once used, the bats returned back to whatever they happened to be doing before they had been so inconveniently summoned.

The bats dropped Treacle off in the shadows precisely where he needed to be, as always. The small, little home of Mr. and Mrs. Hammerstone was also in the shadow of the night, but these shadows were not still. Instead, they all seemed to be slowly gravitating toward 32 Upper Screw Lane. Treacle wrapped his cape around himself to obscure his shape. Since the street was too exposed to cross over directly in front of the Hammerstone's house, he crossed the street a couple of houses up. This manoeuvre also gave him the advantage of now being behind a group of professional hit men. As far as Treacle could discern, they were all walking with knives drawn, but their knives did not reflect any light, and the men walked with a practiced style that made as little sound as possible.

Treacle crept up behind the first, dispatching him as quietly as possible with a quick snap of the neck. He then took the thug's place in formation. Once the shadowy group reached the alleyway to the back of the Hammerstones', Treacle made fast work of the remaining two in front of him. A knife flashed red across the neck of the first thug closest to him, who gave a little squeal in death. As his partner turned to see what had happened, a set of teeth clamped his windpipe.

Once he was certain that the would-be assailants were down and out, Treacle quickly made his way to the back of 32 Upper Screw Lane, and tapped out a tune on the back door so that Clump would know it was him. A few seconds later the front door of the home was forced, to screams from nearly everyone -- some in horror, some in pain and some in bloody hatred for the intrusion into the family's home. Treacle knew one should never enter a house unless invited, but that rule of etiquette was never envisioned for life-or-death situations. Thus he broke in the door and flattened himself to the wall just in time to avoid a crossbow bolt whizzing past him, unleashed by extremely angry Clump standing in his shorts, his face full of rage, and afraid he would be obliged to fight an attack from two directions.

Treacle nodded at his partner. "Three down this side," he said, as reassuringly as possible. To Treacle's great relief, Clump saw through his blind rage and lowered his crossbow. Now Clump concentrated his defence on the onslaught from the front door. Grabbing a rolling pin from the kitchen table, he bludgeoned the first thug to thrust his head through the doorway.

Treacle circled around to the front of the house, and saw the last man starting to run away, leaving his second companion being flattened by the same rolling pin that scored the first. Clump's strength left him as the thug hit the floor, He steadied himself against the table as his wife began treating him like her hero.

"I would suggest you go to the station, but I know both of you would prefer not to sleep in the cells all night, so you're invited to stay as my personal guests at my rather modest home," Treacle stated. "I believe the guest room has been refurbished by Mrs. Etherington for such occasions. I think your wife would find it more than acceptable." Clump knew he couldn't refuse; him being a nob's son, only god knew what sort of trouble his refusal could cause his future career plans. In any case, Treacle was very handy in a tight spot, that was for sure.

Harvey returned to the house to find Mr Etherington wearing a full-length, waterproof green apron. His shoes were completely wrapped in scraps of cloth to stop his smart, shiny new shoes getting scuffed. He certainly looked like someone ready to help start moving dead bodies to a more advantageous location within the grounds of the house, which would help define everyone's thinking to reach the rightful conclusion of self-defence during the oncoming police investigation.

Harvey had seen vampire-like influences on the minds of people before, but it had never been as subtle as this. Normally it was the plain variety of "What am I doing here and where did the last five minutes go?" Not as good as that being shown by the Etheringtons at this moment. Maybe Treacle had a gift for it. If so, he'd better keep checking himself in the mirror each morning but, if it was not a vampire-like influence, they were one hell of a pair of good servants to play along with this charade. The first bowman must have enjoyed his food a bit too much because he was carried with some effort back to the house, where he was placed in a position that appeared to be in support of his colleague who had entered the back window. After getting their strength back in order to move the second body, Harvey could see Mrs Etherington preparing to run to the police station to report the event. The moment they were half way across the road, Mrs. Etherington could be seen disappearing round the corner on her desperate run for help. By the time she could return, the second bowman would be relocated onto the lawn next to the front door. Before long, she returned with a group of officers in tow who were mightily relieved that they had arrived just too late to get involved in a life-or-death struggle.

Stagnation sets in

In town for the season - tethered goat

Harvey turned and found himself face to face with one of the most beautiful women he had ever set eyes on for a second time. "I say, good man, may I suggest a quick slash to his throat to remove the obvious evidence? If you don't have the stomach for it, I will do it," she said as she pointed at the two puncture marks on the bowman's neck.

Harvey knew not to rock the boat, and did what he was told, while Etherington retired to the house before he was sick all over his shoes. "Tell me, good man, where is your master? It obviously looks like he is out of his depth again," she said without expecting a reply.

"Miss Stagnation, I believe Mr. Tanner is dispatching several other opponents as we speak. I believe the phrase is 'You can't make bread pudding without breaking eggs.'"

"How do you know my name?" she asked.

"Harvey's the name, miss," he replied. "I know you, Miss Aleasia Stagnation, because when I was a young lad I attended the blood moon festivities in Nocte Mortis where I was captivated by the most beautiful young lady I had ever seen. Now here you are, looking as young and radiant and as beautiful as you did that day I first saw you."

Aleasia knew only fear in the face of the men she normally met in dark alleys late at night when she fancied a quick bite, but never had anyone complemented her before, and especially on a second meeting. Harvey watched as Aleasia slowly blushed, no mean feat for a vampire to achieve, especially with an anaemic complexion. From that moment, he knew he was not going to be mistaken for a light bite.

He would have invited her into the main reception room, but since he heard Ethrington in there, involuntarily coughing up his lunch, Harvey hastily decided upon on an alternative destination. On such short notice, the kitchen would have to do. As they made their way down the hall, he noticed the hem of her dress around her, it was more smoke than cloth but as the dress rose around her it slowly became a shimmering ball gown while still somehow maintaining a solid black colour. Harvey supposed she had tradition to uphold and black was so good for hiding in dark alleyways while awaiting a quick bite.

In his best gentlemanly manner, Harvey pulled back a kitchen chair for her to sit down, it was the gentlemanly thing to do before placing a glass of the nearest bottle of red in front of her. He thought it would quench any thirst she might have after her long journey, as well as improve the conversation a little.

"Thank you, kind sir," she said, surveying him up and down as if measuring his fluid capacity. "So you are not a servant then?"

"I would describe myself more as a companion," Harvey replied. "I do jobs the master, shall we say, cannot be seen to be undertaking. Plus, I have many contacts that a young, upstanding gentleman such as Mr. Tanner should not be seen in the company of."

Aleasia laughed, setting Harvey at ease. Why she laughed or even followed her expression of mirth with a smile, she couldn't say.

In short order, the bulk of the police constabulary arrived in full force, followed shortly thereafter by Chief Constable Quern in a dashing armour and pyjama ensemble. He very quickly took charge, demanding a quick count of the dead and living and the cost to both sides. Then the question arose -- "Where is Treacle Tanner?" Quern's query was filled with trepidation; he feared the young man's death would suck him into a political maelstrom from which he couldn't extricate himself.

Treacle heard Quern's distant voice and answered from almost the other end of the street, which he regretted immediately. He should have waited until he was a little closer, so as not to reveal that he possessed that superhuman sense. Several hours of questioning ensued in the main reception room followed by the mandatory re-enactment, which was then followed by what felt like another hour of being reprimanded for breaking police protocol by moving the bodies from across the street. It was not the fact they were dead -- what thoroughly got Quern's goat was that the bodies had been relocated. When the police finally left with the flotsam of the night's little escapade, Treacle took the opportunity to descend into the kitchen, only to discover Clump and his wife had been plied with so much medicinal whiskey for their nerves, that they had successfully lost the feeling of nearly all of them. Mrs. Etherington was trying her best to help them into a downstairs guest bedroom, before she and her husband retired for the night.

Then, to complicate matters even further, there was Aleasia and Harvey encamped around the kitchen table, sharing a bottle of wine. Their general happiness seemed at odds, not with what had happened, as both liked a bit of blood-letting, but with everything Treacle knew about Aleasia. She despised anyone who was not a clan member and then barely acknowledged those who were. She was more of a singular, galloping woman-across-the-moor type of personality, with a possibility of thunder later. She was not an open and honest 'it would be all right on the night' sort.

He pulled up a chair and joined them and very quickly realised that he had been mistaken. Their conversation was not really a team sport; it was more tennis. It took an "accident" with his red wine to extricate himself from the situation, and the spill down his front gave him the perfect excuse to politely make his excuses and leave.

The next morning, he was actually surprised to see Harvey join him for breakfast without Aleasia by his side. Harvey stared at him over his breakfast, and Treacle knew there was a question just waiting to be asked.

"Just say it Harvey, I won't take offence I promise you'. The request hanged there for a while, then a carefully phrased question was raised in return,

"Is your strength hereditary or is there another reason?' Harvey asked.

Treacle displayed his broadest smile in an attempt to put Harvey at ease, as he fumbled for the amulet around his neck and pulled it free from his clothing.

Harvey immediately recognized the little gold amulet -- it was only given to pupils from the prestigious school of Wong Zu. He knew it was genuine, as anyone caught wearing one without actually attending the school was a good way to mark yourself for death by all of the school's alumni. That would include a majority of royalty in these parts, as well as a lot of the travelling monks who moved from town to town, telling people to "be good to each other or else --." This religion believed that once in a while a cleric was required to slap its congregation meta-physically back onto the straight and narrow.

"Is it true that they starve the pupils and let them sit in the snow without hardly any clothes on, as well as teaching them to break a man in two with their bare hands?' Harvey enquired.

"No," Treacle shot back. "They teach the appreciation of regular meals and a warm bed for the night. The students who do decide to become travelling monks after they leave the school, are taught to withstand the extreme cold as part of their religious studies." Treacle gave Harvey an obliging smile. "It's said they sit closer to God on the high mountain tops, a common misunderstanding, but that's gossip for you." "And the martial arts?" Harvey queried.

"Yes, it's a study I have undertaken since I was a young boy," Treacle replied. "It enhances any natural talent one may have, and if you're naturally a little bit stronger than most, then you will always be a little bit stronger. It also teaches you to have the strength of mind to survive a variety of physical and metal challenges. I am sure you understand," Treacle concluded, in a tone that indicated he was finished discussing the topic

Harvey recognized Treacle's words for what they were. The clan had not sent some bumbling country vampire into the city like a tethered goat to the slaughter -- Treacle was a vastly intelligent and highly skilled member of their clan, here to stir the pot. By luck or circumstance, his side had been chosen for him against all comers.

"Harvey, I have a task for you today," Treacle said. "I believe a large delivery will be arriving at the docks and I need to know more. I am sure Aleasia would also like a tour of the city as well. You know -- what's good, what's bad and the general location of everything -- that sort of thing." Treacle waved his hand to cover almost anything else he might have forgotten. "Personally, I will be guarding Clump while letting him believe he is guarding me, as we both guard the house together. The builders will be here as well, as I think some more improvements are required to enhance our security."

The builders arrived on schedule -- they really didn't have a free choice in the matter, after all -- and set to work immediately repairing the second floor that they had left half-finished the day before, leaving Treacle at peace in the dining room to read the local paper. The headline above the fold focused on the price of wine, and how it was expected to drop when the much larger cargo capacity vessels arrived, which the port could now accommodate. Count Alexander had invested heavily in dredging and deepening the slips, intent on having port improvements completed for the new season.

As for his nocturnal adventures, the story was buried on page six and described two raids by the police-flying squad encountering extreme violence and protecting themselves against several known violent criminals. Later paragraphs bemoaned the fact that deadly force had been required to arrest them. The story had the touch of Mr. Easy all over it, thought Treacle; it enhanced the standing of the police force while cleverly scaring the criminal element.

After reading between the lines of the story for the second time, he heard a murmur from behind his paper, followed by the noise of elbows hitting the table. The sound had the very particular resonance of someone nursing the mother of all hangovers, readily informing him that Clump had surfaced. Treacle folded the paper so that only the relevant story showed, and handed it to Clump. After watching Clump contort his face in an attempt to focus his bloodshot eyes while trying to make out the story from the cartoons in the headline, Treacle recognized that his partner's reading comprehension was non-existent.

"Let me tell you the gist of the story if you can't focus this early in the day," Treacle said, giving no hint that he knew Clump couldn't read. After recounting to him all the details, plus his thoughts about Mr. Easy contacting the paper's editors before the morning edition had hit the presses, Treacle handed the paper over to Clump so he could appreciate the cartoons in a new light.

Despite his throbbing head, Clump smiled as he recounted a story from his experience on the force. "'It's like that time Officer Ginger was walking past Principal's Bank and fell in on those robbers digging into the vault. The newspaper said he found them through diligent investigation and a stakeout over several days."

Even Treacle had to grin at the audacity of the story; it had a ring of truth that sounded much better than falling down a hole in the ground. That's how it's supposed to work, he thought. Tell the people the truth they want to hear, not what actually happens.

"Well Clump, my old mucker, you can stay here in my house as my guest, where you will be totally safe from everyone, I can assure you," Treacle said.

Clump gave him a concerned look and let slip what Treacle already knew was worrying him. "Does this cover Miss Aleasia?"

"Yes, even she will respect my wishes in my own home, my friend. Although I must admit she is a bit scary, but shhhhh!", Treacle put a forefinger to his lips, "Don't tell her, though," he said with a reassuring smile and a wink.

In the meantime, the builders worked at their rapid and hypnotised pace, finishing the floor and all the shuttered windows. They even added extra fire-resistance everywhere Treacle required, leaving them only the final task for the day of reopening the well in the cellar. Treacle tried his best to get the family Hammerstone to relax, but he recognized that a house full of vampires inside, while outside an enemy willing to slit your throat, was not conducive towards a relaxing environment. He decided the best option was to simply leave them in peace. Thereupon, for the remainder of the day, Treacle made himself scarce by either consulting with the builders or engaging the Etheringtons with domestic duties, leaving the Hammerstones to themselves.

Fashion on Parade

Painted Lady – Pinch the Cloth

Drink on the Wild Side

M abel's career, if it could be called that, was improving again with a new assignment from her agency. This time it was to be a model at the prestigious Franco-side fashion shows where she was to model some of the "one-off" pieces of clothing from the number one fashion designer, Larry Futon. He had a reputation of being "new and cutting edge," insider speak for making loads of money by changing fashion so radically year to year that it was impossible to wear last year's clothes without looking hopelessly old fashioned. Mabel was a bit of a fan of his designs as his clothes even made her look good. The assignment would not be too much trouble as she spoke Franco-side, mandatory in the curriculum at Mrs Higginbottom's academy.

The local Fashionistas were travelling from the city to the venue at 'Seau De Port' on the private yacht 'The Lady Marie Jane' which, for all her refinery and frippery, still packed a stealthy 16 guns under her very discreetly misshaped portals. Piracy had mostly disappeared since the ship owners had banded together and hired the worst pirate they knew to hunt down the rest. They could easily have afforded the best pirate, but the best pirate would have taken the money and created a new world order, whilst the worst pirate -- 'Half a Beard Pete' -- just settled old scores and harassed as many pirate ships as he could.

The Lady Marie Jane made good time on the crossing, and the canapés and generous refills of wine eased the passengers into a gentle slumber. When Mabel awoke, they were entering the harbour's mouth. On the dock-side the local fish mongers were plying their trade -- she heard their cries of "fresh fish", and their wares could be smelt on the air.

Awaiting them on the dockside were three carriages decorated in the finest gilding, each eagerly pulled by two white horses which conveyed them up into one of the nine hills of 'Seau De Port.' At the top of this hill stood a very impressive castle which seemed to be two castles in one -- the outermost castle was built for defence with heavy walls, turrets and battlements, while the inner castle was more a fashion artist's idea of what a castle should look like. It had a very ornate entrance with a door made of teak so paper thin one wondered if it bent in the wind. Mabel could not help smiling to herself at the absurd beauty of the whole spectacle.

The carriages came to a complete stop in a large courtyard, and she could see the grand staircase leading up to the first floor of the inner castle complex. It was made from the finest marble, covered in the images of long-dead sea creatures, forever preserved in mid-death. Mabel considered the scene the most beautiful sight she had ever seen. At the top of the stairs stood their host Larry Futon, dressed in the finest silk suit, in shades of lavender, its colour created from materials gathered from all three corners of the known world. He was very keen to get his guests into the grand hall, styled to resemble a large tent, due to all the fabrics draped across the ceilings and walls. Each piece of fabric had been chosen from his new collection, and had been arranged in such a way to give him inspiration, he announced to his guests, who always asked.

Once she was inside this fine room, Larry skipped up to Mabel and held her face inbetween two warm little hands and gently squeezed, forcing her lips to pout. He then released her from his sweaty little grip. "Perfect! Just perfect, my dear Mabel. You have di look Iz want; we will make history together."

The evening was filled with a lot of self-congratulation and wine. Mabel thought the party was getting a bit out of hand when Larry ordered another dozen bottles of wine from his cellar. They did have to work tomorrow, after all. So she made her excuses and left for bed. The route to her room meant travelling up the main stairwell with its small window overlooking the fields beyond the castle walls. There she paused for a moment. In the distance she could make out a large encampment of soldiers sitting around fires singing songs in front of their tents. Mabel stood and listened a while until she felt the lyrics where getting a bit too explicit. If she listened any longer her flushed, red-hot cheeks would explode.

Mabel was awakened by the market stallholders below her room calling out their wares, as the encamped army on the other side of the village barked out commands for their early morning drills. She dressed herself and arrived early for breakfast, fresh-faced and ready to start modelling.

Their host Larry Futon apologised to his guests for any distress the dragoons might have caused, but the army was on summer exercises, and the soldiers would soon return to their villages for the harvest. Mabel paid no heed -- she was much more interested in all the clothes hanging along the walls. Each garment was organised into colour and style, awaiting the upcoming show. The morning was full of fittings and re-fittings until lunch, which came as a total relief. She didn't know it was such hard work trying on clothes and standing still, as pins were accidentally placed where they shouldn't be.

The afternoon was not much better, with the hair-stylist and make-up artist each, in turn, criticising her hair and face. The hair-stylist declared that she had the wrong facial shape for her hair, while the make-up artist announced that her hair was the wrong colour complexion. Lucky for me I'm so thick-skinned, she thought; otherwise these puffed-up old fools would be getting right on her wick by now. As show-time approached, and her "fools" congratulated each other on the beauty they had created, Mabel looked in the mirror and realised these guys deserved to be in fashion -- they could have been with the salesman who sold the Emperor his new clothes. The whole fashion parade moved down into the courtyard where a huge tent had been erected. A runway ran along its length for the models to show off, well, whatever they could show.

When the morning, started Mabel had felt a rush of excitement for her first foray into the fashion industry. But after her first walk, down and turn with look, and back again, her image of fashion was brutally destroyed, when a personal assistant grabbed her arm and pulled her this way and that. As fast her feet could trip between clothing, shoes, hair and make-up, she was then cast back onto the runway again.

This happened again and again, until the curtain closed at the very end of the show, whereupon she pushed her assistant into a dark corner of the dressing room and clocked him with her right hook. He felt nothing else until they dunked him in the horse trough several minutes later. Mabel imagined that this would be her last trip into high fashion. She hadn't liked it much; she was sure her arms would turn black and blue from the manhandling meted out by the assistant. Yet everyone around her was so excited, and the models proceeded to split the seam of their dresses as they gorged themselves on puff- pastries and champagne.

She decided an early night was in order to avoid being sucked into this unhealthy lifestyle the others had seemed to have perfected. She still had a huge slice of chocolate cake unfinished and some shortbread left from the day before, which she would pack for her return journey home. That was the problem with Franco-side cooking, she groused. If it wasn't the garlic, it was the ridiculously small portions. The amount of food served here was hardly enough to keep one warm at night. On the long march up the stairs towards her room, she glanced out of the window. Curious about the troops' preparation to leave, Mabel watched as they packed equipment into what appeared to be specially marked wine barrels. Did their week of playing soldier make the country safer? she wondered. Or was sleeping at night a bit easier, knowing the man next door was watching out for the safety of his family and neighbours?

Harvey almost couldn't believe his good fortune; he had been awarded the dream job of escorting Aleasia around town. When it was in his mind, and when he went to raise her from her slumber, to his pleasant surprise he found her awaiting his knock. She was clad in a girl-about-town sort of way, or at least what she believed that choice of garb to mean. She even gave up black for the day, dressing in pastel colours. Yet her hair remained black as night and she still wore make-up. In fact, she was wearing a lot of make-up. Her white silk gloves covered any possible portion of skin in danger of exposure. The city was in its usual smoggy state, so that one could walk its entire length in the middle of its largest boulevard without seeing direct sunlight. After some consideration, Harvey decided that the gloves might be some sort of fashion statement. A burlap sack would hardly protect anyone better from the sun than the city's customary smog.

They casually walked and chatted, as they slowly made their way down to the docks. Their conversation resumed seamlessly from the night before. To his surprise, Aleasia was still single. It was very hard to meet that Mister Right, she said, mainly because the candidates couldn't help but feel they were but one wrong step away from being lunch. As for dating a vampire, well, they were so vain -- always wondering if the right colour silk handkerchief went with their eyes. She also loved racing across the moors, a fast stallion below her, risking life and limb on each jump, as she dodged the unchartered areas of quicksand. That was living on the edge, she said, and not many men she normally met liked living that close to death.

Harvey pointed out the city's famous landmarks to the young beauty draped on his arm, such as the spire in the park and the numerous fashion boutiques -- everything he thought a girl about town would wish to see. But like Treacle, she was mostly interested in the new methods of security at the port, with the high walls and towers facing into the city. She even mused aloud regarding the sort of force it would need to take the gates once they had been shut and bolted. Is this like talking to a general's daughter? Harvey wondered. All ponies and ballistas? Once they had arrived at the dock, Harvey truly was at a loss. What would interest this fair lass, visiting town on a trip from the country? Luckily for him, at this point Aleasia requested that he purchase a bottle of wine to bring back for their evening meal. So they visited most of the emporiums, tasting wines and making a list of potentially suitable brands. She placed orders for her very personal stock back home.

Gradually it began to dawn on Harvey that he was enjoying a much better time than she was. The wine was not having the same effect on her. While he was on the other side of squiffy, she still had not reached giggly. Then he wondered -- Are vampires capable of getting drunk? That thought was about three drinks too late in his case. He had not got one over the eight in quite a long time, and was obliged to ask Aleasia to support him on the stagger home, which she did for a second or two before letting him drop into the street. "I think you are trying to take advantage of my good nature to get close to me, Mr. Taadpole," she said primly. "Let that be a lesson to you." She offered him a hand to get back on his feet. He was rather expecting a dainty tug on his arm, while he did most of the effort of rising to his feet. Instead, he received a steely grip which almost picked him straight up off his feet, and put back down right-side up.

They both made it back home in time for Harvey to get a nap and recover before the evening meal, which was steak a-la Franco-side. In essence, it was raw meat with a seared surface to keep all the juices within. The dish was a suggestion from Mrs. Etherington, who wanted everyone happy without the bother of cooking two sets of meals. The Hammerstones also joined them Having discovered they were not part of the household's menu, they had confidence to be seen in company. What Clump didn't know, was that once one was invited into a vampire's home, it was his duty as a host to protect you at all costs. He certainly couldn't invite guests to tea if they were to be the main dish -- that just wouldn't be cricket.

Following the meal, they sat around enjoying a large glass of red wine from the very nice bottle Aleasia had brought back from the dockside. As the conversation turned to the best wines from Treacle and Aleasia's vast vineyard experiences, a knock sounded at the front door. Brushing aside Etherington's complaints that it was not proper for a master to answer his own door, Treacle left the dining room, and returned with a man dressed in a well-tailored dark suit. Clump instantly recognised him as Mr. Easy, but what was he doing here? Mr. Easy did not make house calls ever, not even to Chief Constable Quern. A house-call meant he was outside his home turf and not in control of circumstances. The arsenal of little tricks he had spent years perfecting weren't available to him outside of his office.

Mr. Easy politely bowed, but it was only low enough to keep everyone in the room in his line of sight. "I do apologise for intruding at such a late hour," he said. "But I was just passing by and wanted to check on how you were all doing after what happened last night. I know the truth and have read the most recent reports, and I thought I should inform you that another attempt on your lives will be made tonight. I am sure of it. I would ask the police to secure the area for you, but we would only lose some good men." Mr. Easy gazed at Clump before continuing. "Policemen, I have learnt, stand in the shadows, but only when they believe no one is there to see them. They are too noisy and are usually found smoking a cigarette." Clump wanted to argue, but he knew Mr. Easy spoke the truth, especially concerning the night-shift lads, and he didn't want a friend risking his life while he was safe behind ironwood tree doors and windows. "Anyway," Mr. Easy continued, "I think the type of individuals that you will encounter tonight can handle themselves pretty well and are real professionals. They're the sort of people who take pride in their work, if you know what I mean. But when they find no officers of the law in attendance, it will slow them down a bit. Your enemies will worry, wondering where the police are located, and what they are doing, rather than attending to their own quick slaughter. Second, as they take their time trying to find where they're hidden, I will have some professionals of our own deal with as many as we can. I think you will have to deal with one or two who make it to your door. I recommend Harvey Taadpole should use the full collection of Auntie's toys." He shot a look at Harvey. "Which we are all well aware you possess, Mr. Taadpole, as we have seen the receipt. If you use them only tonight in this sanctioned event, the government will take a blind view on this matter.

Harvey was mighty impressed -- he had heard that no one came out on top when meeting Mr. Easy but, all considered, he thought he had achieved the best possible outcome for his first encounter with him, and hoped it would be his last. Mr. Easy was the type of man you threatened you kids with meeting, if you wanted them to go to bed early and didn't mind them having nightmares about the dark for the rest of their lives.

Mr. Easy nodded to Aleasia. "I see Miss Stagnation has graced us with her company and I hope no bad feeling will follow her from Trotter's Bend." Aleasia quickly managed to blurt out, "It was only cultural differences ---" before she was silenced by Mr. Easy, who raised one finger to his mouth. She didn't like Mr. Easy but she respected the fact that he was from the old country. Anyone who could live as long as he had without getting killed deserved respect. No doubt he must be totally ruthless and as sly as a fox.

Mr. Easy gave everyone one last look as they sat around the table. "Good luck," he said. "I hope I will see you tomorrow." Treacle returned to the table after he had escorted Mr. Easy to the door. He said, "Well, that was nice of him to come by in person, don't you think?"

Domestic Violence

House Breaking – Board Silly

Who's Truth

Harvey lit a very large cigar and, when no one raised a complaint, he sat back in his chair. "I think Mr Easy is verifying that he is being told the truth, whatever that is these days." As Aleasia caught a whiff of the cheap cigar, she shot Harvey a look. "I think I better smoke this outside," he said, rising to leave. Treacle put a hand on his arm as he walked by. "I think today we can make an exception. I get the feeling that if you stepped outside you would never get to finish that." He nodded at Harvey's cigar before turning his gaze to the domestic. "Etherington, check all the locks and windows. We need to know that only the windows we open are the ones they are going to come in through."

"That's a dangerous game you're playing there Treacle', Clump interjected. "I think it's the best game in town, though. People like to find weakness and exploit it to their advantage. That's where we will get the edge or, more truthfully, that's when they will get the edge."

Treacle smiled indulgently at his guest. "I think we'd better get ready. I suggest Mrs. Etherington and Mrs. Hammerstone take a frying pan and rolling pin and maybe a knife block down to the cellar." They both stared at Treacle. Mrs. Hammerstone screwed up her face before saying, "I am not going to hide in the cellar like a scared little girl, Mr. Tanner, especially while my husband takes all the risks." "No, no, you misunderstand, Mrs. Hammerstone," Treacle replied. "The well in the cellar has been opened up and I know we have placed a grate over it, but it will be our escape route if it all gets a bit hairy up above. So I would like you to protect our escape if you could, ladies. You both look quite capable of taking on any ruffians who may try to enter." They both smiled at the flattery and the importance of the job.

Then I would suggest myself and Clump take the top floor, as I am the only one he knows he can trust," Treacle continued. "Etherington, can you protect the main room and the entrance to the cellar? Don't worry about anything else. That leaves you, Aleasia and Harvey, to protect the ground floor." A look of bemusement crossed his face. "Let's hope they have heard about Trotter's Bend -- it might save us a lot of unnecessary slaughter. Aleasia now took her turn to stare at him with a look of annoyance, but Treacle had many years of experience of ignoring her, and quickly moved on.

184

"Now, is that okay with everyone?" he asked. Despite the gravity of the approaching crisis, his guests assembled before him at the dining room smiled at his gesture of courtesy. Everyone fully realised there weren't any other options; their fate had been sealed. Each group departed to their assigned areas as Clump and Treacle trudged up the stairs and down to the very end of the long hall. "I suggest we lock all the internal doors and windows, except this one at the end of the hall," Treacle said. "Then we will retreat to the top of the stairs, which will give us a rather long distance to protect ourselves with these." He removed a set of very small crossbows and quills from behind a picture hanging from the wall. "We will get the better of them" he said confidently, with a wink of his eye. Clump stared in awe at the weapon in Treacle's hands. Even he, a law enforcement professional, had not seen a weapon like this before, due to the fact its manufacture had been totally banned in six states. After quickly studying how it worked, he judged the killing distance was very short -- a hallway's length would be about right.

Treacle mischievously smiled at Clump. "Let's just hope they won't have any crossbows, and we might have the advantage along the length of this hallway." Below them Harvey and Aleasia were heard assembling the flying dagger bow. By now Aleasia had changed from her evening attire back into her black dress of smoke-like quality. Her hair was pinned back and she had armed herself with a few little accessories for the coming night. For his part, Etherington was equipped with an assortment of weapons. None of

185

them would be effective against a determined assault but they all looked very threatening.

While enduring the calm before the storm, Clump just had to fill the oppressive silence permeating the house. He asked, "When were you bitten? Treacle smiled again. "It happened about half past two as I remember." He chuckled. "No, but seriously my friend, I have always had this advantage in life. I was born a vampire to parents who were also vampires."

"So no digging yourself out of a coffin then, after you died?". "Now Clump, you don't believe those stories, do you?" The look on Clump's face told him he did. Treacle supposed if a story was told often enough, people would believe anything, and Clump completely believed. "Let me tell you something that will scare you to the point where you will need to replace your shorts. The number of vampires buried alive is a very small proportion when compared to the number of normal people buried alive. Only we have the strength and the lung capacity to dig ourselves out, compared to the rest of you." Treacle let that thought settle over Clump's consciousness, then added, "that's country doctors for you. They have so little knowledge that they don't even know when their patient is alive or dead." Clump felt a shiver run up his spine. Were normal people really buried alive or was Treacle pulling his leg again? He certainly looked serious enough. "Don't worry my friend," Treacle said in the kindest voice he could summon. "We will make sure you're stone dead before they bury you when you die many, many years from now."

This attempt at reassurance did not have the effect of putting Clump at ease as Treacle had expected. Personally, he had felt mightily relieved when he was told that story and what his friends would do for him.

After a few hours of uncomfortable silence, waiting at the top of the stairs, both of them feeling that anything they said could harm their delicate understanding, Treacle and Clump heard the sound of the window shutters being gently pushed with something sharp and metallic. The sound slowly eased down the hallway as each shutter in turn was tested. At the end of the hall, the very last one moved just enough to indicate that no lock had been fitted. Then the gentle pushing stopped.

Treacle signalled to Aleasia from the landing, that attack was going to kick off in just a minute, only to receive the signal from her. Meanwhile, Mrs. Etherington was in the basement doorway, shouting at them both that she too heard someone coming from down below. Quickly Treacle realized his enemies were coordinating their attack from a number of directions at once.

At that exact moment, pure instinct took control of Treacle; there was no time for reasoned thinking. He grabbed Clump and, over the officer's vehement protests, dragged him forward into the hallway. The double-strength, reinforced ironwood shutters above the hall which had been cross-braced for extra security -- shattered into a rain of deadly splinters, turning the landing area into a bed of nails. At the end of the hallway, as the window's shutters were blown inward, a large sword came thrusting forward. Clump had already sent a bolt flying, not bothering to watch where it went, before flattening himself against the wall and reloading his crossbow. Treacle only needed to hear a crunch of wood behind him to let loose a bolt. His pure instinct, as his other hand went to a sword he had only worn previously for ceremonial duties. He chose it for use on this occasion for practical applications, and not for the gilt that beautifully lined the blade's edge.

The first attacker who had managed to open the window at the end of the hall now slumped backwards. With a loud groan, he could be heard sliding down and off the slated roof of the veranda. Before the body had hit the ground, he was replaced by a second attacker waving a large crossbow, which he discharged the moment a shadow fell across the hallway. The bolt flew past Treacle's ear and embedded itself into the wall. Treacle's sword moved so fast that Clump only realised what had happened after his crossbow fired as a sword fell across the trigger mechanism. The bolt took out the intruder who had been forcing his way through the window, sending him backward. He landed dead, with a sickening thump on the ground below. Treacle exchanged his own loaded crossbow with Clump's spent one and threw it at the open window. It connected with someone peering in to see if the coast was clear. Behind them they heard two men jump down from the roof window. The assailants instantly discovered that ironwood splinters could easily penetrate the soles of one's shoes. As they screamed in pain, Treacle and Clump dispatched them at once with a swing of their swords. Suddenly Clump lifted his bow and fired toward the roof. Treacle had just enough time to stumble back between the splinters before another attacker fell dead at his feet.

Down below, burning rags thrown up from the well filled the basement with smoke. The idea was to produce enough smoke to cause panic and confusion, while hiding the assailants' foray from the well entrance. Mrs. Hammerstone had taken refuge in the corner of the cellar; it had been all too much for her, whereas Mrs. Etherington was taken back to her childhood back in her father's kipper smoking room. Knowing how to cope with a situation like this, she had placed a wet cloth across her face to prevent most of the choking smoke from entering her lungs.

The lock on the grate over the well entrance had been easily broken open with a small crucible of molten iron. Now an assailant climbed out of the well, only to discover a frying pan slam his head into the wall several times. His head exploding in pain, he released his grip on the brickwork, falling upon his disgusted comrades beneath him. They made no attempt to catch their comrade, instead allowing him to drop unimpeded to the deep water below. The attackers had no sympathy for their fallen companion; his absence meant more money for their success. When the second assailant desperately struggled to pull himself out of the well and into the smoke, he found his vision obscured. He saw nothing but smoke, until a rolling pin suddenly appeared from nowhere and slapped him viciously across the face. Knocked cold, he fell backwards into the well and out of sight. The third and last man almost ran up the ladder - he was determined not to be caught like the others when he reached the top. But when he leapt clear of the well, a large lump of wood resembling a knife block materialized from the smoke, catching him square between the eyes. His fall down the well sent him to the grave with his other companions.

On the ground floor, Harvey and Aleasia had managed to drag Etherington and themselves under the dining table, before the shutters in the dining room and kitchen simultaneously blew in with a tremendous noise. As Etherington gazed at the dining room wall, he thought it should belong in the house of the most unsuccessful darts player ever -- splinters from the shutters were stuck in the wall, pointing in all directions.

Harvey didn't care about the damage incurred, or any destruction he would inflict upon the property. In his book, any fight one walks away from is a success. From chest high, he aimed the flying dagger bow in the direction of the kitchen and, in a wide sweeping arc, he fired as many daggers as he could into the smoke rolling in from the kitchen door. Once his daggers were spent, he drew his sword and ran straight into the screams, smoke and general mayhem he had just created. Inside the kitchen, he was a whirling dervish, going berserk, plunging and swinging his sword into anything that moved. Harvey wasn't going to play nice, not today.

For her part, Aleasia decided that if someone wanted to take on the vampires, they would find out why vampires had really been feared throughout history. Anyone who moved whom she didn't recognise got dragged in through the now-open window. She then proceeded to discover how quickly she could bite someone across their windpipe and rip out his throat in a single motion, whilst using the unfortunate as cover until she could find her next target for slaughter. When too many killers suddenly appeared all at once, she would throw one to the wall and let the iron wood splinters do her job for her. Then, with her peripheral vision, she watched Etherington pick up a battle axe. Twisting it in his hand, he lunged at a large assailant in front of him. Instead of making contact with the attacker's body, he swung the axe on top of the man's foot, crushing it beneath the heavy blade. But it did the trick, the attacker screamed in pain as he dropped his weapons and hopped around madly, holding his foot, thus giving Aleasia the opportunity to drive one of the several hair pins holding back her hair into his neck. He fell to the floor, lifeless, as his heart stopped.

Now Harvey returned from the kitchen in search of the fearsome siege-breaker. Finding it, he aimed the weapon at the front door -- through the open window he had spotted a throng of men huddled around the entrance, packing black powder into a cannister. No doubt, by now they had already ignited the fuse, so he had but a few scant moments before the inevitable explosion. Harvey swallowed hard, closed his eyes and pulled the trigger. Half of the city heard the sound of the door being obliterated and then the secondary explosion of the main charge detonating early, making a suitable echo. The remains of the door now sat on the wrong side of the explosive, turning them into a thousand little pins of ironwood flying in all directions up the garden path. They left a smouldering trail of destruction running away from the house, up the path and into the street. The thugs who survived the initial concussion and ballistic material had no choice in the matter of fighting -- they were all shredded with splinters from the ironwood door, incapacitating them.

Above the sounds of the injured, writhing on the ground, shrieking in pain and calling for their mothers, police whistles screamed, heralding the approach of the city's officers. This was the last straw for many of the mercenaries remaining at the back of the house. They scattered to fight another day. If truth be told, most of them would prefer that day to never come and, if it did, the people they encountered inside this house tonight would be elsewhere.

Aleasia searched the wreckage looking for Harvey, or what she presumably thought would be the remains of him, only to find his body had been thrown across the dining room through the wall, coming to rest on a pile of debris in the back room. Remarkably, Harvey was still conscious but he knew he had passed far beyond that point people would call "being on your last legs." For starters, he couldn't feel them anymore -- he was sure it was a blessing, because looking at the mess laid out before him he was sure his legs would hurt like hell if he could feel them.

As Aleasia held his hand, he whispered to her, "I can't live like this. I've had a good life, full of many adventures." He blinked and his eyes widened as he searched Aleasia's face. "Whatever god wants from me once I'm gone, I will accept with grace, but there's one last thing you can do for me and please make it quick."

Aleasia now had tears running down her face. Struggling to find the right words, she leaned forward so their noses almost touched and gave him one last kiss. Looking down at her hands, she proclaimed, "Damn, I have broken my nails!" Then she sunk her teeth into his neck. Once Treacle had decided it was safe to leave his post and that no lingering attackers would drop in from above, he and Clump made the walk down the stairs very carefully, choosing their path to avoid all the splinters protruding from each step. from the bottom steps he could see Aleasia sitting there in the back room next to the lifeless body of Harvey. She wiped away the blood from his face, as she held one of his hands in her lap.

Aleasia wiped her tears away. "I think he is going to be in better shape than my nails, look at them," she said as she held up her hands. "Bloody ruined that manicure I had." Clump readily saw the puncture wounds on Harvey's neck as he took his pulse from the rapidly cooling neck. Before long, he felt no signs of life. Looking up, Clump shook his head at the crowd huddled at the door. Treacle glared at him in frustration. "And you call that taking a pulse? What did I say about checking to see if people are dead? This time, use this mirror and see if he's breathing." He pulled out a small mirror case made from highly polished silver from the breast pocket of his jacket and gave it to the police officer.

Clump placed the mirror above Harvey's mouth and looked for any condensation from his exhaling breath. "I can't see any misting," Clump said. "Do you see his reflection?" Treacle asked. Clump bent down and tried again but instead of seeing Harvey's reflection in the mirror Clump, as he described it later, saw Harvey if he were made from smoke.

"Then he is not dead yet, just resting," Aleasia interjected. "He will need a lot of rest and may I suggest some nice pork blood pudding. Maybe it would better if you held the pudding and just give him the blood. It will perk him up no end due to its iron content." "I have a bottle of 'Old and Very Peculiar,'" Etherington piped up. "That will do the trick. It's full of iron, or so they say. I keep some in the kitchen for medicinal purposes only, of course." He left the room and returned forthwith with bottle and glass in hand, leaving a trail of bloody footprints. "I dare say the floors need a good clean, sir," Etherington suggested as he opened the bottle and prepared to pour it into the glass he was holding. Slowly the very dark, viscous liquid tumbled into the glass, as if the law of gravity did not apply to its movement.

Treacle gave the contents of the glass a wee sip, just to check. It really did have a massive iron content and he instantly felt a headache from the Old and Very Peculiar's extra kick of adrenalin. "That would be a perfect medicine for his condition, I would suggest," he said as he tried to shake the headache off. Clump knew

Harvey now had a second chance but what a chance to have. That's the sort of luck one wouldn't wish on the next fellow. Mrs. Etherington looked down the cellar steps and suggested to Clump that he go comfort his now-hysterical wife and stop her from coming upstairs before most of the blood and bodies had been removed. If she was in shock now, what state she would be in if she saw this mess?

Now assured everyone was still alive, Treacle wandered out to the front of the house, holding his head as it throbbed from the heavy mix of blood-lust and Harvey's medicine. In the middle of the street, plain as day, well, actually it was more like dusk, was Chief Constable Quern, Mr. Easy and a rather old, military-looking gentleman whom Treacle didn't recognize.

On seeing Treacle stagger a little, Mr. Easy stepped forward. "Are you hurt lad?" he asked.

"No, it's a headache from all the excitement," Treacle responded.

Well, in that case, let me introduce you to Lord McCoughland, commander of the irregulars," Mr. Easy said as he guided Treacle toward the old man.

"It's a pleasure. I don't think I have heard of the irregulars," Treacle said as politely as possible, as he and the commander shook hands.

"How are you, my lad?" Lord McCoughland croaked in a raspy voice.

"The police use them on celebration days when manpower and a preponderance of numbers is the name of the game," Mr. Easy explained. "Luckily, tonight they were meeting at the Pork and Pie Inn just down the road. They were just leaving when all hell broke loose and they didn't want to miss any of the fireworks." He laughed. "When the historical question will be asked, 'Where were you when that battle happened?' the irregulars will work on the principal of responding truthfully." Mr. Easy's voice slipped into the vernacular of a working class news seller. "'I was in the centre of that, lad, and anyone who says otherwise is a damn liar!'"

Once Treacle spotted them, the irregulars stood out like a sore thumb. Their customised armour and weapons, designed for younger men, was a defining feature. One look at the face of Lord McCoughland, which was a road map of old battle scars, indicated that the irregulars had received their positions by the sweat of their sword arms.

Leaving Mr. Easy and the commander, Treacle took the opportunity to see if he recognised anyone from amongst the dead. There was a slim chance he might have seen one of them before in his travels around the city, but he had no such luck on that score. Most of the men were well-tanned, as if they had been in the sun for several months -- a benefit the great smog could never provide. The smog could slowly turn a man's skin black due to its ingrained dirt suspended in air, but a tan was certainly out of the question. As treacle slowly walked the line of dead bodies the officers had dutifully laid out, he suddenly felt a presence at his side. Just by the measured and sure-footed pace of the man, he instinctively knew it was Chief Constable Quern. "Recognise anyone, lad?" he asked. "No, not yet," Treacle admitted. "A bit odd -- we have thirty four bodies here and Constable Sims informs me we have enough legs for thirty five. So I think it's safe to say lad, at least thirty five people wanted to kill you, and please don't tell me you have no idea why." Quern kicked a sword lying on the ground in front of him. "Don't tell me its mob mentality. No mob goes tooled up with weapons like this." He paused and gave Treacle a sombre look before continuing. "I know mobs, lad. I have faced them down, and I can tell you that they generally use pitchforks and kitchen knives. As for those men killed back there in the alleys and those little dark corners, you are going to be in so much trouble, my boy, for those men were obviously killed up close and personal-like. It's one thing to kill them in the street as they're kicking in your door but what happened here is just plain common murder."

At that point Mr. Easy beckoned Chief Constable Quern over to him. Treacle saw a very old man scurry away from Mr. Easy as Quern approached them both. By his body language it was very obvious that the old man certainly didn't want to be anywhere near Mr. Easy and Quern in conversation, but as he left, he gave Treacle a wink, a sly little wink, and Treacle was sure the old man's walk was a jaunty one at that. Sometime later, after a rather animated talk between the two of them, Chief Constable Quern returned with Mr. Easy at his side, who apparently was acting as some sort of schoolboy monitor. Treacle could see they were obviously not the best of friends, but they certainly respected each other.

Chief Constable Quern spoke first, and his words had the sound of officialdom wrapped around them. He cleared his throat before speaking. "Treacle Tanner, the investigation into any misconduct on your part in this small domestic disturbance has been concluded, and it seems you don't have to worry. Following an investigation by the irregulars into your case," Quern continued through his clenched teeth, "It has been discovered that all of those killed in the back alleys and on the rooftops died from falling on their swords in all the excitement. In some cases, they must have been very excited, as they committed this act several times.

"Thank you, Chief Constable, for your most thorough investigation. It's good to see the irregulars are doing such a good job," Mr. Easy said in an earnest tone of gratitude.

As Mr. Easy signed a sheath of documents presented to him by a young government runner, who had suddenly appeared from nowhere, the Chief Constable leaned in toward Treacle and out of earshot of the venerable civil servant. "It seems lad, the irregulars' special operations team were, oddly enough, on active service last night without my knowledge," he murmured. "They were supposedly on a training exercise in this area when luckily, they happened across what appeared to be attempted murder, and acted accordingly."

The Chief Constable turned this way and that as he collected his thoughts, letting his brain come off the boil before returning to the practicalities of life and staying alive. "I think lad, you should get some sleep, if you can find a bed. My wife and I will have the Hammerstones to stay as our house guests. Treacle quickly responed, "That's a very nice thought sir, but might I suggest you wait a while before we relocate Mrs. Hammerstone, at least until the most of the mess is cleared. She seems to have a delicate temperament, and I am sure you and your good wife would not like to deal with the aftermath of exposing the lady to any more gore." Treacle turned back toward the house but, after a couple of steps, Chief Constable Quern shouted a query at him.

"Is Harvey Taadpole still alive?"

A bit taken aback at Chief Constable Quern's very firm grasp of the situation, Treacle responded, "He was when I left him."

When Treacle reached the entrance to Aleasia's bedroom, he saw that Harvey had been carried on the remains of a door, which now lay discarded in the hallway outside, to his cousin's bed. She had strapped Harvey into one of her whalebone corsets, at which Treacle couldn't help but raise a smile. His expression did not escape Aleasia's notice. "I know you think it's funny," she snapped. "But you remember Uncle Hector when he broke his neck. The only thing that stopped him living with his head on his shoulder for all eternity was a large ruff which gave his neck time to heal. It's exactly the same principle."

Treacle nodded -- there was nothing he could say that a nod couldn't convey a hundred times better.

Aleasia sprang to her feet. "Well, shall we go to that brewery then? Mrs. Etherington knows to give Harvey a small teaspoon of that concoction every two hours. He will soon be up and about."

"The brewery can wait for another day," Treacle said, giving Aleasia an option to stay. "I think he might be as high as a kite on that dosage," Treacle added.

"No, it can't and you know it, my cousin," Aleasia replied. "This is a once-in-a-lifetime find, and it's best found whilst one is still alive."

Old and Very Peculiar

Odd Brew – Hard Deals

Card of Chance

The so-called street was nothing more than a yard that opened up onto the back street of a back street. It took Treacle and Aleasia quite some time to find. He couldn't believe there were streets one could only reach by an alleyway. It was all very quaint in his estimation. The building had no name, just an empty beer bottle hanging by a string above the door hinted at its purpose. In the light of the open door sat a very young man drilling buttons. Thousands of bags of buttons. Bags of them un-drilled one side completed the other.

Treacle and Aleasia, unsure if they were at the right address, approached the lad, "Hello there. Can we see the owner of the brewery?" Treacle asked. "I believe it's a Mr. John Watson." He pointed to the label of the bottle he had brought with him.

The lad laughed. "I am the owner, but John Watson was my grandfather, the inventor of the great family secret of 'Old and Very Peculiar.' Of course, it's made to my recipe now."

"Did you change the recipe to cheaper ingredients?" Aleasia asked with her most engaging smile. "No," replied the lad. "It's a family secret, see, but he died before he could tell anyone. So now I make it from what I remember seeing when I was a young lad."

Artfully, Aleasia hid her laugh in a coughing fit. Treacle knew the difference between this lad's age and the time when he saw the secret ingredients measured. He reckoned that it must have been less than ten years ago at most.

As Aleasia wandered up the alley, still coughing, Treacle tried to move the conversation forward.

"Well lad, what's your name?" Treacle inquired.

"James," he replied. "But everyone calls me Jim."

"Well Jim, I would like to buy some of your beer."

"It's not beer sir, its stout. Very similar to the uninitiated," Jim said.

At once, Treacle knew he was in danger of becoming immersed at great depth in the complexities of brewing. "Well, can I buy some stout then?"

Jim's smile broadened. "No, not this time of year, sir. It's only made for Saint Fhriven's day or, if you will, Mild Winter's Day. No demand, you see, this time of year.

"Well, what if I ordered a special brew. How many bottles could you fill?"

Jim looked confused. "How many bottles do you have sir? Each brew batch would fill about a hundred bottles, if you have them."

Treacle stroked the label of the bottle in his hand and realised the label had been applied over a pre-existing bottle label. Coming to grips with the situation, Treacle asked, "So I take it you have no bottles available?"

Jim leaned back, placed a large roll of labels on the table and nodded. "That's the last of them. I'm afraid after that you will have to make your own."

"So let's see if I understand this correctly," Treacle said. "You make two hundred bottles of beer a year but you don't have any bottles, and that roll is the very last of the beer labels left in existence."

Jim smiled. "That's right, mister. You got it down the first time."

Rejoining the conversation after her stroll in the alley, Aleasia looked stunned. This lad should be swimming in cash with a drink like this, she thought. It was a pure vampire energy drink. It would make a fortune for its creator. Treacle looked Jim up and down as he contemplated a course of action. He couldn't buy Jim out. It wouldn't be right and besides; he knew nothing about the brewing business. So he made him an offer he thought no one could refuse. "Jim, would you be interested in a partner for your brewery?"

"No," Jim responded. "Grandfather Watson always said this would make our fortune, and not to sell any part of the brewing business. In fact, it's in his will. Aleasia bit her lip, a sure sign of her growing impatience. Treacle attributed her edginess to the fact she had ripped out a couple throats already today, and was still strung out from the natural high. Treacle was suddenly struck with a flash of inspiration. "How about the distribution rights? Anything in his will about them?"

Jim scratched his head, and a look of uncertainty crossed his face. "I don't think he mentioned anything about distribution rights. What are they?"

Treacle smiled. "That's where I make a single payment for an area such as the Upper Plains, where I have exclusive rights to sell your stout."

"What's the catch?"

Treacle made a face of someone thinking hard. "Well Jim, you won't be able to sell any stout in the Upper Plains, that's for sure, and you couldn't tell us what price to charge for it either."

Jim thought about this for a moment. "How much would I get paid?" he finally asked.

"Well, you will have enough money to buy a thousand new bottles, labels and ingredients. Then, when the bottles are delivered,

I would pay a reasonable sum for them that allows you to make a thousand more while paying yourself a wage that doesn't amount to buttons." This lad seemed to be quite sharp for a boy that worked for buttons, Treacle thought. Jim hadn't taken very long to ask how much he would make from the deal.

"Well, does that matter?" Jim asked.

"When you receive the payment we agree to, remember the amount you earn goes up the more we sell, as your profit will be a fixed value on each bottle," Treacle answered.

Again Jim had a long think about it before replying. "To tell you the truth, I don't know how much any of these bottles and labels would cost. I really don't think I could give you a price at this very moment." Aleasia placed her hand on Jim's arm. "I am sure a clever lad like yourself could investigate how much all this would cost and give us a figure per bottle. We will pay for a thousand bottles cost upfront for the distribution rights, and that would allow you to start straight away without worrying about the money. Then we will pay cash on delivery, either at this door or in the Upper Plains if you wish, and you can charge us carriage costs."

Jim looked at her sceptically. "My old pal Badger put you up to this, didn't he? He's always playing these little jokes on me. You can tell him he really had me going there." Treacle placed a gold coin on the table. "I do not know this Badger fellow and if I did, I am sure if he played a joke about my business I would rip his throat out," he said with a smile, exposing a fang. Jim almost wet himself. He had heard about vampires coming down from the mountains for young maidens, but he couldn't remember any stories about them coming down to play tricks on people. But investing in breweries? That would explain a lot about the people who ran the beer trade. Nowadays the beers were getting stronger and stronger, which left people sprawled out senseless in the street, helpless to protect themselves from anything. Yes, Jim considered, it did seem possible that all breweries had a vampire in control, using potent brews to slowly dull everyone's senses with alcohol. It made total sense to his thinking.

"What was the partnership gain?" he asked. "I'm interested in learning more details." Jim wanted to hear more, just as long as becoming a vampire was not part of the offer.

"Well I thought your grandfather prevented such an arrangement in his will," Treacle remarked. "If truth be told, it only covers those bastard brewery companies that tried to cheat him out of his recipe so many times," Jim said. "The terms don't apply to anyone outside of the brewery guild. Are you perhaps members of the guild," he enquired.

Treacle smiled. "Those bastards, no, I think we would stand well apart from them. I propose the partnership would be an equal split three ways. At those words, Aleasia pulled Treacle aside. Following a short discussion in a language Jim couldn't understand or even comprehend, Treacle returned. "Jim it would be a fifty-fifty split," Treacle said. "Half for you and half for us and we will invest enough money for you to make a rather large brewery. Your skills and our money could make this business go far. We are not people," he added. "There will be enough money for all of us." Raising his eyebrows, Jim sat down in a nearby chair and pondered. As he sat and thought, Treacle could hear the gears of the world turn. This lad certainly was deliberate. For certain, Treacle could hear Aleasia yearn with exhaustion. After great length, Jim stood and faced them.

"I have three questions," he said. "One -- do I need to be a vampire to be a partner? Two -- will I ever have to obey you? Three -- if you're not greedy I would like fifty five per cent and you can have forty five per cent!"

Aleasia laughed long and loud, the likes of which Treacle had never before heard from her. He shook his head in exasperation and took a nearby seat, sighing as he placed his hands on his head in exasperation. She turned to Jim wiping her tears away. "Let me answer you," Aleasia said. "I think I can speak for Treacle on this one when I say there would never, ever, be a day when I would even think of making you a member of my clan or a vampire, if you will." She regained her composure and turned serious. "Anyone who thinks like you would be way too dangerous, and as for your second question, I have already tried to control your mind with an order and we see the results." She opened her hands to signify the position in which she and Treacle found themselves. "Regarding your third and last question, we are not fools. Young men like you with big ideas want to feel in control of their own destiny, so I suggest fifty one per cent for you forty nine per cent for us. And now," she said in a tone of finality, "If you don't mind, I haven't slept for a very long time and I am getting tired."

Jim knew he had pulled off an advantageous deal and thrust his hand forward immediately. Treacle grabbed it as quickly as he could, and shook it before Jim could whack on a few more per cent once he realised what was going on.

"I will need to start the brewing process immediately if you want the first delivery as soon as possible," Jim said. "I will need five silver coins for the ingredients and firewood." Treacle flicked the gold coin in his direction, only to have it snatched from the air as it was still travelling upwards. That's some lightning reflexes on the boy, he thought, and wondered if vampire blood ran somewhere in Jim's family tree.

Staggering back to Upper Reach Lane from their lack of sleep, Aleasia and Treacle nonetheless laughed at the deal they had made with Jim. They would have taken no interest in the brewery, just to get the clan drinking Jim's brew rather than blood. His concoction could integrate them into society, if the drink was in every bar on the continent.

Upon reaching their street they discovered some of the irregulars had decided to play cards on their veranda to pass the time, while the builders worked on the doors and shutters, making the place secure again. In fact, Mr. Easy himself had issued the plans directly to them. The irregulars believed if and when trouble started anew, they wanted ringside seats. Yet it would be rude to sit and stare at the house and its occupants all day, so a seat on the veranda would suit them just fine -- having a butler who kept them supplied with drink and snacks was an added bonus. Treacle was too tired to argue with his uninvited guests, especially when they were so well armed and primed for action.

As much as every fibre in his body screamed for sleep, he knew he still could not go to bed, even if Aleasia could. He had to write a letter immediately, for the clan would never forgive him if he accidentally died in his sleep without giving them a complete update. So he wrote down everything, from the battles on his doorstep to the remarkable beer that could free the vampires from their restrictive diet. It all went onto the page; he didn't really care whether the sentences read properly as long as the facts were there for the clan to read.

As soon as he finished, he stepped out of the house to post his letter. On the veranda, he acknowledged with a nod the men there playing cards. Immediately, he recognised one of the players as the man he saw last night speaking with Mr. Easy.

Looking up from his cards, the old codger saw Treacle and the letter in his hand. "I say there squire, if you wish, I can post your letter for you," he said. "I work at the sorting office and I'll be there later this afternoon."

Treacle didn't put up any resistance to his offer. The thought occurred to him that the irregulars might take exception if he insinuated that they couldn't be trusted, not even with a letter. "That's very kind of you, sir," Treacle said. "I leave it to your capable hands to ensure that it will arrive safe and sound."

"Don't worry; it will reach its destination. Not snow, not rain and all that rubbish," the old man said as he returned to his game.

Another of the players looked up from his cards at Treacle. "Oh, just so you know, the irregulars are holding a card tournament tonight on your veranda," he said. "Mr. Easy put up a substantial cash prize so we're expecting a very high turnout. We didn't think you would mind, sir."

"No, I don't mind," Treacle replied. "Knock yourselves out." He was sure that many of them would reach unconsciousness, but only through the vicious blow of having that one drink too many.

Lost in the city

Model Beach – Harbouring Evil

To Do List

Mabel rose early for breakfast to find her host giving out large bags of make-up and perfume, all made by his own shop. As she later discovered by the way each was presented, this was payment for all her hard work. She wasn't even allowed to keep the dresses tailored specifically to her body shape, as they were considered too expensive for payment.

She realised Larry Futon's purse squeaked as he walked, it was so tight. Now, to add insult to injury, for the final insult she had to attend the anti-climactic beach party. The prospect of such a gathering sounded as bad she imagined it could ever possibly be. The other models seemed happy to receive their gifts, and she thought for the sake of the peace she better start sounding appreciative. Gilded coaches ferried them to the beach, where little tents had been erected behind a large table and chairs. First, however, Larry wanted the girls to wear items from his new beach collection. He described them as generous gifts; conveniently, small changing rooms awaited them down on the beach.

Once all the models had changed into their swimsuits, they emerged from their changing rooms to see that a volleyball court had been marked out on the sand. With suspicion, Mabel listened as Larry announced that the photographer, who did seem very professional, would take a few snaps just for the record. At once Mabel saw the scam for what it was -- a cheap photo shoot and another chance for Larry to rip off his models while playing the pretence of the perfect host. He was a slippery as an eel, and as devious as they come, Mabel decided. This exploitation of his models was totally polished, a dubious skill only attained after many years of practice. The meal seemed to take for ever to prepare, while the photographer wanted to take as many pictures as possible. The food was described as a five course banquet but the servers didn't pile anyone's dish high with succulent delicacies. Instead, the food was served in such small portions she could swear some of the models tried to eat the plates decorative motif by mistake. Mabel knew that when she got home she would mark Larry Futon's card in her address book with the words "a horse's arse."

Now, as their meal came to an end, three large ships came over the horizon and dropped anchor in the bay in front of them. A small row boat came to the shore to take them on board to return to the

Great Smog -- or so she assumed. No one actually mentioned their destination. For all she knew they could have been white slave traders.

To her surprise, on the return trip they were not allowed to go below decks. All the models had to sit wherever they could on the deck while still wearing their swimsuits. They tried to cover their modesty and any other part of their skin that flashed underneath their towelling robes from the ogling crew, who acted like Winterfest had come early this year.

As they neared the coastline and their destination of the great smog, Mabel noticed the smog of the city had much more of a blacker hue than normal. Obviously something had been burning, and it must have been in the richer part of the city, she surmised, as the poorer side would have completely burned to the ground if something had caught fire in that tightly-crowded residential area. The boats seemed to take forever navigating the berths as, for some godforsaken reason, they had been squeezed into the furthest corner of the port. Each of the models were given back their bags full of clothes and escorted to the gates of the port where Mabel was unceremoniously dumped with the rest of them. As she checked the contents of her bags to make sure she had everything, one of the models hovered over her, intent on asking a question.

Mabel smiled warmly. "Can I help you?" she asked, recalling the young girl. She had been placed at the far end of the table from her at all of Larry's meals so Mabel hadn't the chance to properly make her acquaintance. Then again, she instantly regretted speaking to the models to whom she had spoken. They only talked fashion, as if their life depended on it. It was a personality type she despised.

"Hi, my name's Shamel Midgepot," she said, as she looked around with an expression of worry on her face. "I was wondering if you could tell me where I am." "Hi, I'm Mabel." She smiled reassuringly. "I know the port area might have changed a lot recently but you're on Portside Road, and just up there is Broken Bottle Road', she replied.

"No, I think you misunderstand. What city are we in?" Shamel said leadingly.

Mabel made a mental note to adjust the notation on Larry Futon's card to "a horse's arse." She tried to get the model back into the port as she was obviously in the wrong place. But for some reason, the gates were now locked shut and the guards wouldn't let anyone in.

"Well Shamel, you better stay at my place while we sort out this mess," Mabel declared. "But before we go, let's get some meat on those bones of yours. You look starved and I'm feeling faint." Mabel walked them to Esperanto's Cafe and Bar, where she ordered curried eel, her favourite dish. Much to her annoyance, Shamel chose salad with fresh fish. Over their meal Shamel began confiding in her. She spoke of her wish to earn enough money to return home a rich woman. Shamel wanted to help her family purchase back the family farm and bring back the former glory of its heyday.

In between taking orders from his other tables, the waiter recounted yesterday's events in the city, but Mabel was sure she wasn't hearing it correctly. Why would a street gang attack a police officer's home? That would be a suicidal long-term career move -- someday their luck would run out. No wonder the irregulars were on the streets. The bit in the story about the whole gang dying in the attack sounded like a cover-up to her. At least the criminals will be on sabbatical today, so the walk home from the restaurant would be the safest walk home she had ever had in the city.

Treacle slept soundly through the irregulars' card tournament, even though fifty men sang battle songs above the coal chute to his cellar at one point during the proceedings. He knew his neighbours must be thoroughly annoyed, but who was going to complain that fifty drunken police officers were disturbing the peace?

He ascended the stairs as the sun rose, to find Lord McCoughland playing patience on his dining table, no small accomplishment on the heavily damaged top bristling with an assortment of weapons. Judging from the specialised nature of the armoury, it was obvious someone had been shopping at Auntie's Emporium.

Lord McCoughland, whose first name turned out to be Bruce, beckoned to Treacle to join him. "Laddie, you did a fantastic job last night, there's no denying. But next time, if you need any help against impossible odds, come down to the Pork and Pie Inn. Okay?"

Treacle gratefully acknowledged the generous offer. During their conversation, Etherington managed to present a breakfast, arriving with a small glass of stout and the news that Harvey was healing but still not regained consciousness.

"No doubt he's tough as a boot," Bruce commented. "Your man Harvey appears to be one resilient sort, and those scars will get him the odd drink or two someday, as people listen to his stories."

As McCoughland continued his banter, Treacle sat and reflected as he listened to the old man. I need a day of rest, Treacle thought. But it's best to keep one's head down in a city that moves this fast. The past will soon be forgotten, because there's too much of the present occupying everyone's life. As Treacle exchanged pleasantries with Bruce, he took the opportunity to size up the old man. He must be one of Mr. Easy's right-hand men, or more accurately, right hand swordsmen. Suddenly Bruce leaped up as his hands dived into his pockets, setting Treacle on edge.

McCoughland exclaimed, "I have a letter for you! I didn't put it down anywhere -- I was afraid Etherington would throw it away with his meticulous cleaning." He presented Treacle with the letter. "Here it is."

One glance told Treacle who had written the elegant, embellished curlicues on the letter. It was from Uncle Ruud, but what a time to take receipt. He had to read it now in front of Bruce; it was too important to wait. After quickly scanning the page he placed the letter in his pocket.

"Not bad news from home, I hope," said Bruce appraisingly, who seemed to talk from past experience.

"No," Treacle replied. "Just Uncle Ruud telling me to be safe and keep my head down."

Bruce smiled. "We are who we are -- some stand and fight and some sit under the table."

"I believe there is a time for each," said Treacle. "It's all a matter of timing."

Bruce clasped him on his shoulder as he left. "Keep yourself alive and the world will turn, my boy," he said.

About mid-morning, as he re-read the letter for a second time to Aleasia, who had only left Harvey's side for light meals since returning from Jim's brewery, they heard a knock at the front door. Treacle instructed Etherington to answer the caller, as he deemed it was now time to maintain proper standards, after the assault on the premises.

After a moment Etherington returned. "A young man called Jim wishes to see you, sir," he announced. As an aside, he added, "I must apologise about the state of the wooden floors, sir. Some of the bloodstains are very difficult to remove."

Aleasia replied almost instantly. "What you need is Mr. Tweed's Soap for All Occasions in a water mix as described on the tin, it removes everything, and what remains will give the floor some character. It won't remain red very long," she added knowingly.

"Thank you, ma'am," Etherington replied. "And the lad, sir?"
"Let him in, Etherington," Treacle said. "He is my, er, rather, our new business partner."

From the tone in his master's voice, Etherington knew not to argue. He said, "Yes, sir" and turned sharply on his heel to show the lad in. A moment later the brewer appeared by the table.

"Well Jim, how's it going and how did you find us?" Treacle asked.

"Very well, sir," Jim replied. "I came by to give you an update. I have ordered the bottles and the new labels, and decided keep the traditional design for both. At the moment, I have a thousand bottle mash brewing. The Friends of the Peculiar -- that's the people who buy the brew when in season -- are very interested in another couple of hundred bottles as an off-season special. They think such a large brew will taste even better. May I sell some to them?" Treacle and Aleasia both smiled. " We will sell to anyone and everyone Jim, and I have a five thousand bottle order here." Treacle waved Uncle Ruud's letter in the air. "So don't worry about starting a second mash. Your brew is already in great demand."

Jim mentally juggled the order in his mind. "That will take about five hundred days to complete even if I get the second still cleaned out and the chickens evicted," he said. "When do you need them?"

"That was only to keep production going before the big order comes in, I think," said Treacle, noticing Jim mentally calculating delivery and production schedules. "I reckon thirty gold coins will get us started. By the way," he added, "I did notice the old warehouse in Turnip Street is for sale. Maybe we can use that."

"Well, the equipment won't come cheap and the guild fees will go up," Jim said.

Treacle undid a money belt from his waist and gave it to Jim. "There you go, a hundred gold pieces. Keep the receipts for the accountants," he instructed. "I believe we will engage the usual firm of 'Mr. and Mrs. Book,' the double bookkeepers. They are very trusted from where I come, and they have never failed to get the final figure we wanted."

"Is there anyone you wish not to employ?" Jim asked. "It seems there's always people not employed by the breweries in this town, mostly out of spite or family hatred or some ethnic reason that doesn't make sense."

"All that matters to me is that those in our employ expedite the product into the bottle and out the door," Treacle replied. After watching his partner secure and disguise the money belt, Treacle dismissed him and his head full of production estimates.

Aleasia looked at Treacle. "You know; he really is the most dangerous person I have ever met. We better not let him even think about becoming a vampire or we will all be in trouble. It would only take him a couple of weeks, I'm sure. And when were you going to tell him the truth about that letter?" "The poor boy has enough to think about," Treacle said. "I don't think the truth will put him at ease or even in a mood to brew fifty thousand bottles."

Aleasia smiled. "Did you notice he didn't tell you how he found out where we lived? He's a sly one, I tell you. "She rose from the table to return to Harvey's side. "By the way, who did Ruud assign to young Jim?"

The brothers Phileas and Belleas have orders to watch over him, I believe, and to protect him at all costs."

Aleasia's face reflected everything Treacle was thinking. "Phileas is very good, but I hope he can control Belleas. He does have a temper and a blood lust with it." "We can only hope," Treacle said, as Aleasia left to play doctor and nurses.

Etherington returned with rag in hand. "Sir, I hate to bother you, but the wife and I were wondering if you have any suggestion on the removal of blood from tiled floors and plasterwork. I tried Miss Stagnation's suggestion, which worked wonders on the floor, but it seems to remove the paint from the walls sir."

"I would suggest a repaint then is in order, after you have cleaned the majority of what you can of the walls," Treacle said. "Don't worry about the cost. I was thinking about changing the colour anyway."

Etherington realised he was being politely let off any of the damage already done. Just try my best, he thought. The painters could sort out the mess that remained.

At mid-afternoon Chief Constable Quern arrived on what he called a "diplomatic mission" on behalf of Mr. Easy, informing Treacle of all the news on the streets. Quern acknowledged that everyone believed a street gang had been massacred for attacking a policeman's house, which meant the men on the beat were in no mood to take prisoners.

"But most interesting of all is the fact that not one officer recognised any of the attackers, and not one piece of identification was found on any of the bodies," Quern said. "It's indeed a mysterious twist to matters. I've brought a number of policemen in from the outlying villages for identification of the bodies, and still nobody has recognised them. Mr. Easy still doesn't know who supplied the gunpowder, but it was military grade."

"Which means, it all actually worked as designed," Treacle remarked.

"If it's not too much trouble, would you mind if I took a look in on Harvey?" Quern asked. "There's a nasty rumour about that he died last night. His body was reported being carried away on a door."

With a trace of discernible regret in his voice Treacle said, "Sadly, that's not possible. He's convalescing and under constant medical attention. Anyway," he added, "A bit of mystery where his health is concerned would only give us an advantage." Treacle changed his tone, moving along to other matters. "Has anything strange or untoward happened over the last twenty four hours that I should know about?"

"Funny you should mention that," the chief constable replied. "A request passed across my desk earlier today from Count Alexander requesting as many officers as possible to protect his guests at this evening's gala event, whereas everyone else is expecting one of the quietest nights in memory for the city. It hasn't been this quiet since the 'Ivanhoe' sailing ship broke up at Miller's Point. Half the city was down there all day and night, carting away anything they could get their hands on."

"There's not really a lot to work with, is there?" Treacle said. "I do have friends in the Upper Plains who could look at pictures of the dead and see if they recognised them, but I don't think it will help. I suggest, Chief Constable, that you go and smell them. I caught a strong smell of sweaty garlic myself. Maybe they visited a Franco-side restaurant before they visited us. It's the only clue I have, but it's better than what you've got."

The smell of garlic? Quern wondered. Well, that was something a vampire would be sure to notice, whereas the guy on the beat would dismiss the odour as just spicy cooking in the air. As this thought ran through Chief Constable Quern's head, he quickly reviewed Treacle's words, trying to divine any subtexts to his statement which he could identify. A tiny, almost imperceptible bell began to ring within him. Suddenly his inner klaxon began to shout. Garlic! Garlic and vampires. Garlic, that's the key, but what and where?

Those thoughts swirled in Quern's head until it completely turned upside down. Suddenly he remembered -- a folder in Mr.

Easy's hand that he quickly placed back on the pile of documents on his desk. When Chief Constable Quern's eyes espied it, it was upside down, but no matter. He long ago had mastered reading from that direction; it was a skill that helped a copper rise through the force. Now, he strained his memory. What did that paper say? "The Study of...." Yes, that was it! A scientific paper of some sort. "The Study of Garlic-Based Silver Polish' -- yes, that was the start of it, he remembered. It was such a strange topic that it stuck with him, but he could now see the document in his mind's eye. There was something missing from the title -- some icon. Suddenly the entire title formed in his mind; if it had been a street sign it would have been fifty feet long in capitals with flashing neon lights. The title was "The Study of Garlic-Based Silver Polish on Religious Symbols." This would explain the potency of a silver cross. He was sure people would be permanently silenced before spreading this highly dangerous piece of information. Damn that report! he fumed. Now he had to struggle to keep his thoughts from polishing the door handles and window latches of his home, instead of ascertaining why he had thirty five unclaimed corpses in his cellar. Quern decided to take his leave to go clear his head. Otherwise he would never solve this case.

Count Alexander did not let the loss of thirty five of his best men change his plans. In truth, he had no choice in the matter. He had spent many months of meticulous planning before setting his scheme in motion. He had to let events play themselves out as he had soldiers arriving from all directions, some travelling for many days.

Their deaths only hardened his resolve to see the teeth pulled from these troublesome vampires. Once he became ruler, what could the clans say about any accidents in battle? Previously, the clan had always stayed out of the politics of mortal men. Involving oneself in politics meant aligning on someone's side, whereas everyone knew vampires were a side of their own, fending themselves against all-comers. As long as they stayed rich and lived in grand houses on the Upper Plains nothing would ever change.

It was now even more important to keep on track with his plans, than to worry about the fate of two country suckers, the Count decided. So much remained to be done, before springing the trap on the city. Already he had three fully laden ships in port that needed unloading, and their cargo distributed around the city. Then there was the matter of the couple of hundred mercenaries to be housed, fed and hidden from the authorities -- not really much of a problem at the port where a new warehouse had been constructed on the site of the now-razed neighbourhood on Portside Road. He had made arrangements to surreptitiously hide his men behind large bales of wool stacked in the storage facility. The warehouse provided enough room to organise and distribute his men throughout the city, but like any other fully functioning garrison, it required extraordinary amounts of supplies to keep it running. Whoever said "an army marches on its stomach" wasn't wrong on that point.

But tonight he was going to hold a party that no one would ever forget. Once he had gathered all the powerful and influential people into a single room, with one bold flourish, he would remove them as a threat in a single stroke. To that end he was meeting with his conspirators, the usual crowd who wanted power but didn't think hard work or even loyalty was the fastest way to the top. In their opinion, a large guillotine would sort out any dissent to their right to rule, and it would be all done in the name of the people, of course.

The mercenaries where slowly dispatched in twos and threes across the city, with a local escort in case the police stopped them for a bit of routine questioning. At least someone would be present who spoke the language, could steer the conversation away from anything incriminating and keep them out of the clink. Throughout the day their weapons were included with the normal cart deliveries of wine across the city. Everything was hidden and ready for use, waiting for the moment when the blade would fall.

The first thing he had planned on his 'to do' list after he had grabbed the throne was to get rid of that civil servant Mr Easy, the jumped-up little mandarin. A decision that had only been reinforced by this morning's last and final tax demand, informing him that criminal charges would be brought, as well as the seizure of his assets if he didn't pay. Taxes, in his opinion, were for the little people. Didn't his businesses pay enough tax on their behalf for him not to?

An Invitation They Should Have Refused

By Invitation Only – Feeling Queasy

L ater that evening, Harvey came round; more like passing from comatose to delirious, as Aleasia described it, but she thought it was a massive improvement. Treacle tended to agree with her as it was the shortest route to a quiet life. Mostly Harvey talked in his delirium about a beautiful black haired girl, assurance to Aleasia that she had made the right decision in her choice of cure.

Treacle wanted to look one more time at the city's maps -- he had a very good idea what was happening -- but how it would play out was still a mystery to him. Would it all start at the port? The mercenaries would have to fight their way uphill and even the most gung-ho soldier would not want that. Attacking from outside the city gates? A viable option given the calibre, so to speak, of the soldiers posted on the city walls, but the mercenaries would still run the risk of being seen and losing the element of surprise. That was the trouble with the city wall patrol, thought Treacle. They never followed orders and they never kept to a routine. They might walk the walls at any time, day or night. Some days they even ate their sandwiches as they made their rounds.

So Treacle eliminated the likelihood of an assault from outside the city walls. That meant attack from within the city somewhere, but not at tonight's party, especially with extra security everywhere and private bodyguards accompanying the city's established families like lapdogs. Since the first wines of the new season would arrive in the next couple of days, Treacle's best guess was that a diversion would be created when the town was flooded with strangers. Those in power would be detained and dumped in a keep somewhere or, if the assailants were ruthless, dumped as don't keep out at sea. He decided not to walk around town since thirty five men had besieged his front door. He would keep his head down until a couple more friends were in the shadows. And shadows were everywhere -- one could walk down the street at midday at the height of summer without getting a tan in the city's smog.

Mabel decided to take Shamel under her wing for the foreseeable future, as it seemed to be the thing to do. The young lass certainly needed both charity and a friend. Luckily for the itinerant model, Mabel had an invitation to a party later that evening. Shamel would meet the upper crust of local society, while Mabel hobnobbed with a wine-glass in hand and a friend on her arm. Mabel's closet had a large selection of dresses, outfits she modelled in her photo shoots on the condition she display them whenever she went out on the town. However, Shamel couldn't wear them -- people would think she had been cavorting in her mother's wardrobe, as the clothes would drown her short little figure. The meagre bag of possessions she carried certainly didn't have an evening dress within. So Mabel put her education and resourcefulness to work and, after a moment, inspiration struck her when she suddenly noticed her curtains.

"A bit of creativity and a large wooden brooch and we will have the whole room talking about your sense of ethnic style. Don't you worry," she said, as she styled Shamel. "You have an exotic look anyway. Where are you from?" "Scrumble County in the New Territories is my home, but to be a success in our business you have to live in Faris," Shamel replied. "That's where all the fashion houses are based."

"I don't think they care what's being worn in Faris," Mabel said. "In this city they only care about what the girl on the street corner is wearing. Well, maybe the girl a little further up the street, if truth be told."

To procure a large coach to ferry them to the gala, Mabel sent a note by runner to the local picture desk at the paper. Their transport arrived at their door with photographer in tow. At the party, the rich and powerful would all be part of the woodwork unless the women wore a fabulous dress or the men were especially handsome. What was fashionable just seemed so arbitrary, thought Mabel, watching the city roll by from the coach window.

Outside 'Le Castille' the coach pulled up, and Shamel rose to open the door only to find Mabel placing a hand on her leg to restrain her egress. "Wait for the cameraman," she instructed. "He will only take a minute to set up and then we can exit stage left and make our grand entrance."

From the coach window they saw Davy Hailey busily setting up three cameras along the red carpet for an action shot of the girls' arrival. He waved to Mabel, and the two girls exited the coach and skipped along the red carpet, as the flashes from his cameras caught the girls with smiles on their faces. At the door, Mabel turned back to see a grinning Davy give her a thumbs up. He quickly put his cameras back on the coach and rushed off to catch the first edition of tomorrow's paper.

Mabel hooked arms with Shamel and escorted her through the double doors. All eyes in the room turned to them as they swept through. As they arrived at their designated bar, Mabel gracefully procured two glasses of wine for Shamel and herself, without breaking step. The bar was populated with the crème de la crème of the fashion industry, including Lady Jane Fortesque, fashion editor of the 'Times,' who raced over to meet them.

"My dear girls, what beautiful outfits! I believe yours, Mabel, is a Karl Lageronfield, and yours?" Lady Jane looked at Shamel. Without hesitation, Shamel jumped in with both feet, and replied, "It's a special creation by Mabel, part of her 'New Seasons' range."

Lady Jane was impressed -- a top model from Faris, obviously brought in at great expense to show off Mabel's first creation, and what a creation it was! Simple and elegant, with a large floral print, just right for the summer months. This could take a whole page, with photos, if she wrote it right, the fashion editor thought. Maybe a headline like "Local Girl Captures Heart of Fashion Industry." The piece would write itself, but then history always did.

From Lady Jane's gushing praise, Mabel realised that a trip to the curtain shop followed by one to an ethnic brooch maker was now on the agenda for tomorrow -- she had just been anointed a fashion designer. She wondered if this was how so many others had broken into the industry. A fashion reporter takes a shine to you, writes one good piece and voila! A career is born. At least the design business wouldn't bruise her arms as fashion modelling did. Nor would she have to jump into fountains to get noticed. Merely make something nice for a young girl to wear around town and suddenly, Mabel was an overnight success.

As Shamel gave Lady Jane a little pirouette the way only a fashion model can, without tripping up on her own feet, Gustav, principal of the shop 'Gustav,' ran up to kiss her hand. He was a rather self-centred man, Mabel thought, judging from his animated conversations with others in attendance. Before she could even say hello she heard his broad accent, which she could only imagine came from where every spoken word was charged by the letter.

"My pet, do you 'ave a place to sell you' rags?" he asked. "Luv, I can throw them together and give you forty."

Mabel presumed he meant forty percent but she wanted clarification. "I presume you mean forty percent of gross sales," she said.

"I," Gustav replied.

They shook hands on the agreement. It seemed like a good offer and since the design was already complete, no more work would be needed -- a considerable weight off her mind. The more she saw of this man, the more she wondered if he had spent too much time around his clients. His hair was lightly curled, and his eyebrows were sculpted and waxed, she was sure. His mannerisms and the weakness of his handshake could only be described as effeminate.

Gustav, whose real name was Larry Sludge, chose his nom-de-guerre to inspire the clientèle he wanted to attract. In a flash of marketing foresight, he started calling himself Gustav after a pet dog he saw in a Faris park when he was young. Counter to the Latin saying "Brevis esse laboro, obscurus fio," he thought a single name made him more memorable. Indeed, his career had taken off, and now he dressed all the rich and famous in these parts. One truly had to be rich and famous to sample Gustav's wares -- it was the only 'by invitation only' shop in Great Smog, and not a single piece had a price tag. The cost was calculated based on the measure of the patron's wealth or fame.

Not surprisingly, Gustav knew everyone present at the bar, and promptly decided to show off his new designer and her model. Shamel had never had so many people compliment her before. Usually she heard she was too fat, too thin, too tall, or too short, but never how stunning she looked and how elegantly she walked.

The night flew by as if on wings and regretfully, for both Mabel and Shamel, time came for them to take their leave. As they left 'Le Castille,' Mr Hailey was there to catch their assured and nonchalant departure on film for the late night edition of the paper, before he escorted them home in the coach. Inside Mabel's house, exhausted and exhilarated, they both flopped into the armchairs in front of the hearth. Mabel had been so excited by the turn of events at the party she didn't even take time to finish a drink, let alone taste any of the delicious catered food. Shamel had hardly eaten -- Mabel remembered her pecking at a dish or two. As for alcohol, she was sure not one drop had passed Shamel's lips all night.

"Time for a drink, I think," announced Mabel. "What's your poison?"

"Do you have any water?" Shamel asked.

"That's not really the safest option in these parts," Mabel said. "How about a light lager?" She fetched a beer for Shamel, and opened a bottle of red for herself. She reckoned she didn't deserve it but who got what they deserved in life?

Treacle came down early to check on Harvey, who had lapsed back into unconsciousness, giving Aleasia time to inspect the tension on her whalebone girdle. As she repositioned it to realign Harvey's spine properly, Treacle asked her, "Have you thought about what Uncle Ruud will say when he hears about this?" He waved his hand in Harvey's general direction. "You know he will hit the ceiling, and I don't want to be around for that. I don't think opening your eyes wide and flashing your lashes at him will work in these circumstances."

Aleasia smiled. "No, I will just tell the truth -- he almost gave his life to protect us from all those nasty men who want the demise of every vampire who ever existed."

"That's stretching it a bit, don't you think?"

"It's possible Harvey did believe that at the time," she replied. "We don't know."

"Good luck with that one," he said before going for breakfast, a meal which now included a pleasant course of "Old and Very Peculiar," served in a small glass. The effect of the early morning beverage gave him a spring in his step right from the off. During his meal, Treacle felt himself almost jump from his seat as he suddenly heard someone batter the front door with urgent force. Etherington answered the summons with what was becoming his normal efficiency.

"A Mister Hammerstone for you, sir," Etherington announced, as Clump pushed him aside.

You have to come quick Treacle, the Chief Constable has been taken ill and is asking for you, I think it's serious'. Treacle immediately jumped up from the table. Before leaving, he grabbed a selection of small knifes and tucked them into very discreet places on his person. Confidence always came from being thoroughly prepared, he observed. As they ran across the city Treacle found himself making up ground as Clump set a blistering pace. Arriving at a huge house in a posh area of the city, Clump perceptively guessed Treacle's thoughts. "The house is a city-owned residence," he explained. "They found that the best officers tended to be the poorest, so the city gives them a home in line with their importance to the city. The nobs respect the house and the prestige of the address, even if they don't respect the Chief Constable personally. That's why the house is so important."

As they walked up the front path, Treacle caught a whiff of fresh polish imbued with garlic emanating from the windows and doors. He stood behind Clump, waiting for the officer to open the door so he wouldn't burn himself by touching the handle.

As Clump swung open the door, he said, "I invite you in. Is that right? By invitation only?"

"Yes, something like that," Treacle said.

Crowded around the downstairs wash-room were two officers awaiting their arrival. One nodded toward the wash-room door as they both made room for Treacle and Clump.

"I'm here, Chief Constable," Treacle cried out.

"I think its food poisoning, but I survived the cooking on the battlefield at Five Elms without even a twinge. Now the whole household is ill," came an anguished reply from behind the wash-room door. Of course Treacle knew of the Five Elms war -- nearly everyone alive had heard of the conflict. Half the army died from food poisoning and deplorable hygiene before the battle ended.

Treacle looked Clump up and down. "Are you feeling well?" he asked.

"No problems for me, but the wife wasn't feeling too hot when I left her," Clump replied.

"Did you not eat anything yesterday?" Treacle wondered if the whole household had been poisoned, or just particular individuals.

"Well there was that foreign muck from that party I gave the wife. It had too much garlic in it for me," Clump scoffed.

"What a brilliant idea," Treacle said abstractly, collecting his thoughts while he considered all the implications of what he had just heard. "I know just what you mean." He patted the officer reassuringly on the shoulder. "I don't mean poisoning your wife, Clump," Treacle said. "It's so clever, isn't it? First thing to do in a power grab is remove all the people who make the decisions. You could kill them but that's messy, noisy and could cost the lives of your soldiers. Or you could round them up and imprison them, but that requires the capture of a jail or dungeon and the control of hundreds of people. That's going to take a lot of men. Or... you make them all ill with food poisoning. They can't leave the bathroom for more than a minute without making a public disgrace of themselves, and if you need them later for any reason like controlling a rampaging mob, they're still alive to do your bidding."

A muffled groan from the bathroom indicated Chief Constable Quern's agreement with Treacle's analysis. "I think the Chief Constable wants me to take charge during this time," he told Clump.

"Treacle, my life and that of my family is in your hands," Quern's voice echoed from the bathroom porcelain.

"Don't worry, sir. They have already lost the element of surprise." Treacle turned to the officers in attendance. "Right, you two lads by the door, you heard the Chief Constable. I am in charge." He pointed to one. "You run round the stations and tell them to empty the cells, barricade the internal doors and get ready for an attack. You," he indicated to the other, "Run to the nearest house of a member of the night watch and see if any food was donated to them last night, and if they ate it. If you know no-one on the night watch, go to the station and ask someone who would know a member of the night watch. Now off you go, both of you, and come back here when you're done."

From Clump's erect bearing, Treacle could tell he was awaiting orders. "We will wait and protect the family and I think we will use Plan 'C,'" he said.

Clump was taken aback -- he always had considered Treacle a man of instinct. "How many plans are there?" he wondered aloud.

"I have a few and if I told you some of them you would be in charge within the week," Treacle smiled. "All you need to know about Plan 'C' is that we have to wait until their trap is sprung, and then we can smash them. I imagine we're dealing with a hydra-like organisation." Treacle paused for a moment. "That's a multi-headed beast," he explained. "So we have to see who the heads are before we cut them off, metaphorically speaking."

Clump knew what type of organisation Treacle meant; the officer had dealt with the local collection agency before. He thought for a bit before speaking. "But we really need the army."

"Don't worry about an army," Treacle said. "I have that already in hand." For the next twenty minutes Treacle sat patiently and watched, while Clump paced backwards and forwards like an expectant father. "You must learn to relax, my friend," Treacle advised. "Everything happens in its own time." At length, Clump finally sat down, shifting in his seat, ready to spring into action at a moment's notice. Only a couple of minutes passed before he was up and about again, peeking through the peephole and answering a knock at the door.

"There's a wine cart with some very well built men outside," Clump directed his voice toward the bathroom door. "Where do you want the delivery?"

"I didn't order any wine -- aaargh! My bowels," moaned the Chief Constable.

Suspicious, Treacle looked out of the window at the "delivery men." They were certainly well built, he noted, and just the sort to control a policeman. "Small hiccup in the plan," he declared. Giving a confident smile to Clump, he pulled out two knives and tucked them into the back of his trousers.

The two largest men from the cart started up the path to Quern's house, a worrisome development in Treacle's view -- he hated for someone on the street to raise the alarm when he saw his comrades come to a sticky end. The survivor would return with an army in tow and kill everyone in the house. Even if he could rally to protect the house, how long before the attackers would get smart or bored, and just set fire to the residence?

The door took the full force of someone's beefy shoulder, without the courtesy of a knock. As it fell flat, both Treacle and Clump saw the point of a crossbow bolt directed at them. No doubt these knaves had done this before, Treacle thought. Eyes glued to the weapons, Clump and Treacle retreated toward the wall behind them. This was not supposed to happen -- what they needed was a bloody miracle and Treacle knew to never rely on those. You were always left disappointed. -- Treacle had survived deadly situations before. Most people didn't know how to check if someone was dead; they just assumed if you had a large hole in you, you must be dead. However, Clump certainly wouldn't have the advantage of a vampire inheritance to save his bacon. Once normal people were down, there was no getting back up.

As their assailants hesitated, perhaps weighing the wisdom of killing their prey, a shadow fell across the room. All we need is rain, Treacle thought. At least they wouldn't try to cremate me if it was raining. Just a mass burial in a ditch somewhere to dig yourself out from. He expected the hole had already been dug, knowing the time and work spent in the planning of this attack.

For some reason the shadow unsettled the mercenaries. One of them kept turning around, but everything looked the same. Their guide waved back from the cart, the street was quiet and the day was bright with a light smog as always, but there was something wrong. Something was out of place, and neither ruffian could decide what was amiss. -- Finally they decided to disregard their apprehension and stepped into the house, after first checking to see if anyone was lurking behind the door. At that exact moment, two extremely well dressed young men dropped down behind them from the second floor balcony. Clump expected to see throats being ripped out with the hunger of a pack of wolves. Instead, two crossbows flashed little daggers, and Clump saw the men in the doorway crumple up into a pile on the floor.

The men with the knives were obviously vampires, Clump surmised. They had thick black hair slicked back into short ponytails at the nape of their necks. Both wore black and white polka dot bow-ties and something very similar to capes.

One looked at the other and said, "We better move them. That's a rosewood floor and the devil to remove stains from." The other agreed, and they dragged the lifeless corpses outside to bleed on the grass.

"A little help required here, I think," said Treacle. Clump turned and gaped to see him pinned to the wall by two bolts. One was imbedded in Treacle's thigh; the other had entered the top of his shoulder. Both bolts well and firmly affixed him to the wall. "Well, don't look at them! Pull them out!" Treacle shouted.

Recovering his senses, Clump grabbed the bolts and made the extractions as quick and painless as he could. "That was my very best casual jacket, that was,". Clump apologised.

"It's not your fault," Treacle said. He steadied himself by grabbing Clump's shoulder. "I need a drink," Treacle declared, as he made a bee-line to the drinks cabinet and threw the doors open. The Chief Constable must have inherited some libations with a house this old, Treacle conjectured. Lo and behold, there at the back of the cupboard covered in dust was a six pack of 'Old and Very Peculiar.' Treacle pulled out three and opened them one by one with his teeth. He then proceeded to drink a whole bottle in one go. The effect was instantaneous -- his hand went to his forehead as his face contorted, and a blinding headache set in from the rush.

Clump inspected the bottle. "No wonder you're not feeling well. This is at least ten years old," he remarked.

By now the two vampires had returned, cleaning their knives on red silk handkerchiefs and looking very pleased with themselves. Treacle offered them each an open bottle of 'Old and Very Peculiar.'

"Here, lads," Treacle said. "Take a pull if you really want to know what you're fighting for." They both took a gulp and reacted as if the season was full summer and the drink made of pure ice. Both he and Clump watched as they both shook slowly all the way down to their feet. "That's just in case you had forgotten," Treacle said. He turned to the policeman. "Clump, this is Hugh and Dew. Down there on the street is Lou -- the vampires three. They're the sort of friends you need in an extremely tight spot." Treacle turned back to the newcomers. "When did you arrive?" he asked.

"We were flown in at dawn," Hugh said.

Treacle gave him a very hard stare. "I think you mean you flew in at dawn, and the rest of...." he managed to say before he was interrupted.

"They will fly in at dusk, as you would expect," said Dew.

"Can I trust you to protect everyone in the house?" Treacle asked.

Both the vampires laughed heartily in reply. Treacle knew the house was now as safe as a bank only wished it could possibly be.

"Next time lads, could you try to get them to miss me?" Treacle asked as he placed his finger in the hole in his trousers.

"We were trying our best to make them miss your friend, the mortal," Hugh said in a tone of voice Clump considered would be the same if the vampire referred to a pet.

"Come Clump, I will be needing your help," Treacle stated. "Your wife is very safe here, unlike most of the inhabitants of the city." Treacle started to walk, then jogged and finally broke into a run as they proceeded towards the main police station. Clump found it hard to keep up, giving him new respect for the endurance of a vampire, especially as a moment earlier Treacle had a hole in his leg as big as a finger. They both stopped at a street corner and peered round to see a horde of mercenaries besieging the main station.

"I think we need an army to attack that place. Any suggestions?" Treacle asked.

"We can wait till dusk," said Clump.

Putting on a Show

Giving a Show - Let's Charge

M abel set an early morning alarm call to deliver the dress to her new found friend Gustav. Instead of staying in Mabel's small, dingy flat all day, Shamel decided that accompanying Mabel was much more fun. Besides, Gustav had called her a "canny lass." She didn't know what he meant by that description, but she was sure it was a compliment, just by the way he spoke the words.

Mabel placed the dress in one of her sturdier handbags to protect it from the elements, and the two of them set off on foot across the city. Mabel held a fistful of coins just in case they met anyone untoward -- she had been taught in a bit of a scrape to drop the coins and run like hell. It always worked, or so she was told. They noticed the streets were quiet, but paid no attention to this ominous detail. As they walked down Pin Street in the fashion district, Mabel saw two heavily armed men standing next to a cart of wine outside the Pin and Cushion Inn. Naturally she concluded the new season's wine had arrived early this morning, which invariably sold for a premium in all of the city's bars -- for the first week anyway -- before everyone remembered they much preferred beer. She didn't think the wine needed all these weapons; each man had a broadsword and a dagger on their hip. On the cart two fully armed crossbows sat at the ready. Despite all of their armaments, Mable felt sure the men wouldn't bother them. People who looked that serious never did. Well, never while they were on duty, anyway. But when the two girls drew next to the soldiers, one grabbed Mabel's bruised arm, which happened to be the one holding the bag that contained her dress.

"Surrender," he said in his heavy Franco-side accent, which Mabel understood only because she had the benefit of several years of school lessons. "This is a Franco-side city now."

Out of pure instinct, and with her blood boiling at the impudence of the man, as well as several years of expensive schooling kicked in, Mabel hit him with a left hook out of nowhere, using all the strength she could muster. The force of the blow lifted the man from his feet and into his compatriot, knocking both their swords from their hands. Mabel placed her bag on the cart and took a stance, showing she was ready to fight, no matter that the other man now held his knife out, ready to pounce.

Mabel's school lessons in combat technique suddenly came back to her in a torrent. Her teacher was Isabella Blackbird, the famous lady with the lamp, or so the story went, who walked the battlefield of Five Elms on her wedding day. She was famous for tending to the wounded while wearing her wedding dress. As she encountered each injured soldier she would tear off a strip of cloth to staunch their wounds. After she finished attending to his needs she would continue her search for her missing husband until she heard another wounded soldier cry for help. So by the end of the battle she was said to be a sight to behold. True or not, the tale was repeated by all the soldiers on the battlefield that day -- at least to their grandchildren anyway.

Isabella Blackbird took rather a novel approach as to how a young lady should deport herself in a fight. The first lesson: some battles one couldn't run from, so you better be proficient at tearing the enemy's heart out. As for fighting a man armed with a dagger, Miss Isabella had arranged for a travelling monk to come to Mrs. Higginbottom's Academy to teach the girls combat moves, some of which Mabel now intended to use. She quickly grabbed the man's wrist holding the knife. With one violent twist, she disabled his hand and then she pulled him close to her and swung her hips, dropping the ruffian to the ground. A quick blow to the man's neck rendered her assailant unconscious. By golly, it worked just like the monk showed her, she marvelled.

Shamel gawked to see two men lying unconscious at her feet. She had never seen that many men felled by a woman before. Taking a broadsword in its scabbard from one of the fallen men, Mable gave it to Shamel to hold, and was pleasantly surprised to see her put it on in a military fashion.

Noticing her admiration, Shamel said, "In the 'Military Weapons' magazine swimsuit edition, they believe the models must attend a week's training to hold the weapons properly. Otherwise we get awful complaints."

Mabel shrugged her shoulders; sticklers for accuracy was understandable. People took their weaponry very seriously, particularly on a dark night in a lonely road. It might be the only difference between living to an old age or laying dead in a ditch. She found putting on the scabbard was trickier than it looked, especially trying to appear dignified and ladylike while tying it around her calf. It seemed to her the low window sill of the Pin and Cushion Inn looked the perfect spot to place her foot, whilst balancing herself as she put on the scabbard. From within the bar, Mabel noticed about twenty faces watching the show she seemed to be staging for what appeared to be their amusement. The bar denizens looked to be mostly police officers at the ready and awaiting orders. So she availed herself of another part of her school lessons: when using a good, clear voice with nicely rounded vowels, everyone will give you the benefit of the doubt.

"You chaps look like a captive audience," she remarked.

"We were," piped up an officer. "Those mercenaries had us penned-in here for the past three hours. It's like an occupying army has taken over the town. We're without weapons. Well, the bartender keeps a blackjack behind the bar, but what good would that do us?"

Instinctively Mabel knew if she stepped away, someone else would take control. Power was like that; someone always wanted it. She could have easily let one of the officers take charge from this point onward, but that option was contrary to everything she had been taught at Mrs. Higginbottom's Academy. Maybe her reluctance to relinquish leadership came from the fact that most of her classmates would one day rule over fortunes or estates, or control business. Whatever the reason, she had the mind-set of the ruling class.

"Right lads, there are two crossbows and some daggers sitting here on the street. I suggest you take them," she instructed. "And does anyone know where we could procure more weapons?"

"There's George's pawn shop round the corner. He always has a few things in the window," someone announced from the back of the room.

"Okay, why don't you go and get them then? Write him a receipt or get an invoice -- he will be more accommodating if he knows he's going to get paid for them." Mabel turned her gaze to a couple of slightly built policemen who appeared to be fleet of foot. "Right, you and you, run to each end of the road and a keep a look out. The rest of us will check the street for more volunteers."

George the pawnbroker reluctantly surrendered his stock of weapons although he really didn't have any choice. He had never seen so many police officers in his shop looking this way and that. He was totally unsettled; who knew what they might notice? The fact they requested an invoice just made him more determined to give them every weapon he had.

Mabel recognised that she needed a plan. Standing around wasn't going to help matters, and finding more men would be helpful. It wouldn't do any harm to outnumber the enemy at least two to one. Now that the time for action was needed, Mabel was amazed at how she could put her school lessons to actual use in the real world. She dispatched emissaries to the local bars; the pubs were always good places to find belligerents fortified by drink, ready to fight. Once the lads had returned with some of the more troublesome members of society, selected mostly due to the highly documented instances of their use of violence against individuals, she knew it was time for a rousing speech. They needed some red meat, so to speak, to inflame the blood. Standing atop the overturned wine cart in front of the Pin and Cushion, Mabel faced the milling, muttering mob, while Shamel stood to one side, gaping at the spectacle.

"My friends!" Mabel cried. "Our city faces a time of crisis. We could choose to surrender...." Boos rang out, mostly started by the drunks at the back of the crowd, and jeers quickly spread through the assemblage. "Or..." She raised her voice even higher and paused for effect. "Or we will fight them for our families, fight them for our city and fight them for our country!" Mabel raised her sword above her head to remind them the reason why they were there. As the mob roared a throaty cheer, Mabel smiled in triumph. That was a good speech, she thought -- it had been short enough for the angry drunks to follow. Once the huzzahs subsided, she gathered the crowd around her as they began marching en-masse to the local police station.

The station had been besieged for most of the morning without much movement from either side. Those inside knew to follow orders and wait for reinforcements; those on the outside were in no hurry. The besiegers knew the police officers would surrender, given enough time, and then they would have the Chief Constable's head in a basket. As Mabel and her assailants approached the station, she dispatched those with crossbows and longbows to strategic vantage points. By now the crowd, swelled in number while marching toward the station, could sense something historic in the offing. Bystanders joined the mob just so they could tell their grandkids of their part in the event.

The crowd had grown to the point where people spilled over into the neighbouring streets running parallel to the one on which Mabel and the mob marched. All streets led to the station; its centralised location at the intersection of several crossroads made it easier for the police to see trouble coming. As they neared the station, Mabel slowed the crowd's momentum, reorganizing the various tactical assets available to her as they marched. First, she placed in front those who had brought a kitchen table (lighter than the sink and much better at stopping an arrow). Following behind them came anyone with a weapon, then those who had raided their kitchen drawers for knives and rolling pins. Last were the stragglers who had joined so they could brag about their participation in the attack.

Just as Mabel, Shamel and the mob reached the bend in the street, from which they would be in plain view of the police station, she stopped the procession. As loudly as she could, Mabel screamed out her speech again before setting the mob loose. She had never seen tables move so quickly as they formed a wall of woodwork -- the sight reminded her of an armoured creature she had seen as a child in the Academy's gardens.

The crowd pressed ahead, pushed on much faster than she had first realised. Suddenly she recognised that if she didn't start running she would be left behind. When the crowd's forward flank rounded the corner, crossbow bolts began splintering their wooden tables. The sound resembled the splattering of raindrops at the start of a storm, Mable thought. As the crowd drew closer, the enemy began firing in earnest for their lives but there were too few of them and too many of the angry mob bearing down on them. Mitigating their misery, the besieged officers began throwing all sorts of unpleasant objects from the station windows. The mercenaries were now fighting on all four sides and had abandoned the crossbows for their trusted swords and daggers as the enemy closed ranks on them.

One last scream of encouragement from Mabel, while standing on what was now a discarded pile of tables, whipped up the attackers for the final push. But her cajoling was unnecessary. The mercenaries had surrendered -- there was too much determination in that voice for them to fight on.

The Spire

Opening a Gate - Getting a Tan

Having a Picnic

Treacle decided to wait until dusk before attacking the main police station, but to do nothing while he waited was to lose everything. So he decided a small show of force was required -- something to help reduce the number of men on patrol might be very advantageous later on.

Treacle nodded to Clump, indicating to him to retire back up the street into the darkness of the alley they had just passed. When they arrived, Treacle explained his plan. "We must take back control of the walls of the city, if not the gates. It will stop the city from becoming a boiling cauldron of brutality and give an escape route for the citizens." He stared momentarily at Clump, who appeared stunned by the orders. "What are you waiting for, an invitation?" Treacle said as he pushed Clump forward into action.

The both ran to the nearest gate house located at the northern wall to find it unguarded. It didn't need to be, as the doors of the house were wedged shut, due to at least a couple of carts worth of boulders heaped against each door, making escape impossible. Treacle glanced at the main gate to see it padlocked shut. The small door in the main gate was also padlocked shut, and the main opening mechanism to the heavy city gates had all of the handles removed.

"I think we should move these boulders, don't you? Treacle asked, as they both scrabbled at the rocks. Voices began to rise from inside the keep, giving them encouragement to keep at their task. It took a bit of time, but Treacle and Clump managed to open the door. Inside, they found ten men grateful for their release, but none of them knew of a quick way to get the padlock off the small door in the city gate. Treacle soon discovered that the lock certainly didn't belong to any of them. Also, they never kept any spare handles for the main mechanism. One of the guards, struck by inspiration, suddenly spoke up.

"What if we unhook the chains and open the gate by hand?" he suggested. "It will take a lot of effort." In fact, it took eight of them to accomplish the feat, but now that the gate was open, Treacle wanted to keep it from closing.

"Anyone have any padlocks?" he enquired.

"We have few in the office for emergencies, but there is nothing to padlock the gate to," a more senior guard replied.

"We can double a chain's length and padlock it short to hold the gate open, can't we lads?" Treacle said, inflecting his voice with confidence to inspire the guards. They all agreed, and opened the main gate enough to make it impossible to close. They wrapped the chain around the gatehouse short enough to stop the gate from being shut. The senior guard pushed the padlock shut and gave Treacle the keys.

"Listen lads," Treacle said, distributing the keys to two of the guards. "You and you keep a key each. I don't need to diminish your responsibility for the safety of the gate, and I would suggest you all come with us for your safety." Treacle knew anyone left behind would be tortured mercilessly by ruthless inquisitors in a desperate attempt to find out the identity of the key holder and his location. He looked into the eyes of the men around him, hanging on his every word as if their lives depended on it, which it most probably did. Assessing the situation, Treacle's military training told him that if he and his companions attempted an attack on major points of control and command, such as a police station, their efforts would be completely futile. Most of them would never make it back to their families if he guided them on that path. "Right lads, what we need to do is find out what's happening in the city without getting caught." He looked around his companions. "Any ideas?" Treacle had some of his own, but a dozen heads were better than one, he had always found.

"There is the Spire of Yurt," one of the younger men said. Treacle had seen the spire -- it had been a marvel of its time. It stood as high as the tallest tree in the highest spot in the city, but completely constructed out of what appeared to be solid stone. He had once or twice wondered how long it would take to climb, if one wanted to reach the top.

"Good idea but we can't climb that," Treacle replied. "We will be spotted straight away."

"Not if you're inside it, you won't," came the response.

Treacle took a second to look at the tower, piercing the sky with its domination of the city's only park. It looked as solid as the stone from which it was constructed.

"The tower is really hollow, with a stone staircase of sorts inside," the young guard continued. "My father showed me when I was a boy. The land there is very soft and couldn't take the weight of a solid spire."

"Right lads. Thanks to...?" Treacle gave the young man an inquiring look.

"Crispin".

"Right. Thanks to Crispin we know what to do, so let's go." Treacle led the small group into the midday shadows, hugging the edge of the gloom until they reached the edge of the park.

"All this land not long ago once was a rubbish heap," Crispin explained for Treacle's benefit. "But to stop the flies and the odd drowning, it had been grassed over for the good of the city. Could you believe people used to try to get across this area at night, teetering on precariously balanced planks after a heavy drinking session in the pubs?" The entrance was located somewhere in front of a dragon, as far as Crispin could remember from his childhood, which Treacle thought wasn't that many years ago.

The base of the spire had a plinth sitting on each side, with a mystical beast draped upon it. Even at close inspection the spire still seemed to be constructed of single pieces of stone, stacked on top of each other. Certainly no hints of its hollow centre could be seen.

"I think the dragon is looking at the entrance of that small gardener's hut over there," Crispin said, pointing to a small hovel half hidden in the gloom. The little stone hut had a very substantial door, locked with a chain and padlock. Treacle ran his hand down the door's old engrained wood and then looked at the broken roof-tiles sitting directly above it. He stabbed the door with his dagger and, moving it from side to side, he quickly splintered the wood to expose its sodden and rotting core. Before long, he made a hole big enough for a firm hand grip and, with one good pull the door was ripped in two.

At the foot of the door was a set of steps going down into the dark. The steps were very steep; each was so thin, they found it necessary to turn their feet sideways to support themselves. Anyone thinking they could take the steps at a run would end up as a crumpled broken heap at the bottom. Ahead of them they could make out a dim circle of light shining down from the top of the spire. Nobody moved, as they let their eyes adjust to the darkness. Treacle reckoned there was about one hundred feet of unlit space between themselves and the halo of light on the floor.

Not surprisingly, Treacle's eyes adjusted first. "Well lads, there's a great big hole in the floor half way down this corridor so take it easy," he warned.

One remarked, "I can't see anything down here, not even my hand, and you're telling me you can see something about fifty feet away?"

"Yes, well, I always eat my carrots," Treacle replied with a modest laugh. It was a complete lie -- there weren't many vegetables he hated more than carrots, but the phrase, without fail, dispelled any further inquiry. Why, he didn't know. Turning to the matter at hand, Treacle announced, "Me and Crispin will go ahead. We don't need all of you to climb one tower." Crispin felt a hand firmly grab his arm firmly. "Come on, lad," Treacle directed.

Treacle slowed down. "Ok, can you see the deep trench running across the width of the passage way in front of you? It's there by design you know".

"All I can see is the light at the end of the tunnel," Crispin said.

"I think if you stepped forward any more, that would be the last thing you would see," Treacle replied. He grabbed Crispin's other arm and guided him to the wall. "Feel up there," he instructed Crispin. "There is a rail. Grab it and work your way along the wall. Keep your toes pushed into the wall and you can slide across." After a few moments, Treacle asked, "Excuse me, but why have you stopped sliding?"

"Aargh -- I think I have reached the end of the rail," Crispin replied.

"Of course you have. You can step backwards now -- just don't walk toward my voice." Grabbing Crispin's arm, Treacle escorted him toward the light. When they arrived at the halo, they had a perfect view straight up. Crispin tried to look to the top, and stumbled backwards from the sensation of losing his balance.

The walls of the spire had little stone pegs sticking out in a slow spiral. Treacle looked at Crispin for answer. "Oh, as you get higher there is no room for steps," he explained.

"Right then," Treacle said as he climbed onto the first peg and started upward. The pegs were about the size of his shoes so he didn't worry about them supporting his own weight ... until about fifty feet up when the pegs narrowed in width. Now he had difficulty balancing his feet. Finally he just used the balls of his feet, which slowly started to ache the higher he went. After Treacle climbed another fifty feet he noticed the space grew closer and his feet could now span the gap from one side of the spire to the other. He stopped to look up, to see if his goal was near. Twenty feet higher above him he could see a small stone perch and, just above that was the glass roof which flooded the spire with light. He knew he could not reach the perch if he had to climb that far at the speed he was travelling. Plus, he could now feel the prickling of his skin on his face; it wasn't a good idea to go any further. He suspected he was above the smog and the now unfiltered sunlight was touching his skin.

A few inches above him was the joint from one solid piece of rock to another. The gap was small but it might work. Tapping his pockets, Treacle discovered two daggers still hidden on his body from earlier when he armed himself to visit the Chief Constable. He pulled the daggers out and drove them into the crack as an extra foothold. Climbing atop of it, he very carefully took his jacket off, draped it over his head and secured it, the sleeves pulled as far as possible over his hands before continuing.

The art of mental projection was part skill, part art and part excellent judgement of distance. It could only be achieved across short spans, with a clear line of sight. But this time, if he was wrong it wouldn't be a couple of feet to the ground -- it would be a long, long fall. As he considered the drop, he looked down to get a feeling of what to expect when he reached the top and noticed Crispin below.

"Get out of the light!" he shouted down into the gloom. "I might fall!" As Crispin promptly obliged, Treacle mustered as much concentration as he could manage and focused on the ledge above him. Soon a small grey cloud rose up the spire and suddenly he appeared on the ledge with a panoramic view of the Great Smog. Knowing he didn't have long, Treacle quickly scanned the city, which today thankfully wasn't completely shrouded by smog. He immediately noticed Franco-side troops at the main police station; they seemed to be encased in some sort of wooden structure tall enough to reach the less secure second floor windows. On the other side of the city, the port had never looked so busy. The ships anchored just outside the harbour walls were waiting for berths and all of the ships flew the Franco-side flag. As he looked over the city, Treacle tried to ignore the pain radiating from his hands. Due to the intense sunlight, they were grey in colour and in places already turning black. Before turning away, the last sight he viewed was the Franco-side flag flying over what must be Mr. Easy's office.

Now the pain was excruciating, and the acrid smell of his burning flesh filled his nostrils. Treacle quickly looked down at the flash of steel from his daggers and focused his concentration on standing just above them. The next moment he was there but his feet slipped as he fell an inch onto the blades. His arms shot out to the stone pegs, just catching them with his burnt fingertips, but he could feel himself slipping, and his feet scrabbled for any support. Then one foot found a peg, removing the weight from his fingers. Wasting no time, he quickly found a much more secure position before resting for a moment. Looking down at his hands, Treacle noticed with relief they had stopped smoking but still were a total mess. Since he was still exposed to sunlight, he soon started back down the spire. To his relief the descent was much quicker than the climb up. Once he reached twenty feet from the bottom he pulled out his handkerchief and bit into a small black pudding -- the leftovers of his breakfast -- that he had thought to bring from home. A moment later he reached the floor and led Crispin back to their companions.

"Right lads, it's not mercenaries we're fighting now," Treacle announced. "It's the Franco-side army, if that makes you feel any better. After all that climbing I don't know about you but I think I can do with a drink. I have heard of this perfect little place called the Pork and Pie Inn, which serves a good pint, and we might find some more men to help us." He gazed around the circled men. "Anyone know the fastest way there?"

Meanwhile, in Nocte Mortis the great houses busily packed picnics and prepared their coaches for a day out by the sea. No one could recall the last time all the families had taken a day trip -- it would a day to remember, for sure. The servants had prepared the coaches with the finest wines and the freshest blood sausages the local butchers could supply. Departing just before mid-day, the families' coaches across the plains made a sight which had never been seen before.

The line of coaches merged with more coaches at every junction. They came in all directions from the mountains surrounding the Upper Plains, each joining the flow with one direction in mind. The guests at Gallops End Inn later reported the line of coaches stretched as far as the eye could see and they just kept coming, hour after hour. There was not even a horse's length distance between them for the mail coach to proceed, as it just wasn't fast enough to keep up. Everyone left in the Upper Plains decided it would be a good day to go to bed and get some well- deserved sleep, maybe leave the window open for once. Most considered it the best night's sleep they ever had.

One of Mabel's school lessons had dealt with the topic of crowd control -- the phrase "a boiling kettle quickly cools" came quickly to her mind. She recognised that she needed to sustain the mob's gently simmering rage so she could channel and control their furore. Directing some of the crowd to stand a table up, she clambered atop to address the throng. Instinctively she knew not to waver or show any sign of fear; she just needed to project a grim determination to succeed.   As she lifted her sword above her head, the mob spontaneously turned silent, awaiting her words.

"We have won a great victory today," she began. A huge cheer rose from the crowd. "But now we must save more of our men in blue so they can protect you. I say, 'Let's march!'" She pointed her sword toward another provincial police station as the mob began chanting "March, march, march!" As some of the lads helped her down from the table, she could see the wide smile on Shamel's face. She must be having the time of her life, Mabel thought. As Mabel strode down the street with Shamel at her side, everyone en-mass began following the two women ever onward.

Indeed, Shamel was all aquiver with excitement.   In her pronounced rural accent, she said, "I haven't had so much fun since I was a kid herding the mountain goats on the slopes of Mount Katj while our dog was ill. My older brothers kept sliding all the way down the slopes when they took a wrong step."

Listening to her friend, Mabel pictured an even younger Shamel -- if that was possible – rock-hopping while grown men slid down a mountainside. It was a picture of a home she had never had. All she had was this city and, by Saggie's skirt, she was not going to let anyone take it from her.

The provincial stations were meant mainly for show, a reminder to people that a police force existed to guard the tax offices built behind them. The stations were always located at a junction. People could see that ubiquitous blue sign outside, depicting a truncheon and cutlass behind a portcullis. While the cutlass had long since passed into memory, tradition remained; nobody wanted to change the signage that had maintained peace in the city so well for so long. Just like many legends that no longer were true, it made its own truth from its longevity.

About halfway to their destination, they entered a road, where suddenly a wine cart careened down the pavement at top speed, heading straight for them. The mercenaries protecting the cart wanted to turn and run away, but they were too close for comfort to the angry mob. With so many crossbow bolts pointing in their direction they decided that surrender was the longevity of valour, and slowly placed their weapons on the ground. Mabel could smell the foul stench wafting from the cart where she stood at the end of the street. By the time she reached it, she found the governor of the bank in a very sorry state. He obviously had been very unwell all over himself. The governor thought the crowd would laugh and jeer, but his state was such that everyone felt anger that such a great man should be reduced to a miserable state by these barbarians. It took all of Mabel's persuasive powers to stop the crowd from tearing the mercenaries to pieces but luckily, some of the police officers still tried to maintain some form of control. They quickly stepped in to take the prisoners back to the station. The poor governor was led away to the nearest backyard privy, which he ran to as fast as he could. By now the crowd had found its second wind; when they reached the second station their sheer weight of numbers alone forced its mercenaries to an instant surrender. The mercenaries were in the Great Smog for the money -- they lacked the fervent conviction to have their name inscribed on a plaque saying "Remember the brave few who died here --." They tended to leave that for the losers.

Mabel felt an intrinsic thrill as she savoured her role as leader. As time passed, she found the exercise of power easier and easier. She thought she must have overcome most of the crowd's apprehensions regarding her guidance. But once she was acknowledged as a leader, people tended to keep regarding her as such. Like dominoes, the next two stations fell just as easily as the second. Mabel's greatest difficulty was her grasp of the city's geography. She needed an officer to correct her direction after the fall of the third station so they didn't end up walking into the sea. She needn't have worried; the crowd was in a forgiving mood for anyone who could free them from foreign rule.

On their way to the Pork and Pie Inn, Treacle and his new-found friends crossed Deane Street. The thoroughfare was as silent as a cemetery, with a very unpleasant smelling wine cart abandoned in the centre of the road. When they arrived at the Pork and Pie, the establishment looked to be abandoned and closed for a couple of months at least. As Treacle and his companions ran toward the front of the Inn, the door opened by what appeared to be its own accord. They all dived inside to find themselves surrounded with points and blades.

Bruce smiled from behind his broadsword. "Ah Treacle, my lad," the old man smiled. "I was wondering when the reinforcements would turn up. You also brought the gatehouse lads as well."

"Commander, what are your plans?" Treacle asked brusquely. "You know half of the Franco-side fleet is in harbour, and their troops are on the street. I have seen them all."

"That doesn't change our plans," Bruce answered. "We're all too old for a frontal assault, anyway. Maybe we'll just harass them a bit."

"They do have one weakness," Treacle pointed out. "To protect themselves, the majority are all behind the wall of the port and that has only a single gate."

Bruce stood up and faced his troops. "Well lads, it looks like we will have to save this city one more time," he pronounced. "Who's with me?"

A throaty cheer of agreement came from the men, and Treacle was sure he heard a few women's voices as well. "I saw a wine cart in Deane Street if you want one' Treacle said.

Bruce smiled again. "Defeat them with their own equipment? I like the way you think, boy." While Bruce wore his age on his face like a badge of honour, Treacle was sure he had a few years on the old "boy." The usage of the term would have to wait for an opportune time to be discussed. Bruce looked round the room and, when he couldn't find his quarry, he shouted "Piero!"

A reply came from the bar, and Treacle turned to see a small chap staring into the flame of candle. "We need to burn the docks down completely sir," he said, as he snuffed out the candle with the palm of his hand in a very unsettling way. He turned to face Bruce with a smile normally reserved for small boys at Winterfest.

"Specifically I want to burn the dock gates," Treacle said. "I don't want them totally destroyed, just let them burn for as long as possible with an intensity that will stop anyone walking through them."

Piero lived for days like these. Normally he worked at the foundry managing the furnaces. His job required using the least amount of coal and accelerants to get the job done -- no request he had ever received was this elaborate. Bruce looked at Piero, who was obviously thinking. Finally, the diminutive man chose four assistants to help him once he was ready.

"I got it," Piero announced. "A bit of white metal with an oil-based accelerant, and maybe some white powder for that extra kick."

"Piero not here, not now," Bruce interjected. "You can tell me how you did it later."

"Oh yes," Piero said happily. "When it's finished. Right, where's this cart?"

As Treacle watched Piero and his minions run off in the direction of Deane Street he said, "Actually Bruce, I am a bit parched."

Bruce slapped him on his back. "That's my boy! Look after the spirit and it will look after you." He turned to a serving wench at the bar. "Round of beers, Matilda."

275

Treacle sat and drank, as several fellows came up to congratulate him and Clump on the previous night's adventures. The troops apparently thought Treacle and Clump would bring them luck, given the fact that the two had already slain so many and survived. Treacle didn't want to upset that perception by mentioning that he had had no choice, no chance of surrender and nowhere to retreat.

Soon, one of Piero's helpers returned, drenched in sweat. "Beer please, Matilda" was all he managed to say, before drinking the whole glass down in one swallow. Wiping his mouth with the back of his hand, the assistant announced, "Piero's ready but he says it's just a little volatile." His breath intake before speaking could have extinguished all the candles in the bar. Treacle considered this an ominous sign.

"Right lads, here's another chance to get one of those medals you're missing from your collection!" Bruce shouted across the bar. "You've done enough for today," he said, patting the messenger on the back.

"No way am I going to miss this, sir," the messenger replied. "Piero says it's going to be historic, something to tell your grand kids about." He ordered two shots of whiskey neat, and downed them both in one gulp as well, to steady his nerve.

Treacle began to think that Piero was a man who lived up to his word and maybe understated things a little. They all grouped up on Deane Street, which conveniently ran down to the docks. The cart was fully laden with barrels of all sizes, strapped down tight.

Before sending the cart to glory, Bruce had a quick word with Piero. "Everything okay?" he asked.

Grinning, Piero held up a long roll of cord. "I wouldn't be next to it when it goes off if I was you."

Surveying the docks from their vantage point at the top of Deane Street, Treacle said, "All the wine carts seem to have three men guarding each of them. I suggest that me, Clump and Bruce escort the cart with Piero's slight frame hidden behind it. I believe we can get pretty close before raising any suspicions."

"Well lad, I trust your decisions but we have a small problem -- the gate is open," Bruce said.

"Oh bugger!" Treacle surprised himself by saying it aloud.

"Listen, any commander worth his salt would close the gates on any sort of attack. You know that," Bruce said.

"Let's hope they do," Treacle responded.

Bruce signalled for the bowmen to get ready 'Piero has told me we have only one chance for this, so no pressure my lad," Bruce said with a smile across his face. "I will sort out an attack and get those gates closed for us." Bruce barked his orders out to his very willing troops, who seemed to consider the false attack as a good day's lark, rather than a life and death struggle for survival.

The bowmen started by targeting the tower guards with some success, but the initial moment of surprise was short-lived. Bruce's strategy seemed to gradually increase the amount of people in the fight, spreading them further along the roof tops as the skirmish progressed. Treacle's military training allowed him the ability to see what Bruce was up to -- slowly giving the impression that it was the start of an ever-increasing force of men who didn't even have time to wait for a coordinated attack. It was a strategy only a general with a large amount of men at the ready would consider a good idea.

General Dishevel, placed in charge of the port by his commanding officer, had received his post to keep him out of the way of the real soldiering. When the attack started, he had been lolling in the sun, enjoying a rare sunny day (by the Great Smog standards) and enjoying cheese and wine. Meanwhile, his men slaved to get the ships into port and discharged of their precious cargo of military supplies in time to make a difference in battle. As the general sipped from his wine glass, one of the guards who. a moment earlier had been walking the dock walls, fell dead upon his table, smashing the fine china across the floor. A crossbow bolt protruded from the man's chest and a large red pool started spreading outwards from his fine claret across the floor. In the back of his mind, the general had known that, so far, the operation had been too easy. Where was the screaming? Where was the slaughter? He immediately realised his forces were under attack and it was happening right now.

"Sound the alarm! Get me some troops!" the general screamed as he jumped up. The men scattered under his gaze, not wanting to be volunteered for any action -- they knew they would live longer that way. The alarm had suddenly increased the amount of men standing on the wall defences, which just gave the attackers more targets, but General Dishevel believed it wasn't part of his job to consider the amount of dead and dying. That was for the historians. Rounding up twelve good men on the general's order was harder than it sounded, but a sergeant managed to catch ten decent men and hoped that no one noticed the difference.

"Run down the street and flush out these brigands," the general barked his orders. "They're only local shopkeepers -- a collection of untrained peasants with weapons." It would be easy work, he felt. They were people whose names history would not remember.

Looking at each other, the consigned troops knew they had no choice. Their general was notorious for executing people for not doing what he himself would never attempt in a million years. Resigned to their fate, the men charged. Not a single arrow hit them, as the men ran for their lives to the nearest building and the sheltering cover it offered. The street slowly turned to the left ahead of them, obscuring what awaited them. Again they each exchanged a look, trying to reassure each other that it was a good day for the enemy to die, and then they ran forward as fast as they possibly could.

What lay ahead of them once they passed the curve took them totally by surprise. They had never seen so many arrowheads and bolts pointed directly at them before, and behind the bows were these old men flying the battle pennants of some of the bloodiest wars over the last eighty years.

Bruce, who was one of the few holding a sword aloft, beckoned the ten men forward. "We want to salute such an impressive suicide run gentleman, but let's be sensible. Please, drop your weapons," he said with a wave of his sword towards the ground.

The soldiers knew they had been outmanoeuvred, and dropped their weapons without resistance. Treacle stepped out of the shadows and grabbed the helmets of the two nearest men and threw them as hard as he could down the street. The guards on the wall, who had been so eager to cheer their comrades on, fell silent as the helmets rolled down the hill into their sight.

"Shut the gate!" the general bellowed as the barrier slammed shut. The troops inserted cross braces and wedges to secure the door further against battering rams.

Treacle turned to Piero as he heard the command for the gates to shut and shouted over the noise of people screaming orders. "They're just closing the gate now! Anything I should know before I help roll this cart down the hill?"

"The barrels at the front have the white metal in lamp oil, and if we lose too much oil the whole thing will spontaneously combust," Piero mentioned, in the offhand way explosive experts always seemed to comport themselves. "Ah good, always handy to know. I'll try not to let that happen then," Treacle said, trying to emulate Piero's offhand attitude to instant and total incineration.

In all the excitement, Treacle almost forgot to ask how the thing would be lit -- a detail of omission he later nearly came to regret. Treacle got behind the cart with Piero, the munitions expert.

"I need to ignite the thing," Piero said, as he signalled to the cord in his hand.

They started to push the cart. Its massive weight was very deceptive, since the cart was much heavier than it looked. Once they reached the bend in the road, which slowly sloped downhill toward the dock, they found themselves having to hold the cart back to keep it under any form of control. The high profile of the oil barrels at the front kept them both from resembling a pin cushion as clouds of arrows rained upon them. But unknown to them, the arrows had severely penetrated the front oil barrels -- their contents pouring out across the bed of the cart. When the incline of the road abruptly changed, the oil poured out of the cart over the cobbles.

Treacle hadn't looked where he walked. Understandably he was more worried about dodging the arrows flying in his general direction. As he put a foot in the middle of an oil puddle that had poured from the cart, he slid backwards, forcing him to release the cart in order to regain his balance. Without Treacle's immense strength holding the cart back, the forward motion of the cart was too much for Piero, and the small man had to surrender his hold. With the cover of the cart suddenly gone, they were exposed to the onslaught of arrows. Treacle and Piero escaped unscathed, due to the fact the bowmen on the port walls had been following the cart and couldn't target them before the two found cover. Meantime, the cart carried on in a straight line until hitting the curb side, which redirected it straight toward the dock gates.

The cord spooled out of Piero's hand until it had quickly tightened around his fingers. Then Treacle watched the end of the cord fly off the back of the cart. He scrambled to his feet to chase the cart, only to have Piero push him as hard as he could toward the safety of the little alleyway next to the house on the corner. Treacle could barely make out the words Piero was screaming at him.

"Friction cord!" he yelled. "One rub under pressure against itself and its alight!"

Just as Treacle began to think everything was back on plan, the light from the explosion of the cart hitting the gate illuminated him with pinpoint clarity within the permanent darkness of the alley. He felt his skin burn for a sharp split second, and then the force of the blast hit him. It was not as intense a sensation as the light -- it felt more like a gentle summer breeze.

Piero turned to Treacle and smiled. He licked a finger and rubbed it across Treacle's face, exposing the very pink skin below. "Well, you really picked up the dust there," he chuckled.

Treacle was sure it was his burnt skin he saw on the tip of Piero's finger, but didn't want to contradict such a convenient statement. Treacle grabbed the corner of the wall with his fingers to steady himself as he got up, only to feel them burn from the intensity of the light emitted by the flames of the white metal. He slowly receded back into the darkness of the alley for safety.

Bruce ran over, using the buildings as cover. "Well done Piero," he congratulated the munitions expert. "That was epic, that was."

"I couldn't have done it without Treacle sir," he replied as he turned and glanced down what was now an empty alley. "This is a dead-end, isn't sir?" Piero enquired, not believing what he was not seeing.

Bruce smiled and shook Piero's hand. "I don't think dead ends hinder Treacle. Come on -- you deserve a bloody big drink for this."

The bowmen on both sides had stopped firing since there wasn't anything to be seen beyond the searing white fire and the billowing smoke. The fire at the gate was so fluid in nature it had travelled under the gate. Now a burning line of oil was taking the shortest path downhill, snaking its way across the cobbles to reach the port wall, where it was now dripping onto the ships full of armaments tethered below. The fire quickly spread, leaping from sail to sail as it engulfed the ships anchored in the port. The men trying to beat out the flames found that whatever they used would alight the moment it touched the flames. The light was so intense from the white metal, now burning as bright as the midday sun, that people became dazzled. They found that they could not continue fighting the fire before the extreme pain in their eyes rendered them totally blind for some time.

Treacle had taken the opportunity to lose his entourage to get on with what he did best. When he was last at the spire he had seen that the tunnel had continued onward toward the buildings of power on State Street, and wondered where the passage led. Knowing Mr. Easy's thinking, no doubt it would open underneath his desk.

Treacle found navigating across the city much easier from the roof tops, since from this vantage point the Great Smog appeared just like it did on the maps. He jumped from one roof top to another, making good time across the city, but he would first get some items from home before setting off for State Street.

On entering his house, he saw Harvey sitting at the dining table with Aleasia. "Hello my old friend. Looking better, I see," Treacle said warmly.

"I certainly don't feel it," Harvey retorted.

As Treacle drew closer, he saw they both were drinking a glass of 'Old and Very Peculiar.' Aleasia saw the look of concern crossing her cousin's face. "Don't worry -- I have explained everything, especially about the fact we don't consider killing people for food."

"Just pleasure then," Treacle winked at Harvey

"Don't believe him, Harvey my dear. We only bite people if it's a matter of life or death," Aleasia said.

Harvey didn't have much time to learn the complexities of a vampire lifestyle, so Treacle thought he should mention a few more details beyond what Aleasia had told him. "Whose life and whose death you will discover is always a flexible point."

"Harvey, don't let my cousin lead you astray," Aleasia said, still trying to keep Harvey on the straight and narrow. But it was a path he had never trod continuously before; privately, Harvey knew he never could. He might manage to stagger on and off that path for a while -- everyone needed some morals, after all.

"Well I am only back for some of life's little essentials, as it were," Treacle said, moving toward the cupboard full of weapons.

"By the way, we had a delivery from Hugh Branch while you were out," Aleasia said casually, as she pulled out a roll of leather, the size of which Harvey had never seen before. She dropped it on the table, making an extremely reassuring thump and, without even looking back over her shoulder, waved a hand in the imperious way people do when dismissing domestics. "You are not required, Etherington."

"Yes miss." he replied. "I will be in the kitchen if you need anything."

Treacle undid the clan seal and unrolled the roll of leather, enjoying the piquant smell of varnished wood and well-oiled metal suddenly immersing the dining room. The first item he saw was a jacket as black as night itself, which he eagerly exchanged for the one he was wearing. The outside of the jacket was covered in what looked to be a netting of some kind. Next in the roll were daggers of assorted sizes and grips that fitted into little pockets specifically built into the jacket. The next item was a blow dart, which Treacle inserted into his custom made boots. The last object out of the roll was some sort of crossbow with a strange canister mounted under the stock. Harvey hadn't seen a similar weapon before, but the workmanship was unrivalled in quality. It was pure function, made only to be used and not for show or ceremony. In fact, everything in the roll was made with utility in mind -- not a single piece of decoration adorned the weapons, not even a manufacturer's mark

Aleasia patted Harvey on his arm. "Hugh Branch has equipped our clan for as long as I can remember. He really does manage the very best craftsmen."

As Treacle turned to leave, he called out, "Etherington?"

"Yes sir," came the reply from the kitchen.

"If anyone asks, I am just visiting Count Alexander." With that, Treacle left the house. A minute later a shadow moved across the rooftops. The weather was starting to change, and Treacle knew that it would be dark soon.

State Street had been barricaded on all of its major junctions, and the small alleyways had been made totally impassable. The parliament building was totally protected with men on the roof, and down on the street they were just waiting for trouble.

Treacle circled round. It was going to take a lot of time, but the back door always got forgotten. The parliament building sat in a walled compound, with a large park within its grounds which was now a total encampment of soldiers. Someone was not making this easy for him, Treacle thought.

The Ministry of Finance sat next door to the parliament building. It was almost totally unprotected -- after all, nobody worried about the accounts in a war, except the accountants. Only a few guards roamed the premises, and the back of the building was directly adjacent to a large livery stable. From a window on the top floor of the Finance building he fired his crossbow, and a trailing cable flew out of the canister mounted below the stock. The bolt imbedded itself into the lower shingles on the roof, just above the loft. He secured the cable at his end and tested to see if it would take his weight. The climb out was a bit tricky, but nothing he hadn't practised before. The trick was to have a rhythm, and maintain speed all the way across the span. Yards from the comparative safety of the roof, a guard stepped out for a smoke right below him. Luckily for Treacle he had stopped moving the moment he heard the door open.

Treacle knew any movement would give his position away, so all he could do was release his grip. The guard below him very quickly discovered smoking was bad for one's health. Just as he looked up at the sound falling towards him, he was flattened to the floor. The bite around his windpipe stopped the scream escaping his throat as he lost consciousness. Treacle glanced at the door left open and, seeing it was clear, he crept in with dagger drawn. He could hear voices from the main hall, but they had no direct view of him yet. He kept skulking round the back offices, trying to find his way to the back staircase, as he still had to reach the roof. At the bottom of the stairs, he slipped the blow dart out of his boot, just in case he needed the weapon. Stooping low to hide himself behind the banister, he crept up the stairs, placing each foot at the quietest point on the floorboards. As he neared the top of the stairwell, two voices came from the next flight of stairs. Treacle looked up to see the back of one of the guards. He must have been talking to someone at about the same level, judging from the alignment of his shoulders.

Treacle gripped a second dart in the fist of his left hand, and lifted the loaded blow dart to his lips with his right. Leaping up, he slammed the dart with his left hand into the neck of the guard directly in front of him. Simultaneously, one big blow sent the dart into the second. Even though he was experienced with the weapon, Treacle always found himself impressed by the potent effects of the darts' coating and the instantaneous speed in which they neutralised their targets. From that point forward, he made it to the roof without much trouble. By now he could see the weather was quickly in flux-

- dark clouds, darker than the city's smog, were rolling in from the Upper Plains.

When he reached the roof, Treacle saw that a loop of wire was strung between the two buildings as a method for transferring letters. They were attached to the line by means of a peg, and pulled across the short distance. Treacle gave the line one look, and decided that it certainly couldn't take a great deal of weight, so he reloaded the crossbow with the second spool from the pack on his back, and fired the bolt along the same line into the window frame. None of the guards patrolling below on the street paid any attention to what was going on above their heads, not even the sound of the bolt splintering the window frame. But to Treacle's ears, the impact sounded like a thunder clap.

After the fourth provincial station fell to Mabel's merry mob, she gave a blood-boiling, rabble-rousing speech which stirred the crowd and warmed their hearts, while chilling the blood of any of their enemies who listened to her words. She was sure, even by screaming as loudly as she could, with a crowd this big those at the back of the mob were too far away to hear her speech. The time must be nigh to retake the main police station, she thought. With a few helpful prompts from a cadre of officers who had intimate knowledge of the city's streets, Mabel redirected the crowd toward the main police station. The crowd was too big to march down one road so the officers shepherded the overflow down alternative routes. In this way they would surround the station from all directions.

The mercenaries at the main station were blissfully unaware of the trouble headed in their direction. They started to use their battering rams to pound the shutters on the upper floor windows, ... but the shutters had never been designed to be used with battering rams in mind. The shutters would have been totally smashed, if not for the two large stones mounted into the window frames. In years past, when there was a stable next to the station, the stable lads used to hang out of the window and guide the hay, which was lifted by a pulley mounted above the window, into the loft.

When the crowd entered Broken Bottle Road, dining al-fresco in front of them were the irregulars, who had decided to let their enemy kill themselves by trying to put out the fire slowly consuming the port-side gate. So they retired for a late lunch. At the centre of the merry group was Piero, the hero of the hour, who was discovering that there was such a thing as a free lunch. When the now very merry group of irregulars saw Mabel, they all let out a cheer of support.

Mabel thought this group of old men, although fully armed, had settled in for an afternoon of relaxed dining. She hadn't realised they were waiting for reinforcements to bolster their presence.

Lord McCoughland, presuming Mabel was the leader of the mob since she was out front, shouting and waving a sword, called out to her. "Need any help? We will be ready in a minute." As he spoke, the irregulars downed their drinks as one, gathered on the street and joined the mob at the back. They walked quite quickly, as mobs always do -- one half stomping in anger, the other traipsing along in curiosity, not wanting to miss any action.

Knowing that she would need creative tactics to defeat the mercenaries, Mabel organised the crowd just out of sight of the main police station. The enemy had an ample amount of men to defend their entrenched position, so Mabel remembered her lessons about General Slaughter and his associated tactics. She decided on the general's "False Attack Creates No Defence" classic strategy. Mabel's plan met with the approval of the irregulars, who loved the tactics of General Slaughter, but those of them who could remember him as a man thought he wasn't really a people's person. Following Mabel's commands, the irregulars took up positions on the roof tops, side streets and anywhere they could protect the crowd. Once they took their posts, Mabel gave the signal and, in sporadic fashion the archers began sending their arrows at their foes. This stratagem was a classic tactic of General Slaughter, who had always played his enemies for fools. Sadly, as history noted, none of his plans had ever worked, because he had also considered his officers as fools as well. He was notorious for always countermanding his officer's orders at just the wrong moment, snatching defeat from the jaws of victory.

The intermittent and seemingly random fire from the bowmen gave the impression that only a couple of men were moving around on the rooftops, so the soldiers only half-heartedly protected themselves. Then Mabel blew a police whistle, all the bowman fired at once, and the mob surged forward and broke loose.

The soldiers on the ground could see people coming from every direction -- they just kept coming and coming. The number of attackers reached the tipping point military practitioners always fear, when the ammunition at hand is not enough to repel the attack. From that point forward, the soldiers knew their fate was sealed. They desperately fought for their lives, but the blows from rolling pins, mops and other various kitchen implements quickly started to reduce their numbers. In fact, Mabel was amused to watch a housewife batter two soldiers at once to great effect with her coal-scuttle. The men on the second floor who had been using battering rams on the window shutters found mop and brooms hacking away at their feet, until they too were brought down to street level.

After the mob liberated the police officers from their sanctuary in the station's cell blocks, they all emerged from the building just in time to see Mabel climb onto one of the wine carts that littered the street and make a tear-jerking speech. She spoke passionately about the family that was the city, under whose blanket of protection they had all been sheltered until now, but the time had come to save their freedoms and their great parliament itself. Finishing her speech with a flourish, she pointed her sword in what she thought was the direction of State Street, only to find the cart slowly turning under her to point her in the right direction. Then the mob marched on.

The little town of Pigly Poke was conveniently placed mid-way between the Great Smog by the sea, and the bottom of the mountain range to the upper plains. Today the place looked as though it was holding an operatic convention; the number of people wearing black evening wear had dramatically increased from its usual non-existence, to a sea of black and white suits and colourful ball gowns. Wherever one looked, a crowd wearing evening dress could be found discussing the finer points of silver to doubloon exchange-rate futures.

The indigenous population must have been outnumbered at least ten to one by their visitors, and the local inns were doing the best business in years, especially the posh one with a doorman greeting its new guests outside. Doorman Ron, as he was now known, had found the greeting business hard going. Previously, the tips were just enough to keep him fed, but today was extraordinary: it was as though every one of his birthdays and all the Winterfests had come at once. Ron had received so many tips he was sure he could afford to buy a small farm and settle down. The restaurants were also besieged with a new type of clientele, drinking their best wine and ordering their blue steaks and black pudding. The restaurants had not sold wine with a meal in decades, so they had an excellent aged collection from which the guests could choose. At one point the demand had reached such high levels the local butcher had to be awakened from his midday siesta to reopen his doors. The shop instantly sold out of its entire stock of raw steak and black pudding.

A buzz of excitement ran through the whole town like an electrical current. To a person, everyone felt alive with anticipation and the promise of interesting things to come. The restaurants were grateful their new guests preferred most of their lunch almost raw, which was quick and easy to prepare. Thus it meant their patrons were quite satisfied with the quality of the fare. Not only was business booming from the sheer mass of visitors in town, the speed of tables turning over between various parties coming and going ran the staff of the town's restaurants ragged. Luckily the restaurants all hummed along in perfect rhythm, since the amount of customers queuing outside who wanted a quick bite increased with every minute.

Everyone seemed to be in a hurry for some reason. The local residents who had not been involved in the hospitality business found themselves hired as coachmen, even if they only owned a hay cart -- such was the eagerness of the crowd to get to the city. The mayor was heard asking any visitor he could find why his town had been so blessed. Every person queried gave a different story, but the vague consensus seemed to be that there was some sort of show in the Great Smog to which no one wanted to be the last to arrive. -- it would be such bad manners.

One of those asked who acted like he knew more than most turned out to be Sir Ruud Darknight. His reply, which had the air of someone in on the secret, was that everyone had heard about the famous operatic company The Nocte Mortis players. They were doing a special one-off operatic performance in the Great Smog of the famous play 'Denti al Momento di Coricarsi.' The mayor, never one to miss out on a commercial success, had asked if maybe they would hold the next event in his town next season, Ruud explained that he knew the artistic director, and he was sure the players would consider it a privilege to be invited into the town's homes and hearts.

Walking the Line

Bird on the Wire – Sacrifices

Waiting Time

Just as Treacle was ready to climb out onto the line he had just shot between the Finance Ministry and the parliament buildings, he heard the marching mob shouting at the guards positioned at the barricade at the end of the street. Recognising the echoing shouts as a perfect diversion, he quickly set out across the gap between the two buildings. Moving as fast as possible he made quick work of the gap before anyone could see him from the roof. The shouts from the end of the street sounded much more like fighting now, as he let himself in through an open top-floor window. Nobody appeared to be on the top floor. Most of the windows were set back from the edge of the building or located in the eaves of the roof, with no line of sight to the streets below. However, he sensed the presence of heavily armed men positioned by every window.

Grabbing a sheet of paper from a nearby desk, Treacle lofted it into the breeze blowing through the open window in the office. With a bit of encouragement and manipulation of the air current, he managed to lift the paper up and away, watching it waft out the office doorway and into the hall. He was glad he took the precaution of checking the vigilance of the building's security. Almost immediately heavy footsteps sounded down the hallway toward him. Treacle quickly found cover, hiding in the deep shadows in the corner of the office with his blowpipe at the ready. Luckily, the soldier walking through the doorway was of about the same build as Treacle, which meant that the soldier's armour would be a reasonable fit. He fired; the guard slapped his neck as if he was swatting a flym only to feel his legs collapse underneath him. Grabbing the soldier's helmet and tunic, Treacle put them on but, just before passing through the doorway to go downstairs, a sixth sense told him to don the belt and scabbard to hold the tunic down. He also took the enemy's broadsword -- not really his weapon of choicem but its presence might stop any awkward questions if he caught anyone's eye.

Holding his hand to his mouth as he descended the stairs, coughing in an attempt to obscure his features, Treacle apparently roused no suspicions from the dozen or so men standing by the windows on the second floor. They had crossbows in hand, staring intently toward the sound of the mob, eagerly waiting to punish any civilian who came into sight. As he quickly moved down the stairs to the first floor, Treacle resumed his coughing in time with his foot fall, pausing at times to furtively peek over his hand while searching for other soldiers. He didn't like the fact there was a wall on the right-hand side of the staircase; it meant he would have to walk around a blind corner at the bottom of the staircase. Anyone could be on the other side, even his mother -- a scary thought.

As Treacle's foot came to rest on the bottom step, out of nowhere a hand-axe hit him with full force in the chest, forcing him to drop the sword as he fell backwards. Someone had been hiding in the corridor to the right.

A Franco-side officer screamed, "Bloody coward!" in his native tongue. "I told you what would happen if you deserted your position," he spat as he raised the axe to strike a fatal blow. Treacle used his incredible speed to grab a dagger strapped across his waist, and slammed its hilt against a flagstone on the floor. A stream of liquid burst from its point, quickly turning into a small cloud enveloping the officer's face. He fell to the floor, clawing at his throat in a gesticulation Treacle would have described as a fish out of water, if he had ever spent any time fishing.

Count Alexander must be nearby; Treacle could hear him barking orders from down the hallway. "Kill them! Kill them all!" he bellowed. "I don't want to hear about another citizen in my streets."

Treacle found himself strangely affronted. It wasn't just the fact that the Count had tried to kill him -- obviously the knave didn't know how a real gentleman should behave. Treacle reassembled his crossbow into a new configuration and crept towards the double doors at the end of the hall. The doors were more for show than any practical use, he reckoned, judging by the large gaps at the top and bottom. He gently opened the door by pressing his foot gingerly against the bottom of one, while his finger was poised on the trigger of the crossbow. The door slowly swung open to reveal the visitor's area of a rotunda above the debating chamber on the ground floor. The Count had decided to make this area his own -- he sat in the speaker's chair surrounded by an arc of chairs that normally held the representatives of the people. Now the chairs all stood empty, their former occupants languishing in cells a couple of floors below ground. On each side of the speaker's chair the Count's two bodyguards -- armed, dangerous and certainly skilled at their trade -- crowded around their leader.

Outside, having been beaten back from the barricades, the mob kept themselves out of sight from the highly accurate bowmen perched high up on the parliament building. Mabel and Lord McCoughland huddled in the doorway of the customs house and discussed strategy. Their options were severely limited by the fact that the majority of the city's weaponry was held in the basement of the Ministry of Aggression, just behind the enemy lines. Of course the irregulars had their own custom weaponry -- most of them carried enough weapons for another two individuals, but they wouldn't share. They hadn't become old soldiers for no reason whatsoever.

As Mabel and Lord McCoughland plotted their next move, word came that the fire at the port had diminished from fiery white to cherry red and was slowly being put out. Within the next thirty minutes the troops would be able to breach their flaming gate and storm the city. Mabel turned stony grey at the news and the look on Lord McCoughland's face defied description. "We could storm the barricades but we would lose at least half our people, maybe a couple of hundred," he said. "And that's if we win. Then we would have to face the troops coming up from the port."

Mabel knew sacrifices sometimes had to be made in battle, but she was also taught never to pursue a lost cause. She quickly made her decision. "We will play the waiting game," she declared. "With time comes opportunity; opportunity brings victory. I am sure you already knew that, Lord McCoughland."

He agreed -- opportunity needed time, and another thirty minutes of waiting wouldn't make much difference. It certainly wasn't significant enough to put on your grave stone, he reflected. Lord McCoughland looked out across the city he loved and at the black cloud now at the furthest edge of city walls. "The weather will at least match our mood when the troops break through the port gate," he muttered.

Twenty of the longest minutes went by before a runner from the port reached them with news that the gate had been breached, mostly by troops in ones and twos but the numbers were quickly increasing. Mabel and Lord McCoughland exchanged glances. "We had a good run, my girl," the grizzled commander said. "I think me and my men would have followed you to the end of the world. You showed real gumption, especially the self-control you displayed by not attacking the barricades for a second time, which no doubt would have been futile."

"I suggest, your Lordship, that you and your men disband into the city before it's too late." Mabel said.

"We stand with our leader, ma'am," he replied. "We couldn't have it said that we left you and the citizens to face your fate alone."

At that moment, a sound like thunder echoed across the city, accompanied by a brilliant flash of red light. The main gate of The Great Smog burst open and an assortment of carts and coaches rushed into the city. As the black cloud billowed in above the city walls, thousands of leathery wings beat furiously into the wind, sounding like a gentle breeze blowing through a forest of dry leaves. Mabel and Lord McCoughland heard the noise roar louder and watched the dark mass in the sky move closer to them. Suddenly silhouettes of heavily armed warriors appeared on the rooftops as the cloud slowly rolled past.

"I think opportunity has just arrived," Lord McCoughland stated, the relief apparent in his voice.

A voice just behind his right ear whispered, "No, the clans have arrived and I would say fashionably on time as always."

Slowly, Lord McCoughland turned to see a face he remembered from his childhood before he left the mountains to seek his fortune in the city on the coast. "Good evening Ruud," he said warmly. "I hear you're Lord High Protector now."

"Good evening Bruce McCoughland," Ruud Darknight replied. "I think you can let your sword down now. You are all perfectly safe for the time being."

As he spoke, screams were heard all across the city. Some came from frightened home-owners, distraught at the sight of vampires suddenly appearing outside their windows, but most of the anguished shrieks came from soldiers discovering a new enemy in town. Ruud Darknight looked out onto the street at two very well-dressed men armed with very heavy crossbows, and gave them a nod. Lifting their weapons, the vampires sent two arrows flying over the parliament building. They exploded into fireballs of intense red light, the outbursts resembling large flowers suddenly blooming from darkness.

Treacle steeled himself to jump into the small space just in front of Count Alexander. Should he fall short, it would be a bloody miracle if he didn't break a leg on a salon's chair. Taking a deep breath, Treacle leaped and twisted his body in the air, firing two crossbow bolts before his feet hit the floor. The Count's bodyguards slumped backwards, their bodies pierced by the quarrels, and drew their last breath even before he landed. "Uh-uh, I wouldn't go for that sword. This crossbow has the ability to fire four bolts." Treacle declared. "It would be such a shame to have to kill you twice."

"I can wait, Treacle -- my soldiers are everywhere," the Count said with the air of someone who knew time was on his side.

"Then we shall wait," Treacle said in response. He didn't want the Count to have the last word.

An Evil Brew

Futures a Knocking – personality changes

While busy perfecting the wort for the latest production of 'Old and Very Peculiar,' young Jim Watson heard two loud, heavy-handed bangs at the brewery entrance. He opened the door to face two well-dressed, rather pale-complexioned visitors. "Yes gentlemen, can I help you?" he asked, looking curiously at them.

"Hello young sir. My name is Phileas and this is my brother Belleas," one of the men began, nodding to his companion. "We were wondering out of pure curiosity -- do you know these two men we found snooping around suspiciously outside?" He pointed to two men sprawled unconscious just outside the doorstep. "They both claim to be guild employees looking to assess your forthcoming yearly fees," he continued.

"Yes I do," Jim replied. "Well, no not really, but I know they work for the guild if that's what you mean. Anyway, both of you have told me your names, but who on earth are you really?"

"We're your personal security by appointment-like," sniffed Belleas, wiping his hand across his face.

"Yes it's our job, you know, to keep you all together compos corpos-like," said Phileas.

Young Jim thought for a while, and considered why an unknown master brewer such as himself would need two eccentrics like these two to protect him. Phileas looked thin as a whippet and had the build of a runner who delivered government mail. Conversely, the muscular Belleas looked like someone who broke things for a living. His business partners must value him very highly to assign these two characters as guardian angels, Jim decided. Each looked to be useless as an individual bodyguard but together they seemed to make one excellent protector.

Finally Jim spoke. 'It's very nice of you to go to all this trouble to protect me, but I'm sure the guild will raise merry hell about this when they find out, and I will be forced to pay an extortionate amount in fees to cover dangerous working conditions as punishment."

Phileas and Belleas looked at each other and, without speaking came to the same conclusion. "Don't worry, young sir," Phileas said assuringly. "We will realign their thoughts, making them forget any unfortunate events that occurred today. It's actually very achievable, as most people already want to forget this sort of thing already."

"Subtle-like," Belleas added.

Despite the earnest assertion of his newly found benefactors, Jim wasn't filled with confidence by the description of their method. The first image running through his mind was that of a big hammer bouncing off someone's head.

"Yes, exactly. Subtle-like. No problem. Don't worry -- just carry on like we're not here," Phileas continued, his tone brimming with certainty.

Jim had no doubt his protectors were assigned by his new partners Treacle and Aleasia. How many bodyguards had grey evening wear, buttoned-up shirts and silk hankies protruding from the top pockets of their suits? Always a good idea to befriend your bodyguards, and doubly so if they were vampires, Jim felt. If they cared about you like Treacle and Aleasia did, they tended to be personally invested in the safety and welfare of their charge. A wee bit of 'Old and Very Peculiar' might start his relationship with Phileas and Belleas on the right foot.

While the vampires dragged the two dead weights into the brewery, out of sight of any passing trade, Jim tapped the vat and filled three glasses of his latest brew for his new friends and himself. "A small drink gentleman," he said as he handed each of them a glass, which they threw back in one large gulp. Both vampires adjusted their posture, lifting their shoulders and stretching their necks, before standing silently for a moment. Then each grabbed the other's shoulders and coughed deeply.

"Lad, you're a bit of all right in our book," Philleas wheezed, as he caught his breath.

Knowing he had made two fast friends, Jim was in an upbeat mood as he left the vampires to adjust the memories of the two misunderstood intruders. He inspected the temperature of a fermenting batch of 'Old and Very Peculiar;' by the time he had returned, the two brewery guild men were sitting up, right as rain.

"We have some questions, Mr Watson, to determine your guild payments. I hope you could spare us the time," one stated. Later at the guild house, some of the more aggressive businessmen of the

Master Brewers Guild discovered their two best assassins had returned thinking they were accountants.

Every Cloud has a Silver Lining

The black mass - Huddle of Justice

The large black mass that could have been easily mistaken for a storm-cloud loomed nearer, so close in fact, that parts of it now came into stark focus. It appeared to be an extremely dense swarm of agitated bats. Now the swarm split in two; one half circled and descended onto State Street directly in front of the barricades. Legs, arms and assorted body parts started appearing from the black mass, depositing what looked like the Saturday night crowd one would see around the local playhouse. Everyone wore their best evening wear, and some of the women even wore pearl necklaces shimmering in what was fast becoming a blood red sky. The second half of the cloud slowly moved off down the hill toward the port, leaving the beating sound of leathery wings hanging in the air.

A rather prim older lady emerged from the crowd and approached Ruud, Mabel and Lord McCoughland. "We're all ready, dear, just awaiting your word," she announced.

"Mrs. Flagstaff, as always a pleasure. If your clan MORTALIS will do the honours for me," said Ruud with a heavy spin of deference.

The lady smiled with excitement, and showed way too many teeth from Mabel's point of view. She must have been from the country -- she just had that look of someone who hunted small animals for fun. The lady walked back to the centre of the crowd at the barricade and, holding her arm aloft, screamed, "Leave one for me, you buggers!" She brought her arm down, and the crowd at once turned violent in unison. The clansmen threw off their jackets, the women hitched up their dresses, and together they stormed the barricades. Mabel was sure that almost instantly, the prim older lady had taken a crossbow bolt to the shoulder and had pulled it out without even breaking stride.

Ruud had also noticed the resiliency of Mrs, Flagstaff. "She does so love being in the centre of things. She would never have it any other way." He frowned as several vampires, the first to scale the top of the barricades, burst into flames as they were hit by small bottles of garlic oil shot from the expert bowmen atop the parliament building. Ruud pulled out a gleaming sword so sharp, Mabel was sure it could cut the very soul from her body. "Well Lord McCoughland, Mabel, I don't know about you, but we can't let the kids have all the fun," he said. "I suggest we give them some help."

Lord McCoughland waved his men to follow him into the attack, uttering the immortal line '"Last one to Parliament buys the beer!" Shamel still wore her silly grin, which served to confirm Mabel's opinion about the model, as she blithely waved her sword toward the parliament building. Anyone who still remained, and that included Mabel, soon realised they would miss the show if they didn't get their skates on. She ran into the centre of the street and shouted, "For the city!" and received a hearty roar of encouragement, as she too went over the top of the barricades.

What Mabel saw from the top of the barricades took her breath away. The clans had already dealt with those standing immediately behind the barrier. Even now, the vanquished resembled dried and shrivelled prunes; each precious drop of life-sustaining blood had been drained from their bodies. Beyond them, people were fighting in every conceivable location, but she was not going to linger and admire the view. She jumped down just in time, evading the arrows aimed at her position on top of the barricades. Without hesitation, Mabel threw herself into battle. Seeing one of the irregulars had fallen, she ran to him and slashed wildly at his assailant, who had raised his axe to deliver a fatal blow. The enemy dropped his weapon and fell back, trying to hold his body together. Not waiting to see the damage she had inflicted, she moved on to another mercenary holding his own against an irregular. The mercenary took advantage of his youth and strength to drive back the old man but, as Mabel ran past, she slashed the mercenary's backside with her sword. That diversion was enough to give the irregular the opening he needed; he immediately skewered the mercenary with his sword.

As the battle raged, Mabel eventually found herself fighting next to Ruud and Lord McCoughland. She prayed her fencing lessons would pay off or, at worst, not embarrass her. At Mrs. Higginbottom's academy, fencing involved short swords and multiple opponents. They normally trained in groups of three or four, duelling against each other, or teams against a single individual. To her relief, she found the lessons stood her in good stead as she dispatched two men trying to cut her down.

Despite the fact she was fighting for her life, Mabel found herself awestruck by the success of her comrades-in-arms' contrasting combat styles. Lord McCoughland fought with the broadsword in one hand and a dagger in the other. Both weapons had full hand guards. She soon discovered why -- he had a tendency to fight dirty, intentionally missing with the blade, only to smash the guard into someone with the brute force of a rock launched by a powerful ballista. As for Ruud, he utilised all the flourishes of a practised fencer. A careless opponent would find that Ruud had twisted the sword from his hand. Or, just when an enemy thought he had the better of the fight, Ruud would throw a quick kick to the knee-cap to drop his opponent. Either way, Ruud achieved the inevitable result. Mabel found she was getting an education at least, as she used Ruud's method of kicking her opponent without warning. She quickly realised why the irregulars were so successful -- they believed only fools or the mad followed rules. They fought using their own rule book.

Slowly they battled their way to the front of the parliament building, leaving the irregulars to deal with anyone left alive on their flanks. After half of their soldiers had fallen to the sword, the enemy surrendered, much to the regret of many clan members who hadn't had so much fun for many a decade.

Treacle could hear the screams getting closer, coming from all directions, but he kept his eye on the Count. He was determined that this slippery snake would not escape to fight another day. "You do know, Alexander, that no matter who comes through those doors, they will want to stretch your neck."

"I have nothing to fear," the Count replied scornfully. "I believe that's the screams of the poor being put to the sword by an army of trained professionals, my young vampire." His eyes started to drift from Treacle's crossbow, which slowly swayed back and forth hypnotically in an attempt to keep his full attention. But Alexander's eyes were drawn to something behind Treacle's shoulders -- the way the Count's eyes darted to and fro, Treacle figured a number of hostiles had materialized behind him. The sound of crossbows taken off safety could just be heard over the battle raging outside, but the shape of the rotunda made it impossible for Treacle to determine the direction of the bowmen.

"Well, don't just stand there! Kill him! Alexander screamed. The sound of bows unleashed was followed by the whirring of their bolts through the air. Then Treacle heard cries and groans of pain and the crunch of bodies hitting the marble from behind him.

Harvey's voice rang from the public gallery. "What a shot Aleasia, what a shot!" he exulted. "Did you see him fall? He must have been killed instantly."

"Thanks, Harvey!" Treacle shouted up to the gallery.

"Any time, mate!" Harvey echoed back.

"But he's dead!" exclaimed the Count, pointing a bony finger at Harvey in the gallery. "Everyone saw his body being carried away."

"A good man never dies, but you wouldn't know that, would you?" Treacle said.

The two of them sat in silence, the Count confidently awaiting the inevitable rescue from his troops, when the double doors of the debating chamber burst inwards. Ruud Darknight strode across the threshold with a beautiful young lady on each arm. Treacle was sure one was Mabel Stirrup, the young lady from the party, whose company he had the pleasure of sharing for several minutes. The second looked very familiar, but he couldn't remember where he had seen Shamel before. Next to them was Lord McCoughland -- the sly old dog was still alive and looking somehow younger. Maybe it was the excitement of another battle won, Treacle speculated.

Behind them entered all of the representatives of the clans including Mr. Partridge, who represented the blood-pudding manufacturers and the only non-clan member of the Upper Plain governors. All the other governors represented the banking industry in some way or another. The only people who looked out of place were the two self-described legal eagles, Mr. Loophole and Mr. Technicality -- most considered them a pair of vultures. Both looked to be pushing a hundred and would drop dead if someone dared to raise their voice at them.

Ruud snapped his fingers and made a series of very small hand gestures. In response, the members of the clan surrounded the room. "Treacle my nephew, you are relieved of duty," he announced, and signalled with his hand that Treacle should lower his weapon, which he did. "Count Alexander, it is a pleasure." Ruud spoke loudly to the room, knowing that clarity of speech was paramount on occasions such as these.

"You have no right to hold me. Release me at once," the Count bristled. "Under the Upper Plains accord, I order you to support the rightful leader of the Lower Plains, and I think you will find that is me."

"Thank you, Count, for reminding me of my duties," Ruud said coldly, contempt dripping from his voice. "Mr. Loophole, if you please."

"Ah, yes," Mr. Loophole said, as his dentures clicked. He certainly needed new dentures, Mabel thought, or maybe a better dentist or even his own teeth. He thumbed through a thick, leather-bound document. "Here we are (click). Paragraph 132, subsection 14 (click). The party of the first part, that's (click) the self-governing land of the Upper Plains (click), shall support the legally appointed representatives of the people (click) of the Lower Plains."

"So hacking off the heads of the people's representatives does not make you the legal government," Ruud said. "Someone has to be nominated by the people."

"I nominate Mabel Stirrup," Lord McCoughland said, before anyone else could speak. He knew some wars were best fought with words -- they usually found their target and could go round corners.

Ruud turned to his legal representatives for their reaction. "He is well within his rights, sir," said Mr. Technicality, consulting his own copy of the document Mr. Loophole held. "Being a Lord, sir. Subsection forty two, appointing a monarchy."

"WHAT?" Count Alexander spluttered. "You can't possibly go on with this charade."

Ruud looked round the room. "Anyone wish to nominate the Count?"

An absolute hush fell over the room. Taking the silence as a cue, Mr. Loophole spoke. "The people will need to show (click) support for a queen, sir."

"But of course," Ruud responded. "Anyone wish to second their esteemed Lord and appoint Queen Mabel?"

The overflowing crowd roared from the public gallery and the surrounding corridors. Ruud nodded to Mr. Loophole. "Mabel Stirrup (click), please read the marked passage please."

"I -- insert name here -- swear to be king slash queen for the good of the country or until a better candidate is found" Mabel read from the document handed to her by Mr. Loophole. "I will consider state funds not to be my own to squander; see subsection ninety two."

Mr. Loophole peered at Mabel over the top of his glasses and whispered to her, "Absolutely perfect (click). Let them argue you didn't follow the exact letter of law (click) as it is written."

"This is PREPOSTEROUS!" Count Alexander screamed as Ruud stared him down.

"I think you will find it's as watertight as can ever be achieved under the laws of man," Ruud said, before turning to Mabel. "Your Majesty, may I suggest that under the Upper Plains accord, we have rather more leeway to deal with these matters than does Your Majesty. We can wait for you to organize a trial, swear in a jury, appoint a judge and then hold the trial, or the Upper Plains can act under its own jurisdiction. But let's check the legal position. Mr. Loophole?"

"Ah, it seems that Count Alexander has (click) invoked some very ancient rights by killing representatives (click) on the debating chamber floor during an active session of parliament," Mr. Loophole said. "It appears to me that an argument for immunity from prosecution (click) could be argued, which would only leave the lesser (click) crime of rigging an election by giving himself (click) the only vote on who the leader will be, from which (click) he cannot escape the law." Mr. Loophole continued, "Such a crime carries (click) with it a one year jail term or, if we follow the provisions (click) of the Upper Plains accord, the upper plains could consider it an act of treason against the lower plains (click), it could be argued, which can invoke punishments up to and including banishment (click) or death."

"So, Your Majesty," Ruud said, turning to Mabel, "Your first official action is to make a royal decision on the jurisdiction of the prisoner."

Count Alexander pleaded, 'If you arrest me it will be war. I am a diplomat of the Franco-side court!" Those words were exactly what Ruud wanted to hear -- an admission of complicity with the Franco-side government.

Mabel turned to the room and spoke in a clear voice that carried to every corner of the Parliament. "Indeed, Ruud Darknight, it appears to me that the Count is already in your custody. It would be exceedingly untoward of me to begin my reign by making demands from our allies. May I suggest his fate is for the governors of the Upper Plains to decide."

The governors huddled and forthwith voted to support any decision their Lord Protector Ruud Darknight wanted -- why appoint someone to authority and then not defer to his judgement? "It is decided," Ruud declared as the huddle broke apart. "The sentence is banishment, and I will personally see to it that you, Count Alexander, will reach the Franco-side capitol of Faris unharmed."

"I will return, and when I do," Count Alexander said, pausing for dramatic effect, "I will have a hundred warships."

"The punishment for returning from banishment is death," Ruud replied. "I will issue a kill on-sight order upon your head for these lands, so I would think very hard upon returning." Changing his tone, he continued, "And now I think the time for debating the subject is over." After signalling his guards around the room with a series of finger manipulations, Ruud Darknight seized Count Alexander's arm and forced him up the stairs to the roof. Behind them, the guards sealed the staircase to stop anyone seeing them leave and to stop any escape bid. An apparition of leathery wings descended to the roof from the black mass above the city, picked the two of them up, and carried them onward toward Faris. The flight didn't take long as the bat flies.

After silently enduring the journey across the sea, Count Alexander's fury got the better of him as they approached the capital city. "Why on god's earth would you support that bubble-headed idiot of girl?" he blustered. "I could have given you everything you wanted -- a supply of fresh maidens at your beck and call and a large share of the tax collected across the city."

"Sadly Alexander, I just don't like you or what you stand for," Ruud said in reply. "I don't stand for anything -- that's how I rose to power."

"If you wanted a deal I would have done one," Alexander protested.

"You just don't understand us at all, do you Alexander?" Ruud shook his head. "How could I, as a vampire, support someone who wished to impose a society where the main culinary ingredient is garlic?"

At Ruud's signal, the bats released the Count from their grasp. He considered the Count safely delivered to Faris without harm. The landing, however, was another matter entirely. As he listened to the scream plummeting hundreds of feet to the steps of the Franco-side palace below, Ruud wondered how Count Alexander could not have heard the maxim 'You are what you eat.'

Epilogue

Count Alexander scrabbled to get himself back on his feet, but the wet grey slates on which he found himself laying made standing up difficult.

"Hee hee, that sure was some fall, mister," a cackling voice called down to him from above. "I thought you was going to land on Lady Justice's sword for a moment, but as you got a little closer, I changed my mind to a crash landing directly on her set of scales. Blow me down, you managed to miss both of them."

The man shouting down to him was obviously a workman of some kind. He sat on a lofty perch at the end of a roof as he tapped out ashes from his pipe on the disgruntled face of a statue that stood just below him.

"I survived! I'm alive!" the Count screamed.

"Nobody falls that far and lands on the ample bosom of the old lady of justice and survives. You're dead as a doornail, man. Don't start embarrassing yourself acting the bloody fool."

"But you can see me!" Alexander blurted out. He kept patting parts of his anatomy to reassure himself of his existence.

"Of course I can, man, I'm as dead as you," the workman replied. "I died when I fell from her sword during the construction of this fine palace of justice, and I tell you, that stonemason who carved her Ladyship certainly did have a thing for a well-rounded lady. You really can admire his work from up here," he said as he filled his pipe with tobacco.

"That was 300 years ago!' the Count said in a rather confused tone.

"My fault, really. I should have taken the stairs," the labourer continued.

"That's how you died? Climbing down the statue on the façade?"

"No, you bloody fool, that's how I became stuck here for 300 years. I got up after my fall and saw the light and this long staircase and I chose not to go. So if you see a staircase you better take it, that's my advice."

The Count looked around and realised he was standing on the roof's edge where it met the marble façade at roof level of the grand palace. A wispy cloud slowly drifted through the sky toward them and, as the cloud became level with them, he saw it rolling over an invisible flight of stairs. Each step was highlighted as it rolled off the edge from one step to another. Sitting in mid-air, it stretched up toward the heavens as well as down toward eternal damnation.

As he took his first step he called back to the workman, now happily pushing pigeons from the roof with his foot" Aren't you coming?"

The labourer sat motionless; apparently he never moved far from this spot. "No mate, not going my way." At that precise moment the stairs collapsed, becoming an express slide to hell, and the Count disappeared from sight before he could utter a sound. Mutterings across the palace square could be heard from the end of the roof. "He thought I don't listen," the labourer said to himself as if someone was listening. "He thought old Max doesn't hear things sitting on this edifice of power. He got what he deserved, didn't he, my friends?" He asked the pigeons cooing at his side. "The old lady gave him some of her own justice, wouldn't you say?" The birds murmured softly in agreement.

Mabel, in her quest to find a usable wash room, found Mr. Easy at his desk, working on the headline of tomorrow's papers. It was a job he normally left for the editors, but today's events needed just the right turn of phrase. Mr. Easy considered the appointment of a queen to be a monumental event, one that might not happen again for decades. The transition to her reign needed to be stage-managed to keep everyone believing in the continuation of the power of the state. More importantly, he needed to keep confidence in the power of the servants of the state all the way up to the head of the civil service, namely him. Power had always been an illusion and, in these times of uncertainty it needed to be doubly so.

"Miss Mabel Stirrup, a pleasure to meet you," he said warmly. "Or should I call you 'Your Majesty?' My name is Mr. Easy and I will be your Chief Civil Servant. It will be my job to make sure the city runs smoothly, so you only need to make the big decisions."

"You know, that's a relief. I don't think I could keep the city running all by myself," she replied, adding, "you can call me Mabel."

"I think we will get on extremely well then, Mabel."

"Did none of the soldiers come down here to see you then?" the new queen queried.

"Who would worry about a humble civil servant such as myself?" Mr. Easy scoffed in a light, self-deprecating tone. "And if Your Majesty would excuse me, there is much that needs to be done before morning. The wash rooms are two doors down on the left, if you were about to ask." Mabel nodded and dashed off; nature's call took precedence over any further inquiry.

Mr Easy thought he better improve his game. If that girl could walk any quieter, he wouldn't have heard her footsteps entering the hallway just outside his door. She might have caught him with the bodies of two enemy guards sprawled across his office floor, with tell-tale puncture marks on their necks.

The clans of the Upper Plains rented out every room, outhouse and privy in the city, as they didn't want to return home, now that they had travelled so far to reach The Great Smog. Enjoying the city's amenities, they took the opportunity to catch up with some of the new fashions the city always seemed to generate. They found a much larger selection of goods than they could possibly find at home. The Nocte Mortis players had been encouraged to actually put on a one-night special royal performance, much to their surprise, in the city's famous playhouse. The newspapers' critics later described the presentation as a "cultural experience." They didn't want to be too harsh in their opinion of someone who could rip your throat out if annoyed. More importantly for the theatre owner, the sell-out performance had been the first in a very long time. Every seat in the house had been sold, bolstering his bank account and his belief in the finer things in life. The influx of money into the city, even if for only a couple of days, had certainly won the clans new friends and influence which they intended to exploit at their earliest convenience.

The first of the new batch of 'Old and Very Peculiar' was tapped a little early for the official inauguration dinner. Mabel decided to host the event as a long street party outside the parliament building, due to the fact that nearly everyone was invited. Since a queen had invited them and the meal was free, a large number of guests planned to attend -- once the street had been washed clean, of course. It would be bad taste to feast sitting above the very spot where the enemy's blood had soaked the streets red. Everyone in attendance found the beer rather refreshing compared to its more refined, percolated and reduced version. Treacle had even managed to drink a glass without getting a blinding headache from the adrenalin rush. The free samples encouraged the guests to place orders for thousands of bottles, securing production for the next couple of years.

Aleasia arranged to have her horse Black Bess brought down from the moors so she could ride across the lower plains, since Harvey was still not fit enough to travel. The washboard roads, especially along the back-breaking plains, could cause a coach's seats to seriously readjust a traveller's spine.

As for Treacle, he received nothing for his troubles. Not a single year was taken from his debt of a hundred years of service to the Office of Foreign Affairs. Thus far, he had only managed to complete twenty years before this adventure. As a nephew of Ruud Darknight, he had to be wary of any impression of favouritism on his uncle's part. He even had to return the equipment to Hugh Branch, as it was clan property. The only concession made to him was that he was permitted to stay in the city. Living abroad always had its advantages.

About The Author

Antony Brown has travelled western Europe fixing bits and bytes of corporate databases. From credit cards to the welfare of numerous herds of cows, it's been counted and correlated.

A career like that forces you to travel. He has walked the banks of Lake Geneva, seen the spires in Dublin and worked in such exciting places as Worthing, Reading and Stevenage.

As his job lends itself to a lot of waiting around in airports and staying in hotel rooms away from his family, his frazzled brain sought sanctuary by dreaming of the impossible.